HEARTLESS
in

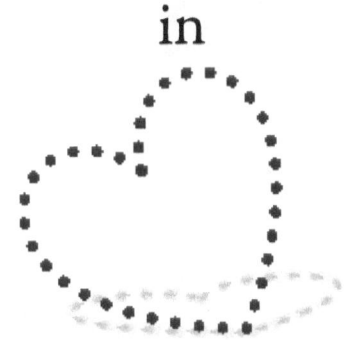

Naperville
-LOVE· NEVER· DIES-

W. Green

Table of Contents

-Dedicated To The One I Love-

Prologue

The California Zephyr slithered through Illinois farmland, the last leg of my cross-country trip from Denver to Naperville. I perched like a bald eagle, comfortable but anxious in my upper deck nest, squinting, my face pressed against the cool green glass. Thousands of bright orange dots flashed along the smoky horizon. Numbed by the heartbeat of the train, my mind struggled to connect the dots until I understood what lay before me. Ripening pumpkins glistened in the early afternoon sun: endless rows of embryonic monsters awaiting their surgical transformations into fearsome creatures of the night. The panorama stirred my emotions and blackened my thoughts as I realized Halloween, the anti-holiday, with all its wonder and weirdness, was about to haunt me again.

As I drifted back in time, those little orange dots released painful memories of my mother's tragic death, her ugly decay, and the unhappiness of my youth. Such were the risks of coming home. I didn't want to return to Naperville, yet I couldn't resist. My father was dying, and I suspected my brother was in trouble. I needed the money that only my father's death could bring. And then there was my lost love, my impossible dream, Kathy. Lustful thoughts had filled every mile of this journey. A decade had passed since she and I parted, and now, strangely, I was also coming home to her. But she was my brother's wife. I quickly dismissed that thought as my eyes were attracted to something above the trees beyond the field of pumpkins. A hungry hawk, searching for the tiny movements of a hapless mouse, circled effortlessly on the rising air, waiting. More often now, the soulful Zephyr horns announced our approach, followed by warning bells that grew louder and faded as we rushed through empty rural highway crossings, relentlessly sliding into my past. I was coming home.

Chapter 1

"The doctor does not approve, Mr. Reinhart, but since it is important...go ahead. But, please, try to make it short."

Otto Reinhart gave the woman a half-smile as he glanced around the empty reception area. Medical people thought Otto, they think they run the world. He connected with his wife's phone. "Hey, Kath. I'm here in the doctor's office..." he cupped his hand around the phone to keep his voice from causing a disturbance, "going slower than I thought. Has Alex arrived?"

"No. I guess his train is behind schedule," she said. "So you're both running late."

"Well, apologize for me, Babe. Pop open a bottle of wine and make my brother comfortable. He'll be worn out after his cross-country excursion."

"I can do that...how long?"

Otto glanced up at the woman behind the desk. Over her half-glasses, she studied him, presenting an unmistakable vision of displeased, entitled authority. He got the message. "No idea. Listen. Got to go now. Bye."

His wife's last words were cut off. He silenced the phone and returned it to the inside breast pocket of his suit coat. The woman at the desk nodded slightly and went back to her keyboarding. Otto resumed his waiting, and he thought about his own clients. Typically, in his business, they were distraught because someone close to them had died. In the natural order of things, death was the end of everything. But his livelihood and life depended on people dying on a continuing and regular basis. He carried a tinge of guilt, knowing good news for him was bad news for others.

As an innkeeper for the dead, his funeral home business offered a certain future for those who now had nothing but a past. He spent his days smoothing and straightening the unknown path leading to the graveyard. Bereaved relatives and friends found comfort in his words. They sobbed, cried out, and sometimes became almost inconsolable, and all through it, Otto Reinhart maintained his patience and understanding.

They might be meeting him for the first time, days, sometimes only hours, after the death of their loved ones, but Otto was a master salesman. He would guide them from one painful decision to another, counseling them and always convincing them that he was not selling anything but wanted only to help them in their time of need. He believed this as truth. Most of the customers of the Reinhart Funeral Home and Crematory, his Naperville neighbors, were traditional people who spanned generations and preferred to do business with the man with his name on the door. The family mortuary was a dignified yet homey, comfortable environment for his clients to make difficult and uncomfortable decisions. And in contrast to the looky-loos who explored the showrooms of nearby automobile dealerships, often only seeking entertainment, his customers were never stokers. They faced a painful situation that dictated their need to buy. As he often reminded his staff of front-office morticians, no one goes shopping for caskets to amuse themselves on a Sunday afternoon.

Today was different; the roles were reversed. Bad news for him was good news for others; the medical business depended on human frailty for its existence, and Otto's doctor's diagnosis pinpointed his weakness. Though never a religious man, he suspected today's meeting with his heart specialist would be a 'come to Jesus moment'. The doctor's office was at the top of the medical mountain, and his gut told him that his appointment with Dr. Ansel Rickenbacker was outside the usual schedule of his monthly medical visits. And that same detection device knew the venue had changed from the typical small exam room to the great man's office, on the upper floor of one of the taller office buildings in town. This was a place where Rickenbacker did business, not the three-story rabbit-warren building where he prescribed, probed, and poked. The location change put Otto on edge and suggested something unusual was in the air.

He felt like a wayward priest shopping for an expensive wedding ring. Inexperienced and nervous, he fidgeted in the overstuffed leather chair, ran his hand through his thinning black hair, and wondered if anyone would see him perspiring. He dabbed his forehead with his handkerchief and waited, breathing with some discomfort. Soon, he would be facing a difficult decision, one which could only be resolved by the medical industry. Otto Reinhart always encouraged his funeral home customers to accept death as the natural consequence of living. And his doctor would use selling techniques similar to his own. But Rickenbacker was in the death-denial business, or at least the death-postponement business. Today, he was selling the possibility of life to a young thirty-year-old man facing his mortality; unknown to Otto Reinhart, he was about to become a potential customer, purchaser, and consumer of one of the most expensive items the medical community offered, a vital organ, a heart.

Aside from the rush of air from the ventilation system, the delicate clicking sounds emitted by the receptionist's keyboard, and the throbbing of his heart, the room was dead quiet. The trim, middle-aged woman with tight black hair, wearing little make-up and dangling half-glasses from her neck, ignored Otto's anxiousness. He studied her for over five minutes, waiting for something to happen. It did when she answered the buzz of her phone, listened for a moment, repositioned the handset, and then beckoned Otto to enter the private office behind her. As he arose, he adjusted his tie and pushed his hair back. Hunched over, he walked the last mile and entered the inner sanctum. The doctor, a tall, imposing man dressed in a suit and tie, faced an expansive window that offered him a heavenly view of the fall-colored patchwork quilt of Naperville suburbia below. He turned to face Otto and greeted him with a weak smile, and the patient reached out to shake hands.

"Beautiful day," said the doctor, "fantastic time of year. It's best to enjoy these days before winter arrives.

Otto nodded. "Right. Enjoy it while you can. A few more weeks, fall will be over, and winter will be back again."

Doctor Rickenbacker, a lion in his world of beating hearts, was not famous for his small talk, nor his scintillating personality. 'Time is money' might describe the business side of his professional mindset. Therefore, as they both took their seats, his smile dissolved, and he opened a discussion of Otto's health and future.

"How are you, Otto?"

"Well, my blood pressure might be a bit dicey today. Today is an exciting day for me," said Otto. "My older brother Alex is arriving from Denver. Haven't seen him in ten years."

"Well, that is exciting," said the doctor. "Don't worry. I won't keep you long. But we do have to cover some important items."

Otto breathed deeply. "Fire away," he said gamely.

"I'm glad we can meet today. You know we and you are doing everything possible to improve and maintain your life. You have followed our recommendations, taken your meds, and on the whole, maintained your diet. A little more cautious exercise would help, but we all fall off that sled." He smiled but didn't let it stick, nor did he appear to expect a verbal response from his patient. Instead, he offered up a solemn declaration. "But...you need to plan for the future, Otto."

Otto did not want to hear those words and that tone of voice. His own end-of-the-road hospitality business was frequented by guests with empty futures, but Rickenbacker managed a hope-business, a help-business, or worst-case, a never-say-die business. The patient summoned some reserved courage and replied, "Sounds ominous."

The doctor placed his elbows on the heavy mahogany desk and steepled his hands. "Quite the contrary. But we are now in a different phase of your care. A phase that may require you to make some difficult decisions."

Otto listened to what sounded like a replay of one of his funeral client discussions, except he was the star attraction of this show, not the deceased wearing a wooden overcoat headed for Cement City. He waited for the punchline.

"We've been over this, but let's review. You have a congenital heart condition. Eisenmenger Syndrome aggravated by your years of recreational cocaine use. We have monitored, mediated, and medicated your situation for about twenty-seven months. Your decision to abandon your addiction and go cold turkey with the substance abuse no doubt saved your life, but the damage is done. Otto, the heart is a remarkable organ. Every day, most hearts beat about 100,000 times. But your heart is beating 150,000 times a day. Even with medication. This increased heart rate, elevated blood pressure, and vasoconstriction put additional strain on the heart and lungs, which could lead to complications. Blood clots, arrhythmias, and even heart failure. That cannot be undone." He paused, but Otto said nothing. "Your heart is not operating like a normal heart." The guru paused again and then spoke the magical words: "It has deteriorated to the point that there is only one viable option...a heart transplant."

Otto Reinhart choked up. He tried to talk, but the words wouldn't come. Those two words, 'heart transplant', were taken as a sucker punch driven hard into his belly. His breathing quickened now, and a surge of adrenaline electrified his body.

Sensing Otto's reaction, the doctor backtracked. "At the moment, it's just a possibility. You would have to decide if that procedure is for you. To some degree, others will have a say-so also, but nothing will happen until you believe it is right for you. There are many factors involved, including health insurance coverage and your overall financial situation."

Otto fell back into the chair; his thoughts muddled, and he stared out the window. His eyes glazed over. "What's the survival rate? Success rate. Whatever you call it?"

Rickenbacker stuck a finger in the back of his starched collar and straightened in his chair. He appeared to think before answering, and each tick of the schoolhouse wall clock above his desk increased the tension in the air. "If you have it done here in the United States, which I recommend, the outlook is quite acceptable. First-year survival rates are over ninety percent, and five-year rates are above seventy. Some patients' lives are extended by fifteen or twenty years."

Dejected, Otto took another deep breath. "So it might buy me twenty years. What about Plan B?" He offered a weak smile. "What if I don't go for the transplant?"

Rickenbacker cocked his head. "Any prognosis would be an educated guess."

"And..." Otto waited for an answer. Not getting one, he looked away from the doctor and stared at the annoying wall clock. Its two flat black hands, shaped like the pickets of an iron fence, seemed frozen in time while the eager red dagger paused and then ticked ahead relentlessly. The doctor was on the spot, and when Otto's sad eyes, pleading for a response, slid down from the clockface onto Rickenbacker's visage, there was nowhere to hide. "Well, it would be all guesswork...you know that your condition deteriorated over the last couple of years. The most likely outlook is more of the same...your heart health will not improve on its own. My best guess...three to six."

"Years?"

"No...Months..." His answer slowly drifted over his desk and died.

Otto swallowed hard and struggled to release the words. "So you are recommending a transplant? There's no other choice?"

The doctor spoke in a quiet voice. "Yes. That is my opinion. But it is your decision. Think it over, Otto. But the earlier you decide, the earlier you get on the national transplant waitlist."

"And the faster I can have the operation?"

"Not quite. Thousands of patients are waiting. Each one has different circumstances. You can apply here, and you can also apply elsewhere, but that doesn't always result in a faster timetable. A donor heart may be available tomorrow or may take months...or even years." He glanced at the paperwork on the desk. "You're thirty years old. That's helpful. You would be expected to recover well from transplant surgery. All things considered, you are, other than your heart condition, healthy. You are not using recreational drugs, a non-smoker, and a light drinker. Plus, you have proven to be a responsible patient. And therefore, the transplant, in my opinion, is your best choice."

Otto nodded. "Heart transplant. OK. I understand." He paused. "It's not a choice. I must have it. Right? I put my name in the hat. And if I can find a heart, odds are in my favor to survive the operation."

The doctor nodded. "You will also have to deal with the uncertainty and waiting. That is an unfortunate aspect of the official protocol. You could get a call anytime. So you would always have to be prepared."

Otto didn't like what he heard. For the first time, he focused on the doctor's smooth bronze tan, elegant grey-streaked hair, and his fingernails, clean, polished, and trimmed by a professional. Anger rose inside of him, but he kept his tone conversational. "I'd be kind of like a backup quarterback. Suited up. Always ready. Always in the game, mentally and physically. Just hoping for the number one to go down...so I can take over...if I live long enough."

"That's one way of looking at it. That's it on your end. It's all about timing and availability. The right donor heart must be available, and you must be ready."

"You mean not every donor heart will work?" he asked, revealing his concern as he began to sense that the difficulty factors were increasing in number.

"No. Blood type, tissue type, location, and the height and weight of the donor must be consistent with your needs. Just like in football, everything must be in sync to increase the odds of success. You have to be a patient bench warmer with a correct attitude." He smiled as he explained the rules. "And...you will always need to be within four hours of the hospital while you're on the heart transplant waiting list; otherwise, you go on the inactive list. But in this case, thousands of other backup quarterbacks are waiting to get into the game." He smiled. "It's best to stay on the active list."

Dr. Rickenbacker checked his watch, pushed back his chair, and stood, signaling the end of the session. Otto took the hint and lifted himself off the chair. The effort drained him.

"Think about it, Otto," said the doctor as he came around the side of the desk and they shook hands. "It's quite a decision, but one better made sooner than later."

Otto drifted out of the doctor's office in a fog. Robotically, he spoke with the receptionist. She handed him an oversized envelope and told him the information would give him an understanding of the procedure and the issues involved. He made the next appointment and exited the building. His mind drifted as he walked almost in a trance. Once in his car, he stared out the windshield. His thoughts locked into a nothingness pattern. Not worried or frightened, he floated in a callous circular pool of What If? and

Why Me? After a few minutes, he shook his head and muttered, "fuck it." Then he started his car and drove off, uncertain of his next destination.

As he drove, thoughts of his brother, Alex, competed with his thoughts about a heart transplant. Otto could use his family to guide him in his decision. But he wouldn't tell his wife Kathy, no point in worrying her. Still, a second opinion from someone close would be welcome. Alex would be one. He had been around the block; he was older, responsible, experienced, and an intelligent risk-taker. Otto's father, Frederick, had health issues of his own, so Otto would not burden him now. Once he decided to move ahead with the transplant, he would tell him. Frederick was not only his father but also the sole owner of the family funeral business. But business was business for the old man, and no matter who was dying, Otto assumed his father would say, "Life goes on until it doesn't." His father's biggest concern would probably be the availability of another person to replace his son. In the old man's mind, people come and go, but the family business, built over half a century, must endure.

The car was moving. Otto drove on autopilot, thinking, worrying, and talking to himself. "Three to six..." He mumbled, failing to shake off the negatives and replace them with counter-measures, alternatives, and hope. Angry, disgusted, and disappointed, he concluded that, in the end, the world was programmed to always deal him a bad hand. He had to take action. Beyond his family, the only other person Otto could trust to advise him would be his personal doctor, one of his few friends and sometimes business associate, Dr. Stephan Jarek was a man devoid of emotion, forthright, and not afraid to provide his version of a straight, pragmatic answer. It was a plan. He would talk to Jarek first.

He drove aimlessly, in no hurry to get home. He didn't want his long-awaited meeting with his older brother to be a depressing experience; his current sour-puss attitude had to be dissolved. He drove to a forest preserve area, parked his car, opened all the windows, and lit up a joint. First, he coughed, but not long after, he smiled and relaxed.

Chapter 2

The train slowed, and I awakened. I closed my book, stuffed it into my bag, and looked about. The handful of passengers along for the ride also appeared as if they had been hypnotized by the rhythmic swaying, clicking sounds, and backward-sliding landscape. But everyone shook off his reverie like a sleepy dog in response to the conductor's announcement: "Naperville is next...Naperville. Last stop before Chicago."

This was my last stop, the nomadic prodigal son returning only to pass on my regrets, collect my inheritance, and kiss the bride. I'll give everyone a pat on the back, a hearty 'goodbye', and a sincere 'good luck'. But tomorrow, whenever it arrives, I will be gone again, dying to start a new adventure and a new life.

As the train rolled to a smooth stop, a few passengers assembled near the door, jostling like anxious cows heading for the slaughterhouse. I lagged behind, carrying a single bag hung over my shoulder, stepped off the train, wandered along the walk, and gathered my senses. Next to me, the train silently slipped away and sped toward Chicago, leaving behind the lingering odor of diesel fumes and a sense of emptiness. I was a stranger in my hometown. I stood on the platform and looked about; nothing had changed. It was quiet, peaceful, and boring. After ten years of abandonment, I was back in Naperville.

The historic train station, red brick with limestone accents, anchored the traditional grassy park across the street, a diagonal sidewalk bisected the square, and a pole with a waving American flag punctuated the center. The park was empty of people, but full of mature trees majestically displaying the rusty foliage of fall. After listening to a thousand miles of train track click-clack, the absence of noise was soothing. Some crows fluttered in the tree tops above, mildly complaining about something, but I drifted into the quiet, peaceful, long-buried world of my youth. I awaited my ride at the curb, stretching my legs and decompressing my thoughts.

A few minutes later, a vintage buff-colored Lincoln town car rounded the corner headed for me, and the driver proclaimed his presence with persistent toots of his horn. The limo stopped. I recognized the man behind the wheel. He popped open the door, flipped his navy blue limo-driver hat onto the seat, ran around the car, rushed up, and hugged me.

"Alex Reinhart...damn. It's really you." He backed off, his arms outstretched and his head nodding, his face in amazement like I was some kind of rock star.

I smiled. I was surprised and pleased by the arrival of my old friend Terry Walker. Stocky and broad-shouldered, wearing a ruddy face with a winning smile festooned with a walrus-like mustache, his forehead reaching to the sky, he was the same guy who drove me to O'Hare ten years ago to send me on my way into the exciting unknown world away from Naperville. "Driving the same shitbox, Terry. I can't believe it." My greeting was natural and uncensored; the words popped out of me without thought.

"You're gonna hurt her feelings, you brute. You loved her when we double-dated at the drive-in movie and folded down those backseats. Those were the days. Right? Anyway. This baby's paid for and runs like a top. Jump in, and we'll roll. Jeez, I'm glad to see you...you old bastard."

I was glad to see him also. I needed a friendly face from the past to welcome me back to Naperville. He tossed the bag into the trunk while I climbed into the passenger side. The car didn't move; we took one look at each other and chuckled. Terry's oversized mitt gripped my left leg just above the knee. "You ready? Everyone's pissing their pants with excitement that you're back."

"What about you? Should I check your pants?"

"That's just for the ladies, Alex." He laughed with gusto, the same old Terry Walker. Wheeling the car out of the lot like he could do it with his eyes closed, he glanced at me and then looked ahead, talking into the windshield. "When your brother called me and told me you were coming. I told him straight off: 'Otto, I'll pick him up at the station. Don't you worry.'"

"I appreciate it, Terry."

My buddy looked puzzled. "Are you kidding? Everything I have I owe all to you. We would have never got our mortgage without you. Hell, we're ten years into the thing now. Another fifteen and we'll have it paid off. It's the wet dream of every suburban homeowner."

"Didn't cost me a nickel to co-sign," I said. "I'm glad it all worked out."

Terry reached for the CD player. "Want some music? Got some super new ska." He didn't wait for an answer. Loud sounds of brass, guitars, and beating drums leaped out and filled the interior. He checked my reaction.

I raised my eyebrows and gave him a look. "I was just settling into the peace of country life," I said in a loud voice.

"Maybe later," he said as he killed the music. "We should just talk now, anyway. We gotta catch up."

I settled down, feeling comfortable now. His chauffeur's license was attached to the back of the sun visor; the black and white mug shot made him appear fifty years old. I tapped on the visor with my index finger. "This your gig now?" I asked in a friendly way.

"You mean first-class professional limo driver?" He rolled his eyes and smirked. "Between assignments. Truth is, I'm a private dick now...an investigator."

"Cool." I smiled.

"This limo job is a cover. I spent three years with the Sheriff's Department. I was a good cop, but the wife couldn't deal with it. Weird hours, bad diet, strange friends...and stranger enemies. So now I drive this rig for pin money for the wife and kids."

"Still married to the same woman?"

"Fourteen big ones last June."

"Sounds exciting. Is it dangerous?"

Terry smiled. "P.I. work or Margie?

"I know women can be dangerous. What about your cases?"

"In Naperville?... You gotta be kidding." He shook his head. "Nah. Lots of peeping, library work, and internet searching. But I'm good at it. And it's a decent gig if you get past the people, the traffic...and the cost of gas." He laughed. "As I said, it's pin money...whatever that means."

We drove south through the historic district, past the college and the cemetery, with me rubber-necking like a tourist, focusing on one place or another. "Looks about the same," I mumbled. "More people."

"How's that?"

"I said it seems like there's more people. I feel like I'm at Disney World."

"You got that right. They're moving here from everywhere. The schools, the restaurants, the shopping, hiking. And they just come to visit. Whatever. Naperville's got it. We've been rated the best U.S. city to live in."

I shook my head in disbelief. "You're kidding."

"Nope. That's a fact."

I was mumbling to myself, now feeling I was lost in America without a compass. "OK, I guess I missed that."

"You're a busy beaver, Alex. No time for hometown pride. But you're a local hero. You spend your time in exotic places showing all of us what's outside our little world." He chuckled. "I've been following your travels. Great stories and photos. Last year, one of them hit the Sunday insert. Egypt...love that mummy shit."

"I didn't realize anyone cared. I've been gone a long time."

"Cared? You got to be kiddin'. You're the talk of the town. But you look thinner in person. They say television makes you look heavier. You haven't gained a pound since you left. Have you?"

"I'm about the same. More facial hair and shorter head hair. A couple of scars."

"And the limp."

"How's that?" I asked.

"You've got a slight limp. Left leg. I mean, I saw it...didn't I? " He smiled.

Surprised by his deductive skill, I gave him credit. "You are an observant S.O.B."

"I spotted it watching one of your TV shows. I am a detective, Alex."

"I'm impressed. I got it when I fell off a trail in *Machu Picchu*. Busted up my left knee in the middle of nowhere. But don't tell anyone. It might affect the adoration of my fans."

"You know I can keep a secret." He rubbed his cheek as he stopped at a red light and looked at me. "Sure...I could tell stories." He laughed. "But I won't."

I viewed the world through the windshield. Left to right, I analyzed my hometown. I didn't get it. For me, it was a larger version of Mayfield or Mayberry or wherever the Beaver lived. Still sleepy. Still filled with little boxes. Still conventional. "All-American," again I mumbled to myself.

"How's that?"

This town. It's the quintessential All-American town."

"And your point is...?"

The light turned green. We drove on. Terry glanced at me. "Otto says your father is having a rough time healthwise..." He waited.

"Cancer. Some kind of cancer. I haven't been told much of the story. I have to talk to him. That's one of the reasons I'm here." I nodded. "Time to make peace with the old man, see Otto and Kathy, and get out of Dodge."

"Hey, Bud, no need to rush. You and I have a lot of blanks to fill in."

"Sure," I looked around, "are we getting close?"

Terry nodded. "Yep. A few minutes. That's right. I forgot. You haven't seen your brother's new digs. You didn't make it to the wedding. Or did you?"

"No. Never did. Everyone still happily married?"

He gave me a quick look. "Far as I know." He snorted. "You're still interested...I can tell. I see your old squeeze every so often." He smacked his lips and nodded. "She stays in shape. Great body. Still turning heads."

Without sarcasm, I responded. "I'll bet."

"Whatever happened to you two? From an outsider's view, it was a thing."

I thought about getting into it with Terry, but tossed out the usual answer. "Too young. Way too young to get serious."

Terry chuckled. "I get ya. Have to pick the fruit when it's ripe."

"Something like that." I chuckled. "You still have a way with words, Terry."

"Well. At least you kept it in the family. Your brother is a lucky guy. But..."

I gave him a look. I doubt he saw it, but limo drivers and ex-cops have eyes in the back of their heads.

"Nothing. I'm just saying. Kathy's an attractive gal," he said as if he was about to let me in on something.

Not wanting to encourage his speculation, I didn't respond. I sensed where he was going, but I didn't want to talk about Kathy's history. People talk without thinking. Someplace other than

Naperville, no one would care, but at its roots, the Big "N" remained a small town with small-town thinking.

We exited the highway and crossed the river passing through a wooden-covered bridge, the tires thumped and echoed in the confined space, and then all was quiet as we exited into a small forest full of mature oak trees. Reaching a clearing, houses popped into view. "New subdivision?"

"For you...maybe. This turf is hot money, Alex. Your brother must be making a killing by burning and burying those bodies. Not my idea of fun. You gave it a pass, right?"

My mind was adjusting to the careless flow of our conversation. "That I did," I responded. "I never liked funeral homes. But someone has to do it. Right?"

"I guess so. The only mummies I like are the ones in those old black-and-white movies. And your TV shows. Otherwise. Dead bodies are not for me."

We drove through a neighborhood full of expensive, but boring, clone houses and headed toward a more exclusive area surrounded by iron perimeter fencing. Terry made a quick right turn onto a narrow road, passing through an entrance gate framed by stone-capped, red-brick piers. "This is it...*Xanadu.*"

Ahead, filling our view, at the end of a long, narrow road bedded in red granite pavers and lined with regimented trees, stood my brother's house, an imposing white stucco Queen Anne complete with authentic leaded windows, fish-scale shingled turrets, and deep wrap-around porches. "Looks like Otto's doing well. You're kidding about the name, right?"

"Oh...that's just my name for all these crazy giant houses. Anyway, you're looking at the original mansion. Renovated top to bottom. Otto and Kathy also put on a large addition in the back facing the river. Sweet crib, eh? Otto's a lucky man...a thriving funeral home business, a historic McMansion, and a beautiful wife. What else could anyone ask for?"

"Got me," I mumbled. "My kid-brother has it all. I'm looking forward to seeing him again."

"And Kathy?" Terry asked with a wry smile under this stash.

He had a point. My brother Otto has everything I dreamed about when I was younger: position, esteem, and money. But that was yesterday. Today, I have no use for mansions, a steady job, or Naperville. But Kathy was a different story; Terry correctly sensed that my feelings for her continued. Like a weak-kneed kid on his first date, something inside me twinged as we neared her house.

Chapter 3

"Dr. Jarek, you have a call...it's Mr. Reinhart. Otto Reinhart." Jarek sorted out the Reinhart brothers in his head and took the phone call. "Hello, this is Dr. Jarek."

"Doctor. Otto Reinhart here."

"Yes, Otto. How may I help you?" He heard Reinhart's strained breaths. "Is everything OK?"

"Sure. I'm OK. As a matter of fact, I've never felt better. But I have some issues to discuss. You remember my brother Alex will be coming in for an exam tomorrow, right?"

"Of course. I'll give him a screening examination and a report for your father's nurse to review. I think it will allay anyone's fears of transmission of disease."

"Excellent...excellent." Another long pause followed.

"Otto...anything else I can assist you with?"

"There is. You know, I saw Dr. Rickenbacker today."

"Monthly visit. Right?"

"Well. It was," said Otto, "or at least I thought so. But he dropped a bomb on me. He advised me in no uncertain terms that I need...well, it seemed to me that I must have a heart transplant. I thought I could talk to you about that."

"It's been a while since I spoke with him, Otto. Maybe a couple of weeks ago. He wanted to run more tests before he would make any determination of the best course of action," replied Jarek.

"Sure. I took the tests. A whole boatload of tests. I guess the treatment program I have been following isn't solving the problem."

"I'm sorry to hear that."

"So I hope you and I can meet to discuss my future with you. This transplant thing."

"We could meet...of course. But this is a decision you must make based on your assessment of the situation and Dr. Rickenbacker's recommendations. He is the specialist. I believe his hospital is rated highly for the approach he is offering." Jarek had no interest in stepping on Rickenbacker's professional toes.

"Look, Stephan. You and I...we level with each other. Don't we?" He paused for a long time. "We may soon do business together. I hope we will be successful partners. So I think you have a dog in this fight. I need to talk this through with someone, and I can't talk to my father. He has no idea about the seriousness of my condition."

"And your wife...does she know?"

"Kathy. Of course, she knows about the deterioration of my health. But not Rickenbacker's latest idea." He coughed. "We share the same bed, so it's no secret I'm half the man I used to be. I mean, just breathing itself has become an issue."

Jarek paused. "Yes, Otto. I am concerned. And you do have a point. But I don't like to let business interfere with my professional responsibilities..."

"Right. Gotcha, Doc," said Otto, "but if we don't make the right move, you and I won't be putting your business scheme into action. I'll be in a box, and you'll be nursing along low-end government patients for the rest of your career."

Jarek shook his head. He wanted to amp up his response, but he restrained himself. "You have a way of making your point, Otto."

"Hey, I'm a guy who's running out of time. If I don't jump on this national heart donor thing, I'll lose my place in line. I wonder if it makes sense. A ton of risks, even if I can find the perfect heart. Rejection. Complications. You do see my concern? You do. Don't you?"

The doctor took a deep breath. He sensed his patient was stretched thin. "You're getting excited, Otto. Settle down. I will discuss this with Rickenbacker. It's only another problem to be solved. Life is full of problems. We'll get past this. Have patience. You and I will meet."

"When?"

"I'll try calling Rickenbacker. His time is limited, you know. Top of the line. Always in demand. But I'll see if I can get a hold of him. OK?"

"How about tonight?" asked Otto, sounding desperate.

"Give me some time to talk with him. And I don't want to meet you at my office," said Jarek. "Is there any other place else we can get some privacy?"

Otto paused and asked: "Can you join me at my club tomorrow...say six o'clock?

"I can do that."

I appreciate this, Stephan. I feel better already."

"For the moment, I would recommend you sit on it for a month. In any event, you're not going to be at the top of the transplant list right now."

"Why not?"

"Because they have a priority list. You're not on life support. You have no VAD implant."

"What's that?"

Jarek thought for a moment. "It's a ventricular assist device. Something implanted to help pump blood from a weakened heart. One possible step in the medical treatment for some. But Rickenbacker must have ruled that out because of your Eisenmenger syndrome. Too many complications."

Otto sighed. "It's almost as if the medical system is in control of my life."

"Otto, it's a major decision. We need to get it right," said Jarek.

"It's the biggest decision of my life. Maybe yours also."

"Try to take your mind off this issue, Otto. Think about how to get our new venture moving as fast as possible. You're the businessman."

Otto paused again, then said: "I didn't mean to push so hard, Stephan. I trust you. Don't worry. We'll do this deal. I'm just losing my focus with my father dying, my wife bitching, and my brother coming home. I've got a lot on the table."

"Yes. Goodbye, Otto. Stay focused. I'll see you tomorrow."

Chapter 4

The road leading to Otto's mansion ended in an expansive, circular, landscaped area. The reflecting pool featured a creamy white marble maiden who struck a standing pose in the center of the circle, her eyes half-closed and face without expression, while a continuous stream of watery wine flowed from the heavy stone water jug balanced on her hip.

Terry guided the limo along the granite pavers, stopping the car a few feet from the mansion entrance. We got out, looked back, and admired the view of the impressive estate. A light breeze, generated by the late summer sun moving out of a stray cloud, eased across the ground, stirring a smattering of autumn leaves drifting atop the pool. The sounds of water falling on water drifted in the air, but something else was present: the faint sounds of geese honking. I shielded my eyes with my hand and studied the sky, searching for the source. Above, almost invisible black blips slowly crossed the clear blue sky. They formed an elongated V-shaped flock of geese flying high, heading south, led by a single goose. As the geese glided away, their muffled warnings of the coming winter subsided, leaving only the lonely sounds of the maiden pouring water.

Then out of nowhere, a never-forgotten soft feminine voice called out my name. I dropped my head and turned toward the building. At the top of the stairs, within the shadow of the porch roof, she stood, her face not yet visible. Step by step, my fantasy became real. My body tightened, and I inhaled before I sidled up the three stone stair steps. For the first time in ten years, we faced each other smiling like two goofy kids. She was taller than the teenage girl

I remembered, now a beautiful woman. Her long auburn hair tossed in the breeze, and her lovely green eyes captured me.

"Kathy..." I said in a voice betraying my suppressed feelings.

"Hey, stranger," she said.

Like sunbeams warming my skin, I felt her presence. We hugged, or was it an embrace, as Terry later suggested? Whatever, we held it too long, and I guess too intensely for Terry. Playing the part of a referee by clearing his throat, we released the clinch. Like a child ignored, Terry made a face, raised his right hand, and wiggled his fingers at her. "Remember me?" His voice interrupted the magic of our moment.

She smirked and nodded. "Mr. Walker," she said, "always glad to see you. Thanks for bringing my Alex home. It's been a long time." She turned toward the door. "Come on in, guys." She escorted us into the spacious hall of her home. An elegant hardwood staircase led to the second floor, an elaborate chandelier shimmered above, and French double doors to the left and right led to the living and dining rooms. The latter featured a curved wall of windows with stained-glass upper sashes. The dining table and chairs seating a dozen for dinner were all modern, in stark contrast to the hundred-year-old period interior of the house.

Terry, his head on a swivel, commented. "First time for me. You and Otto have quite a place, Kathy. Quite a place."

"We call it home," she said, her eyebrows rising as she pursed her lips and nodded, mocking him by suggesting an elevated social status.

"Right," said Terry. "I knew you when you were an innocent high school freshie, walking to school and eating peanut butter and jelly sandwiches for lunch."

She chuckled. "And this guy, Mr. Richie Rich..." she turned to face me, "did his best to ignore our existence."

I adopted a thinking pose. "High school. You can't hold that against me. But I did come around. We're all friends now."

"Friends," she said, "we've got some catching up to do. Your brother will be along soon. He's been waiting." With a light touch of her fingers on my shoulder, she directed me toward the formal living room. "Have a seat. I'll get us something to drink."

"Not me," said Terry. "Got to get back to work."

"Another taxi client?" I asked.

Terry pretended to be offended. "No way. I'm breaking a new case. Big deal. But it's all confidential. Hush-hush. You know."

"Be careful," I warned.

"Not to worry. It's just a keyhole job. Another unhappy marriage. The husband's convinced his wife is getting serviced by the air conditioner service man."

"Is she?" asked Kathy.

Terry smiled. "Let's put it this way. She's hot. He's hot. And he's got the tool to fix everything."

Kathy made a face. "You men are so crude."

Terry gave a little wave. "Gotta go. I'm sure you two have a lot of catching up to do."

I shook hands with Terry and thanked him for the ride. We agreed to go out for beers soon. He headed for the door.

"Terry," she said, "take a photo for me. Ten years from now, I'll need proof the elusive Alex Reinhart stopped by for old times' sake." She handed her phone to Terry and motioned to me to come closer. I stood next to her, and she turned to face me. Her right hand moved up to my face, stroking my beard with the tips of her fingers. "I like this," she said softly.

And I liked the touch of her fingers on my skin and beard. Then I noticed the little gold bell on a delicate, smooth black cord around her neck. Shaped like a polished apple, it had an almost invisible tubular silver striker hanging within. The delicate keepsake fell onto her bronze skin, settling in the folds of the open collar of her tight cotton sundress. "I remember that," I said.

She smiled and raised her hand to her neck. Her fingers delicately held the cord above the bell. She shook it gently, and it released tiny vibes. "Still rings, Alex. My nineteenth birthday."

"Settle down," admonished Terry, "turn to me and say...cheese." We complied with our friend's directions. The camera clicked, and Kathy and I disengaged with a hint of reluctance. Terry studied the photo. "Super," he mumbled. "I'm getting better." He returned the phone and gave Kathy a quick hug. Say 'hi' to Otto."

Kathy and I stood at the door, watching the limo swing around the circle and head up the road. She looked at me, and I looked at her. We both smiled and wandered back into the living room. "Where is Otto?" I asked.

"On the job. I guess. Seems like every day. Seven days a week."

"He knows I'm coming, right?"

"Of course. I think he's meeting with one of his doctors now, but he'll be home soon." She smiled. He told me to make you comfortable. So..."

"So what?"

"He suggested I pop open a bottle of vino. Interested?"

"Red wine. If you have it."

"No problem." She turned and walked away. I watched her leave, leered, I suppose. Terry nailed it. She was beautiful, older, more confident than when I left her, and in every way more attractive. Dressed for a hot day in early October, she wore a simple burnt-orange dress made of clingy lightweight cloth cinched at the waist with a narrow leather belt, her legs bare and tan, and her feet clad in comfortable leather sandals. I studied her body set in motion beneath the dress, leaving little for my imagination. On her way into the kitchen, she glanced back, knowing I witnessed her every movement. Her hair slid across her shoulder, and for a long moment, I admired her profile. "Cabernet...OK?"

Her voice tiptoed in my head. "That's fine," I said, "Everything's fine."

I drifted into the living room, pumped up like a teenager. Ten years was not enough time to snuff out a dream, or was it an obsession? I peered out the front window, watching a murder of crows rising from the distant row of almost denuded trees, and in that instant, suffered a pang of loneliness with thoughts of what might have been. Kathy returned, interrupting my brief regression. Hell, she was here. I was here. Suddenly, I was back on top of the world.

She sat beside me on the sofa, placing my glass of wine on the table. With her drink in hand, she kicked off her sandals, spun around, and crossed one leg over the other, facing me. I reached for my wine glass, nodded, and suggested a toast.

She considered the question. "Yes. A toast to 'destiny'. The creator of everything."

We clinked glasses. I sipped, but she drank as if she needed it.

"It's been one of those days, Alex. But now that you're here, we can relax."

For a minute or so, neither spoke. I admired the striking, bold-colored painting hanging before us; several similar paintings were displayed throughout the house. While the pictures related well to the modern motif of furnishing and lighting, they didn't convey a sense of harmony. Instead, they appeared to be calling out for attention. Then, two old friends talked at once, stopped, and started again. I prevailed. "Are all these paintings yours?"

She smiled. "Guilty as charged. My avocation. My salvation is painting. I am an artist."

I cocked my head. "I didn't know you had it in you."

Her eyes smiled at me over the rim of her glass. "There is much you don't know about me." She adjusted her position for a moment, briefly exposing her inner thigh, which didn't go unnoticed.

"Does Otto encourage your work?"

"It's our home..." her voice had a bite in it, "not his." She looked away. "He's accustomed to running his business, and our home is still a battleground for control. My opinions about the house may count more now, but it's always a hot topic. Over the past couple of years, he's lost some intensity. He's not quite the Otto I married." She paused.

Maybe I was supposed to follow up on her open-ended comment, but I only waited.

"But still, from a control standpoint, he's like your father. He likes to get what he wants. Thank God I've got my little studio in the back. I'll have to show it to you. It's quite comfortable."

I listened to her speak, not to the content, but rather her voice. It expressed her being, smooth, calming, sultry in an innocent way, somewhat controlling, but always unforgettable. Her voice was the one specific remembrance I retained in the ten years that separated today from our past. It settled into a corner of my mind, never forgotten, always available. I sat without speaking, gazing around the room, almost trancelike.

"Earth to Alex...come in."

"Sorry. It's been so many years. Did you ever think about me? About us?"

She rotated back to a seating position, setting her wine glass on the coffee table. Her head lowered as if in thought. Seconds passed before she glanced back at me. "Of course. I reran that tape many times. Did you?" she asked.

"Yes." Our eyes met. "Every time I thought about you, I tried to figure out what went wrong. Or just what happened."

"And?"

I set my glass on the table, reached out, and squeezed her hand. It rested on her knee, waiting. Not looking at her, almost talking to myself, I said: "It was never meant to be. It was the wrong time. I was the wrong me. And you were the wrong you. But knowing that didn't stop me from keeping you in my thoughts more often than I wanted."

"Is that why you didn't come to the wedding?"

The fair question needed an explanation. "You don't come to your brother's wedding wishing he would collapse at the altar." I chuckled to suggest I was joking. "To say the least. That's bad form. From a distance, I could have handled it...but up close and personal..." I shook my head. "It would have been torture."

She put her hand on mine. "Who knows what would have happened? That was five years ago. You were a grown man. You might have swept me off my feet and dragged me to your waiting limo, and we could have escaped."

Another chuckle with a follow-up excuse flew out of my mouth, "Not my style. I've never been the bold, brave hero type. I wasn't too busy, and I wasn't on an expedition. That wasn't the reason. I just found a bar and drowned myself in Scotch. Did you like my wedding gift?"

She nodded. "Napa was a second honeymoon for us, and we survived the hot air balloon flight. But what touched me were the bobblehead German troll dolls in our likeness, except Otto's head was twice the size of mine."

"Nasty. Wasn't it?"

"Fitting but nasty."

Kathy shook off my hand, got up, walked to the window, viewed the fountain, and studied the marble lady frozen in time, caught in an eternal moment of servitude to an unknown dominating male. "What did you mean? The wrong me and the wrong you.'"

I ran my hands through my hair and exhaled with a hint of exasperation. "Just bad timing. We were kids. Even though I'm a few years older, we were both too young to commit to anything. I've thought about this. A lot. And if I think back. I was a different person then. I didn't want to get tied up. I wanted to challenge the world. I wanted to do everything I'd done since then and more. And..." I couldn't disguise my embarrassment, "I think I harbored one of those Madonna complexes."

Looking back at me, she smiled. "You mean a Madonna-whore complex?"

I feigned indignity. "Well, you put it so bluntly. But whatever. I was conflicted. I wanted you, but couldn't commit because I was too young. We were both too young. Maybe I suffered from the psychological weaknesses of a confused young man, but in retrospect, I suspect you were not a Madonna. Were you?"

She smiled. "I'll try to break this to you, Alex."

"Go ahead."

She leaned her head back, searching for words, exposing her neck. "I was just becoming a woman. When we first met, I was eighteen. I was also looking to explore unknown worlds. And you, my dear Alex, were adorable...but a little too cautious."

I dropped my head, pretending to be wounded, and smiled. "Well, that was gentle. But I understand your point. As I said, that was the wrong me. Maybe not the wrong you. I don't know. You were you; I was me. Timing...not so good."

She sat beside me, sliding her body close to mine while putting her arm around my shoulders. "My poor little Alex. Was I too much for you?" She leaned in and dropped a kiss onto my cheek, her eyelash a butterfly alighting and flying away.

I couldn't take it. I kissed her on her neck, then whispered in her ear. "That's a memory I couldn't carry with me. Your smell. Your skin. Your hair." I reached out and grabbed her, pulling her into my chest and kissing her like never before. She responded with her passion unleashed. For a hot moment, we were a decade younger, living in the past, unaware of any restrictions, free of the present, and alive. But I caught a glimpse of something moving beyond the window, beyond the frozen lady, passing through the estate gate in the distance.

"What is it?" She said, gasping for air.

"Someone just pulled in the drive...black Mercedes?"

Her face answered without speaking. She stood, brushed her dress into place, settled her hair, and inquired as if there was more than one answer: "Am I OK?"

"You look marvelous. I wish you were mine."

She sat opposite me on the other sofa, took a drink, and returned the glass to the coffee table. To Otto, it would appear as if two people faced each other and sipped wine while conversing. Kathy slowed her breath and calmed herself. Even though Otto could not have seen us in our unexpected clinch, my heart fluttered. I enjoyed our moment of stolen romance.

The hall door clicked open, and a deep voice boomed out. "Where is he? Where is that rascal brother of mine?"

Kathy popped up to greet her husband while I held my place, waiting. Otto appeared wearing an expensive dark blue business suit, his coat unbuttoned, the collar of his starched white shirt loosened, and his maroon tie hung limply over his middle. He removed a pair of stylish sunglasses, stuffed them in his coat pocket, and surveyed the scene. He looked older, fatter, and paler than I remembered. Thin matted wisps of black hair spread unevenly across his broad, damp forehead, and his high cheekbones supported tired, puffy eyes. All this suggested he was neither fit nor fine. I suspected ten years of working with stiffs every day might do that. Otto had become the prototypical embodiment of a Midwestern mortician.

I see the party started without me. That's only fair. I'm late as usual." Without much thought, he brushed a kiss across Kathy's cheek and moved on to me. "Son of a gun. Give me a hug, Bro. I am happy to see you." We hugged. As Otto stepped back, his face hinted at a recognition of some sort. "Alex, you're looking a bit rough around the edges," he said, "got that mountain-man look."

I rubbed my chin whiskers and smiled. "At least I have some edges. I guess you're settling into married life." I patted my midsection, smiling again. "Regular meals, lawn people to cut the grass, and..." I looked around, my eyes stopping at Kathy. "Things are holding together. I assume business is booming at Naperville's finest funeral home?"

"As I always say, customers are dying to become our guests," said Otto.

I shook my head and smirked. "But those old jokes of yours never die."

"Hey...even my customers like that one. Been here long?" he asked.

I shrugged and let Kathy pick up the ball.

"Terry Walker got Alex," she said. "The train was a little late. But all went well. Alex was just explaining why he missed our wedding."

Otto laughed. "We already know. He was floating around on the Amazon River, fighting off wild beasts and taking pictures. Right?"

"I'm still working on that adventure, Otto. It was kind of a bust. We were all lucky to get back."

"Still thinking about our wedding? You missed that boat."

I smiled and cocked my head. "I do apologize. There is no good excuse. Sorry, I couldn't make it. At that moment, I was lost in a jungle."

My brother took one step and glanced back. "Let's not dwell on it. That was one hell of a wedding gift, Brother...you kill me." He turned again and walked out of the room, talking,

As he walked out, he coughed and coughed again. I had heard that cough before, mostly in third-world countries. It bothered me.

Chapter 5

Later, after eating Kathy's eco-friendly, doctor-approved dinner and washing it down with two bottles of not-so-healthy wine, our after-dinner words diminished. My mind drifted, and I caught myself focusing on Kathy, studying her like a beautiful puzzle to be solved or an adventure to be undertaken. I believed she had more to discuss with me, but her husband, my brother, sat between us at the head of the table. Escape was necessary.

"Well, I'm pooped. It was a long trip, so..."

Otto interrupted. "But could you and I spend a couple of minutes in my study? There are a few items that need to be discussed."

My face should have told him I was out of conversation.

He smiled. "I'll keep it short. Ten minutes, and we'll tuck you in for the night."

"OK."

Kathy got up and began bussing the table, waving me off when I attempted to assist.

I followed my brother into his office and closed the door. His oak desk was positioned in a three-window bay, with a seating area opposite. The walls were decorated with photos of Otto and our father, but none of Kathy. They all appeared related to the world of funeral homes except for a black-and-white Vietnam-era wartime picture of our father, Frederick, and two other soldiers, standing near a helicopter.

I dropped down onto the sofa, and the cushions sighed.

"Nightcap?" asked Otto. He looked at me, more comfortable now. I studied him for a moment, realizing that he most resembled our mother. His face was softer, rounder, and fleshier than mine. I had more of our father's look, sharper cheekbones, a hawkish nose, and an oval face like the old man. However, time was stealing the youth from both of us. In ten years, Otto had lost much of his vitality and strength. Maybe I looked that way to him. Who knows? The obvious after-work tension he exhibited when he first came home was gone; he was more relaxed now, but deep down, he simply looked tired. I was tired, he was tired, we should have called it a night. But we couldn't hide from the topic that had spurred me to return. We both knew it.

"Thanks, no," I answered regarding his offer of a drink. "I'm done for the night. What's cooking?"

"All business, huh?" Otto muttered as he sat next to me.

"Sorry. I'm just tired from the long train ride. Once you leave the mountains, there's not much to see between Denver and Naperville. Hundreds of miles of empty cornfields."

I gazed at him and could tell Otto had a lot on his mind. I waited.

Finally, he spoke: "He's dying."

I glanced down, then back at him. "How long?"

"Not long. Pancreatic cancer. It's terminal. You've come not a moment too soon. He's in a private hospice setting in his house. 24-hour attendants. He's comfortable, sort of mobile, and still feisty as ever."

Seconds passed. "No hope for recovery?"

"No. It's a curse and a blessing. His type of cancer is a quick killer."

"Can I talk with him?"

"Of course. That's why you're here. He wants to see you. You two have ten years to cover. I'm certain he'll also want to talk about money and wills rather than his condition. Unfortunately, you have to jump through one of his hoops to enter his domain. That's what he's like. Always in charge."

I nodded.

"Germaphobic. The fear of death has warped his mind."

"What?"

"It sounds crazy. He knows he's dying, but he screens anyone who visits...including family."

"Meaning what?"

"Well. You need to take a physical exam to prove you are germ-free."

"You're kidding."

Otto shrugged his shoulders. "Not to worry...I've set up a visit with my doctor. Dr. Jarek. Ten o'clock tomorrow morning. He'll give you a quick physical...no charge...off the books. And some kind of written statement proving you are harmless."

I rolled my eyes.

"Humor him." Otto shook his head.

"OK. I suppose a check-up wouldn't hurt. It's been a while. What else?"

"I can brief you on his financial situation."

I jumped in. "The business is yours, Otto. You busted your ass for years, keeping it going. I've never been interested. As far as I'm concerned. That's all yours and Kathy's."

Otto appeared to relax. He pushed back into the sofa, placing his hands behind his head. "I'm glad you feel that way. As far as I know, that's how it's going down. None to Kathy, though. Just me and you. Even though you got your share early and split, you'll get what you deserve. I'm not a mind-reader, but he's not going to stiff you. The old man has a decent portfolio. You're not missing anything. The business. Right now, he owns it. But I run it from top-to-bottom. It's a job...with decent pay, but lots of work. I like the challenge, and I didn't think you would be interested."

"Nope. I like what I'm doing. Casket-filling is not for me, Otto. I'm like Mom. And I'm not driven by money. How about Kathy? Does she work with you?"

Otto slid his hands down, leaned forward, looked toward me, and smiled. "I had a better idea. I built her an art studio out back, and she's quite content to stay out of my business. There's no money in art, but if she's happy...I'm happy. It's her hobby. Every so often, I arrange a show for her. Invite the right people. Some cocktails and *hors d'oeuvres,* and on rare occasions, someone will buy, or I'll find a strawman to buy one. Her paintings are displayed here as she likes. Not my taste, but people say they're quality stuff...not too long ago, she got a write-up in the local rag."

"I like them."

"That's not all you like." He smiled.

"Sorry..."

"Come on, Alex. I see how you look at her. Admit it. You're still carrying a torch. When you and I man-hugged, I noticed you were heavy with her lovely smell."

I didn't miss a beat. I also detected a smell when we hugged. The smell of cannabis, but I kept that to myself. "Hey, we shared a hug. But you got her. You won the prize. That's a fact. I hope you're treating her well."

"No worries. I treat her like a queen. I never say 'no'. My only problem is my health; with my bad heart, I can't keep her motor running. You know how she is." He raised his eyebrows. "You two were an item, right?"

"I'll take your word for it. I have no idea. We just dated off and on for a year. A decade ago."

Otto exhaled. "Well, she's like one of those Japanese bikes we used to ride. She runs fast and hot. I have to work to keep her happy. But I also have to watch my heart. I got medicines to smooth everything out. Too much sex and I might pop a blood vessel or something."

"Is it that bad?"

Otto froze as if he was digesting my question. "We're handling it. But I'll say this...if it became a matter of my life or death...I might let her play a bit outside my corral, but still on the ranch...if you know what I mean. If it ever gets to that, I'll keep you abreast." He chuckled.

I gave him the fisheye. "Kathy might have something to say about that."

He shook off the thought. "From experience, I can assure you she's not that picky. Forget it. It's all hypothetical. So suck it up. I'm not dead yet." He sounded wounded, but thick-skinned.

"I think we're both tired, Otto." I got up. It was a strange discussion, and not kind to Kathy or their relationship. But I was so exhausted I couldn't get any words out.

"Going to bed?" he asked.

"Yep. Long day."

"Sleep well. I put your bag in the bedroom. Top of the stairs. First one on the left."

Chapter 6

The next morning, I ordered a cab to take me to the doctor. I had a slight headache, and I continued to suffer train-lag if there was such a thing. The driver was a balding man, a talkative type in his forties. His head squeezed into a worn Cubs cap; his teeth clenched a dead cigar. He drove through Naperville delivering a non-stop and unrequested guided tour. A little cardboard Christmas tree hung from his rearview mirror and emitted an annoying chemical fragrance. I guess it was the smell of stale vanilla cupcakes. The tour included familiar places. To my left, the venerable mid-town cemetery wore a certain autumn emptiness, and, a few blocks later on my right, the redbrick buildings of the downtown high school appeared. I watched some students race around a track, a few boys tossed a football scoring imaginary touchdowns, and listless others milled about the entrance.

Memories of my hometown returned. Years ago, I departed Naperville determined to replace a boring present with an exciting future, and my plan worked. I became a successful writer and photographer for slick magazines and cable TV shows. Without my father and his business, I might be driving a cab, like my friend Terry. But my father, the indomitable Frederick Reinhart, funeral home impresario, needed someone to take over his business; I was not interested.

Nasty thoughts bubbled up. I relived painful images of my youthful first visit to the white-tiled back rooms of his funeral home. Dead people floating on stainless steel tables, each waiting for my father's trusted right-hand embalmer, Jan Gorger, to clean, powder, and dress them for their final stage appearances. I hated the family business. At the same time, I ended my on-again, off-again relationship with Kathy Price, a delicious dead weight that threatened to chain me forever to the insignificant tombstones of this little town on the prairie, while I dreamed of escaping to the pyramids on the Nile and the burial grounds of the Valley of the Kings. Ten years ago, I decided to escape, and my greatest personal achievement to date remains my abrupt termination of all connections with Naperville.

The driver's monologue continued. My mind wandered, and for fun, I interrupted him. "Remember Butch?"

He stopped in mid-sentence. "How's that?" he asked.

"Butch...Remember?" I paused. "You're a Redhawk, right?"

He thought for a moment, then chuckled. "You too?"

"No. I went to North. Zero-Eight."

"The Big Double Zero for me," he responded. "Hey, did you know Bob Odenkirk?"

"No. He was there way before my time."

"I heard he left town because he thought Naperville was boring," said the driver.

"No surprise there," I commented.

"What's that about Butch?" he asked.

I smiled. "You know the cute little Egyptian mummy sleeping under glass in the second-floor lobby at Central? She...I should say he...just had a birthday. He's about two thousand years old."

The driver pursed his lips. "Oh. That Butch." He joined the game. "Didn't look a day over fifteen hundred last time I saw it. Never could figure out what a real mummy was doing there. But I always thought it was a girl."

"I've done some research. The school ran some tests. It's a boy. Three-foot-six. About eight years old when he kicked the *shadoof* back in the day."

"Say what?"

"That's the name of an ancient Egyptian bucket."

"I get it." The driver smiled and studied his passenger in the rearview mirror. "Say...you're the reporter guy. I've seen your stuff on cable. You do the mummy stories. Sonofabitch. I'm Ted."

"Good meeting you, Ted...Alex Reinhart."

"Hey Alex, I'm sorry I treated you like a tourist. Been drivin' this hack for goin' on twenty-two years. I see a lot of people, including my share of old classmates. Not many famous former students. I guess only a few come home again. Chalk one up for me. Welcome home."

"Not a problem. Go, Redhawks!"

"Go Huskies!" The driver shook his head and flipped up his hand as if to suggest I made his day. " Butch..." he mumbled. "Forgot all about him."

The two native Naperville men rode in silence for a few minutes. "Here ya go, my friend." He pulled in front of a long, plain brick, punched-windowed, two-story façade in downtown Aurora on the banks of the Fox River, straight west of Naperville. I paid Ted, adding a ten-dollar tip, wished him well, exited, and checked my watch. I arrived early and was in no hurry to enter the building.

I had been dropped into the heart of the City of Aurora, second in population to Chicago and full of big-city action; I knew it well, and I decided to walk into my past. The fast-moving Fox River forked around Stolp Island, a modest lozenge of land filled with a melange of buildings: former warehouses and mills, theaters, parking structures, and a riverboat casino. I headed for the nearest bridge linking the island to the land to the east. Aurora was quite different than Naperville. I stood on one of the many bridges and viewed the old Fox flowing beneath me, sliding cold and fast through a shallow canyon of buildings, unlike Naperville's DuPage River, which wiggled through lush forests and rolling glens. Historically, blue-collar workers and their factories lined the banks of this lusty river town. When the natives of my hometown, including the comrades of my youth, tired of Mom and apple pie, they drifted a few miles west to Aurora for a night of exciting entertainment, gambling, and booze. Long ago, it provided me with an introduction to the real world beyond the Naperville womb and helped kindle my quest to travel and explore. The pleasant bit of mental time travel put me in a better mood for the task ahead. I disliked doctor's visits; nothing useful ever came of them. This would be no exception.

As I ambled back toward Otto's personal doctor's office, the older building suggested it was occupied by medical professionals who relied on the backstop of Medicare to create new clients rather than reputation or skills. The lobby elevator door opened, but one look inside the scruffy mini-lift told me it deserved a break. I may have been locked in a closet as a youngster; I've always suffered from claustrophobia, so I climbed the stairs to the second floor. Like the first floor, this one was dismal. Chipped vinyl tile corridor floors, unprotected painted gypsum wall, all capped by a cheap acoustical tile ceiling wearing a grid of surface-mounted fluorescent lights.

I entered through a wood and glass door into a modest waiting room decorated with stock framed images of sailboats, faraway lands, and smiling people, a minimal improvement. At least the place appeared clean. Behind a sliding window sat an attractive, young, blue-eyed blonde woman. She glanced up and smiled. Nice straight teeth, the product of concerned parents, no doubt.

"Alex Reinhart, for Dr. Jarek." I spotted her name on the white plastic badge pinned to the left of the second unbuttoned button of her too-tight white blouse.

"Oh...you're the other Mr. Reinhart?"

I smiled. "I guess I am."

After checking her appointment book, she gave me the usual clipboard, documents, and brochures.

"Thanks, Nora."

She smiled. "Just ask if you need anything."

Sitting in one of the many empty chairs, I flipped through the papers, filling in the blanks and signing without much thought until I reached the last page, an organ donor agreement form. I remembered this popping up before in Denver when I said 'no' on the application for a Colorado driver's license. I was in a hurry then, but I remember evaluating and denying the gifting of my body parts. To me, it wasn't a 'well, what the hell'decision. I returned the completed documents to the blonde but kept the little 3-fold brochures, something to read while I waited. One was labeled *Your Family Doctor*, another *Visiting the Elderly*, and the last and most intriguing was *Life Goes On*. Thinking about my father, I read the words in detail because they had meaning. After all, I was only getting this physical exam to satisfy my father's demands, as usual. The brochure covering visitation cautioned everyone to wash their hands, wear a mask, and maintain one's distance. If my father were to be considered, the writers might have added 'wear boxing gloves'.

The last document provided better reading. It was a heartwarming story about an attractive but ill middle-aged woman who needed a kidney transplant to save her life. She was on the national waiting list, but the demand far exceeded the number of donors. According to the brochure, more than twenty-five people could benefit from a single donor. I didn't think I had that many organs. All of this was new to me. The article suggested checking 'all' rather than specifying body parts. It also noted that six thousand people a year die while waiting for an organ. I was glad I was not hanging on, hoping for such a miracle.

"Mr. Reinhart..." The sweet voice of the young woman brought me to attention. She directed me to enter a nearby door.

I entered and found myself face to face with an imposing figure of a tall man, about six-feet-two, broad-chested, tanned, and muscular, in his early forties. Jarek wore bright white doctor garb pressed and cleaned to military standards. His dramatic face gripped his well-placed bone structure, like a manikin with a pencil mustache. Well-groomed, his dense black hair was cut in the latest style of macho men. He introduced himself, did not offer a hand to shake, and showed me to an exam room.

"Otto always speaks of you with admiration. He told me of your writing and photography achievements. However, my work does not permit me to indulge in many outside interests." He smiled, but his cold, dark brown, almost black eyes offered no glimmer of pleasure. His voice revealed a hint of a suppressed accent.

I said: "I'm sorry to bother you. I'm sure my brother informed you of my father's strange request."

"Strangeness is a common feature of people when they reach a certain age. And those who are accustomed to controlling their interactions with others. I must admit I have some of that attitude, so I can empathize. In any case, I am not your father's physician, so I leave any evaluation to others." With one elbow on the arm of his chair, he put his hand to his chin, almost fist-like, exposing a clunky gold signet ring forced over a knotty finger joint. "But today, we evaluate...you. Right?"

"Sure. Just the minimum to satisfy my father's paranoia."

The doctor nodded. "You were admiring my ring."

I wondered about that but decided to go along. "It's a beauty. Nice etching."

Jarek smiled. "An award I received last year. From the medical association. Physicians who have demonstrated their commitment to patient care through continuing medical education. This ring symbolizes their recognition and my commitment to the profession."

"A caduceus..."

"Excellent, Mr. Reinhart. You are my only patient today. So there is no rush. We'll let's begin."

Dr. Jarek gave me the usual exam. I told him about my last visit to a doctor, over a year ago, in France. Jarek shrugged his shoulders, surmising the exam would not be helpful. He questioned me about my health, medications, and family history and checked my blood pressure, temperature, and oxygen. He keyboarded all the data into his computer. "It is rare that we find someone of your age to visit us who is not taking any medications or involved with chemical substances." He waited as if expecting a response and then continued to enter information.

"The only meds I took were prescribed for me in Egypt. I picked up some kind of stomach bug from the water of the Nile. Couldn't get rid of it. Dogged me for months. But the meds didn't help. Only time fixed the problem."

"All well now?" He asked.

"No problem. That was a couple of years ago. I lost some weight, but most of it returned."

I lay on the exam table as Jarek listened to my heart with the scope on my chest and back, tapped my back with a knuckle, and then probed my abdomen for irregularities. "You may sit up. Please have a seat in the chair again. I would like to take a blood sample if that is acceptable to you."

My facial response must have told a story.

"I'm sorry," said Jarek, no doubt sensing my resistance, "but there's a reason Otto asked me to do your physical. I realize you're visiting your father tomorrow, and the blood sample tests are useless."

"So why do useless tests? I asked.

Jarek smiled a knowing smile. "The test results are overkill, but we are not dealing with a person with normal thoughts. This is a man who is suffering from a death sentence of cancer. He fears communicable diseases. He is hanging on to every second of his life. Blood tests can reveal HIV, hepatitis, syphilis, Lyme disease, malaria, and tuberculosis. You may not have any of these, but your father is careful...maybe too cautious...but his mind is working. Your brother and his wife both had blood tests. Your father's nurse will check everything before you are admitted. I must report that your tests were taken. If not, he won't let you in the door. It's unlikely any of these diseases would be transmitted, even if found. Still, we have to do the tests only to allow you to see your dying father. Now, I have to keep my records proper, which means I will have to report lab results, which I assure you will be negative. Do you get the picture, Alex?"

I nodded. He took blood samples. I wasn't pleased. "Now give me about ten minutes, and I will finish this report and give you two signed copies, and you will be on your way. Satisfactory?"

"I guess I passed the exam?"

"Of course."

We walked out together to the waiting room.

"Make yourself a coffee or grab a soft drink from the refrigerator." Jarek nodded in the direction of the glass-doored mini-fridge in the corner.

I settled in with a cup of coffee and a view of the blonde. As I was downing the last gulp of the coffee, Dr. Jarek returned and handed me a manila envelope containing two report copies.

"Thanks, Doctor. One last question, if I may."

"It all depends. What is it?"

"My brother. He said he was under some kind of treatment for his heart. Can you tell me about it? Is it serious?"

Jarek frowned. "First, Otto has another doctor, a specialist, who is treating him. And," he shook his head a little, "I cannot discuss your brother's health issues. That's just the way it is. Any questions you may have, please ask him or Kathy."

My gaze wandered away from the doctor, and I noted that the blonde seemed to be tuning into our conversation. I turned back to the doctor. "I get it. I'll talk to Kathy. She may be able to help me understand. I'm just concerned about Otto...and Kathy, for that matter."

Jarek nodded. "It is right for you to be concerned, but soon, you will leave town and head back to Colorado. Correct?"

It seemed like he was on a fishing expedition. I clarified my situation. "Even if I'm back home. I can be back here in a day."

"That is comforting. I know Kathy. If anything happened to Otto, I promised I would help her as if she were family. We are all very close."

"Thanks, Doc," I said, holding up the envelope, "for the keys to the kingdom." I glanced over to the blonde as I walked out and gave her a smile and a wave. She exposed her fine white teeth and returned the wave while the sullen-faced Dr. Jarek drifted back into the back room.

Chapter 7

In the backseat of another taxi, I returned to Naperville. Spontaneously, I directed the driver to turn into the downtown cemetery. Since I was coming home and visiting everyone in the family, dead or alive, it made sense. Large elms full of fall color, one after the other, hugged the blacktop roadway edges forming a continuous arch above. Sunlight filtered through the trees, flashing intermittently in my eyes. I squinted and struggled to remember the location of my mother's grave. It was a mystery, but I believed I would recognize it. I sorted the markers, hoping something would strike a chord, granite towers, obelisks, and slabs, but nothing looked familiar.

Almost twenty years ago, in her early forties, she died. Memories of that week spilled out as the taxi crawled through the vast, treed burial grounds. I remember listening to her crying often, alone in her bedroom, drinking, and waiting for Frederick to come home from work or wherever. She talked to herself loud enough for me to discern all the words about bodies, embalming fluid, pancake makeup stains, and comments about his hands 'carrying the touch of the dead.' I was too young to piece everything together, but my parents' relationship was disturbing. The two of them argued often. They were civilized about it, always waiting until the boys were asleep. Otto slept through these battles, but I did not. I lay awake listening, guessing my father was not faithful and that my mother might let that pass, but she hated everything about the family business. She existed in a mental prison. For my father, Reinhart Funeral Home and Crematory was everything. That was clear.

I discovered her body on the floor of our home on the day before Halloween. She sat on the floor with her back to the wall, head down, body limp, scrunched down into a ball of despondent humanity. She left no note, no explanation, but even as a boy, I pieced her last thoughts together before she popped the pills, delivering her to Heaven's Gate. My father, Otto, and I returned from a late-fall week-long fishing trip to northern Wisconsin. When we pulled into the driveway, I jumped out and rushed upstairs to show my mother. I held my trophy fish tight to my chest, a newspaper-wrapped eighteen-inch largemouth bass. I thought my fish prize might stink a little, having been out of the water for a day. It may have, but its odor was lost amidst the putrid stench of decaying human flesh filling the upper floor of our home. When I realized my mother's green-skinned body was the source of the abomination, I dropped the fish onto the bedroom floor and ran out of the room. I never forgot that smell of death.

The last time I visited this cemetery, I was a young teenager, riding in the back of a black Cadillac with my brother and father. Fortunately, the memories had faded. I asked the driver to drop me off at the cemetery office. A few minutes later, I walked out with a small paper map of the area, my mother's grave marked with an 'X', reducing the challenge of finding the grave to a map-reading exercise. I'm good with maps after having worked for two years as a ranger in the national forests of Colorado and later traveling around the world exploring and documenting exotic locations. I found her grave. The pedestal-style red granite tombstone and base read: *Virginia Reinhart, Beloved Wife and Mother, January 17, 1955- October 25, 2003.* The left side pedestal remained a blank slate, awaiting the details of the impending death of my father.

For a few minutes, I stood before the grave, sort of praying, comfortable in the woodsy environment, forgetting my current situation before I remembered my father's death would return me to this same spot sooner or later. I held a quiet, smoldering rage, always seeing her death as a personal injustice. Before leaving, I patted the top of her tombstone and said: "Goodbye."

Chapter 8

The driver dropped me near the marble lady, still pouring water in front of my brother's house. A yellow sticky note on the front door drew my attention: *Alex. I'm in the back. In my studio. Come on down and grab a bite to eat. Kathy.*

I pulled the note off the door and put it into my front pants pocket before wandering around the house on a stone path leading toward the river. As I walked past the back of the old house, I checked out the contemporary addition attached to the rear of the Victorian mansion. It had a large wooden deck that overlooked a wide swath of neatly mowed lawn terminating in a copse of trees at the river below. The glass and stucco structure accommodated all the pleasures denied the original residents: flat-screen televisions, comfortable open spaces, efficient, pretty kitchens filled with time-saving equipment, and upstairs giant bathrooms with whirlpool baths, multi-showers, Euro-toilets, and mirrors ten times the size available to the original turn-of-the-century owners. The final touch was a master bedroom bigger than any slept in by the kings and queens of Europe and an overgrown master closet, a stable for clotheshorses. All this, and somehow, the architect for the addition designed the new appendage to complement the vintage building and not overpower it.

As I walked along moving downhill now, enjoying the quintessential Midwestern fall day, a rare event with temperatures in the mid-seventies and a few random floating fluffy clouds cruising the blue sky. Trees burst with color, and a warm, comforting sun blazed above. This seasonal joy would disappear in a few weeks, replaced by the harsh reality of four months of winter. But today, magic is in the air. I strolled the small clearing in the wooded landscape. To my right, the dusky Du Page River slid along, heading south to seek connection with other rivers beyond. Upstream in the distance, the bridge crossed the river leading to town, but without traffic or noise. The scene was idyllic. Too bad Otto had to spend his days in his funeral home surrounded by death. Today was a special day to be alive.

She stood on the deck of the little building sitting at the rear of the clearing, her studio, a modern-day Marie Antoinette playhouse. Also of contemporary design, the playful box of a building clad in narrow, light-colored wooden boards on three sides had a continuous porch that ran along the front with a strip of clerestory windows above. Three wooden columns supported the porch roof, simple round tubes painted bright blue. A single plane of shiny grey metal sloping down from front to back served as a roof. The façade and its glazing, framed with yellow metal tubing, faced north. Below the clerestory, translucent glass allowed light to pass through but concealed the interior of the space beyond. 'Marie' waved to me. As I approached, I admired her down-home attire, clinging pre-shrunk blue jeans with a red-checkered blouse that pulled tight with each waving movement. I was captivated by the tiny house and its lovely owner.

"I'm here for lunch, ma'am. And I'm a mighty hungry hombre."

"Come on in, pardner," she said with a smile. In the center bay of the porch, two chairs at a round table adorned with a single red rose in a cut-glass base and an open bottle of red wine suggested a romantic lunch. "Let's sit and have a glass of wine," she said as she sat.

"Otto's not joining us?" I positioned myself while she poured the wine.

"You're funny, Alex. He called to say he'll be home late tonight. As usual. A meeting with Jarek. Will you miss him?"

"Late night meeting with his doctor? Seems weird."

Kathy shrugged her shoulders. "Those two are planning something, but I haven't been let in. Anyway, while he's scheming with Dr. Jarek, we can catch up on old times."

I smiled. "Like yesterday?"

"That was a start. Did it bring back memories?" she asked.

I thought for a moment. "Crazy stuff. All those years. They disappeared in seconds."

"That was nice..."

We sat across from each other, our knees almost touching. The grassy meadow sloped down to the river. The river water shimmered as if alive, with the sunlight catching every ripple in the gentle breeze. A couple of white ducks drifted south on the sleepy river. Her voice floated in my head, and I turned to face her. "I'm sorry. Did you say something?"

She chuckled. "Pretty nice out here..."

Lost in a vision of perfection, her flawless face, smile, hair, and mysterious green eyes, I relaxed.

We clicked our wine glasses, "to the most beautiful girl I ever met."

She flipped her head back, filled my view with her wildness, and regrouped. "Wow," she said. "You are a charmer today. Yesterday's little kiss might have awakened old buried spirits."

Was she joking? She was always mischievous. "You know you're playing with fire. Don't you?"

She ran the top of her foot up and down the inside of my calf. Again, she tortured me.

"Kathy...Kathy...Kathy..."

"Yes, Alex," she said, her voice lilting and suggestive.

"What are you up to?"

She giggled. "How about you? Feeling up?" Without waiting for an answer, she declared, "Our lunch. Be back in a second." She entered the little building and returned with two plastic baskets filled with sandwiches and chips. She placed them on the table.

"No fancy cooking out here. The kitchen in my studio is for coffee and drinks. Off and on, we use this as a second seating area. When we have a yard party. People like coming down here to let down their hair." She stopped herself and got lost in thought. "But not so much anymore," she mumbled.

We ate without much conversation. I tested the waters with general questions about her life and marriage, leading to a more open discussion. My brother's health was worse than had been suggested, and clearly, Kathy was, at least at the moment, unhappy and unsatisfied. As I peeled back the onion of truth, I sensed she was sliding toward tears. I didn't want her to cry. I flipped the conversation around and related some tall tales about my travels to Africa, Mexico, and South America. She was a good listener. When necessary, I could tell an exciting and humorous story. The attention-diverting method and the wine worked. Two old friends, not quite lovers, moved closer to a singular moment. The food was eaten, and the wine was absorbed along with the sun, the gentle fall breeze, and a picturesque scene of natural delight. Everything co-mingled to rekindle our latent emotions and increase our anticipation.

Kathy stood. We gathered the baskets, silverware, glasses, and the empty wine bottle. In a schoolgirl voice, she proclaimed, "I'll show you my home away from home. Come in, Alex."

I held the screen door open, followed her, and set the baskets on the counter. I looked around and checked out the large art studio to my left, a perfect place for an artist to create. Diffuse light flooded the room. The plank and beam wooden ceiling and the walls were painted white, and atop the wood-planked floor lay sheets of protective canvas. An easel held Kathy's current project, now devoid of any paint save for gesso. "Waiting for inspiration?" I joked as she turned away from the kitchen counter.

She took two steps and pressed hard against my body, reaching behind me, her hands resting low on my back. She looked into my eyes. "I've been stuck, but now I have my inspiration." She let her hands slide down a few inches, grabbed my butt cheeks, and squeezed. "Right here."

I reached around and pulled her tight. Her soft body met mine. We kissed for the second time, amplified by her right knee, which found its way into my crotch.

"Where to?" I said.

"Behind you," she said breathlessly. "Down the hall. Keep walking until you bump into the bed. Pull off your clothes and buckle up, cowboy."

I followed orders and lay on her bed, staring at the ceiling, watching the rust-colored treetops wave rhythmically in the wind. Excited but peaceful, I listened. She closed the entry door, bolting the lock noisily, declaring our privacy. In some way, her preparation, like a warrior expecting trouble and cocking her gun, quieted my mind.

She appeared, but most of her clothes had disappeared. My eyes filled with delight and lust at the sight of her; her eyes wandered over my naked body, from head to toe, then back to my 'proof of life'. She smiled. "I sense you want to go for a ride." She taunted me by half-bending, reins held, pretending she was riding a horse. Next, she did a little dance, stripping off her bra and panties and tossing the latter in my face for laughs. I grabbed the sensuous morsel and tossed it away, but not before sniffing it for effect. The effect was immediate. "Come here, Kathy. I've been waiting for this my entire life."

She slid into bed and pressed up against my body. We were comfortable, like we had always been more than just friends. But there was something special in our relationship that had been denied for stupid, now insignificant reasons. All was in the past. Our relationship only awaited fulfillment.

She slid her hand down. "Aha...our friend is ready, but are you?"

"Fuck you," I said as a promise and a threat. I rolled over atop her hot, squirming body and delivered the long answer. My response was intense, aggressive, wild, and sometimes controlled, but loving in every way, I think. Our excitement ended in sleep.

The room darkened. Outside, black clouds appeared in the high windows, the wind bent the tops of trees, and the first few raindrops hit the roof. Something caused her to slowly awaken. She was rolled over to one side, one arm tucked under her head, and the other arm outstretched with fingers extended. I sat on the bottom of the bed, toying with the toes of her right foot. It was a pretty sight, well-tanned for a Midwestern foot, and the nails were professionally manicured and clear-coated. My eyes followed the long leg up and stared at the length of her smooth, beautiful body, from her toes to her head, now wrapped in a wildness of auburn hair. It was a unique opportunity to see her completely at peace, her body warm, soft, and satiated. I wanted this memory.

She stirred, stretched, and eased up on one elbow. "What are you doing?"

"I'm looking at all of you. I want to remember this time forever."

"Stop playing doctor. Come here."

I lay next to her. "Weather changed," I said. "It's going to rain."

"Rain is my friend," she said as the drops became pronounced rainfall. "I like my studio. It smells of life...warm and cozy and all mine. Like you."

I rested on one elbow and caressed her. "Don't be so cocky."

"Look who's talking," Her eyes danced, and we kissed again. "You know. When we were younger, you could have had me at any time. It's too bad."

"That's history. I'm a pinch-hitter now. Your star player is injured, and they brought me up from the minors."

"You're so full of it. Alex, you were the only one I ever wanted to play with in the late innings."

"You're the one rewriting history. You loved the pickup games. Pun intended."

She smiled. "Hey, a woman has her needs."

"Whatever."

Kathy thought for more than a moment, gave me a deadpan look, and said: "Maybe we could get rid of him like in one of those film *noir* movies of the 1940s."

"Get rid of who?"

"Otto. Of course. Who do you think? Fate returned you to me. You cannot deny fate."

"You're fantasizing now. Crazy but beautiful. Today you are my love. You've always been my love. But we can't live our lives backward."

"Why not?" Her words drifted out as verbal soap bubbles, floating wisps of hope, popping and fading into reality.

I kept my thoughts close. Kathy, my impossible dream couldn't exist on false hope. We were fellow travelers on the same train. Beneath all her pleasant words, I sensed a desperate need for someone or something to free her from her circumstances. Killing Otto was not one of my thoughts, but anything short of murder that led to a life with Kathy was on the table. What? Thinking about this might kill me. I quit and dropped my head back on the pillow. We lay speechless, our naked bodies touching, lost in our thoughts, listening to the rain tapping on the roof, the wind rustling the treetops, and our hearts beating.

Chapter 9

Dr. Stephan Jarek knew what he liked, and he certainly liked Otto's country club. Their dining table offered a view overlooking the golf course. The rainstorm had blown through, the late evening sun cast deep shadows, and aside from a smattering of fallen leaves, the greens appeared slow but playable. The two men sat next to each other at the quiet corner table, and they watched one of the last foursomes of the day hit their approach shots to the 18th green. The dining room, a gracious, carefully detailed, and comfortable environment, was filled with club members and their friends. Jarek recognized some of them by reputation as movers and shakers. To Jarek, they all had that 'of course, I'm a member of the club' look about them. This was a look Jarek wanted to acquire.

"Kathy and I had our wedding reception here," said Otto.

"This is a wonderful facility."

"Wait until you eat the food. None better," said Otto.

"Can anyone join this club?"

Otto smiled. He raised his hand and rubbed his thumb against the two somewhat fat fingers of his right hand as he answered. "If you have the funds and the board believes you would be a good addition. They may even have a waiting list. I'm not sure. Our family are members forever."

Jarek stopped rubber-necking. "In a couple of years, after you and I have our little enterprise up and running, I would like to join you. I suppose your recommendation wouldn't hurt." He smiled.

"That would be my pleasure, Stephan...I would love to...if I'm still around."

A waiter arrived with a bottle of wine, uncorked it, poured two glasses, and Otto ordered some appetizers. "We want to talk for a while before we enjoy dinner."

"Yes, Mr. Reinhart. Of course," said the waiter who was about the same age as Otto. He nodded and slid away.

"I'll bring you up to date on our property search. All right?" said Jarek.

Otto nodded. "We've got plenty of time."

Jarek kept his inner thoughts to himself. "Well, I have found a suitable building in Aurora. It's just east of the river, about ten minutes upstream from my office. The zoning checks out. The real estate agent gave me a tour. The building appears solid, and it's priced within our budget. It's smaller than we will need, but there's plenty of room on the site to expand."

"Sounds like it should work. You haven't discussed our business plans with the real estate guy?" asked Otto.

"I would not do that. But we should put in our offer soon. And we'll need to deliver an earnest money deposit. Is that a problem?"

"No. Not an issue. How fast can we fit it out?"

"I talked with the contractor," said Jarek, "we don't have that much work to do. It's a substantial open space without windows. But it already has toilet facilities and a few small offices. We'll need to install our equipment. Some new partitions, lighting, electrical, and ventilation work. The building's only about fifteen years old. The current owner uses it as a warehouse for his retail business in Aurora."

"Show it to me next week. OK?"

"Certainly, Otto."

The waiter returned and filled their glasses.

"I'd like to get some cash flow going. Any reason we couldn't start operations by working out of our funeral home?" asked Otto.

"That's up to you...and your father." Jarek's comment was a question and a statement.

Otto sipped his wine, then shook his head. "It's up to me. I'm running the show now. My father is, of course, dying. He is not aware of our venture. And the remodeled space adjacent to the embalming area is finished. We can put that to use at any time. It would be useful to learn the ropes using that space until we complete the purchase and the build-out of the Aurora building."

"That sounds like a plan," said Jarek. "We can run for a few months, in the new improvements area, and then shift over."

"Are your med-tech guys ready to begin work?" asked Otto, his voice revealing his business instincts activating.

"Yes, they are, and the paperwork is settled."

"OK...a little toast to success?" Otto raised his glass, and they toasted. "Now, Doctor, it's time to discuss my problem."

Their waiter returned and set down their appetizers and their dinner orders.

Otto appeared hungry, nervous, or both. He downed the last of his wine, squeezed a lemon slice onto his dish of calamari, and dug in. "So? What about it?" He asked, not bothering to finish chewing his fried squid.

Jarek tried not to watch his friend masticate while he thought of how to approach the next subject. "I spoke with Dr. Rickenbacker. He didn't pull any punches with me, and I won't either. You are not a healthy man, Otto. And your medical situation is nearing a critical phase."

Otto dabbed his mouth with a napkin. "Not much worse than before. I do get short of breath. And I find my fingers swelling at night. But..."

"You have a terminal disease. Period. Rickenbacker reviewed your tests. The results indicate that all the negative symptoms are building. Eisenmenger Syndrome, as I'm sure Doctor Rickenbacker explained, is a process of intensifying pressure on your heart, lungs, and vessels. You have always had the problem."

"Tell me about it," said Otto, chewing on his squid. "You know I had open-heart surgery when I was ten. That was supposed to fix my problem."

Jarek cocked his head. "It's possible it may have arrested the symptoms. But the only current effect of that surgery may be to make it more difficult for you to acquire another donor heart and lungs. Or it might harm your insurability."

"You think I have to have a transplant?" Otto asked the question like he was wondering about the current weather conditions.

Jarek took a deep breath; sometimes it's best to serve up bad news in a cold-hearted manner, and Otto appeared not to have grasped the situation. "Let's put it this way. Without a transplant, the odds are that you won't survive the grand opening of our new business."

"Jesus." Otto leaned back in his chair and stared into space. Jarek didn't rush him. He understood Otto was one of those people who attacked problems head-on, fixed them, and then moved on to the next one. But this problem might not allow another one to appear. He let him absorb the full thrust of his statement. "So there's no way around this?"

"If you delay, your condition will continue to worsen. In some ways, this might increase the likelihood that you will receive a donor organ, but relying on the increased odds because you are nearer death is a risky game. The reality facing you is that even if you do sign up with the national organ donation system, you have only put your name on a list. Then you have to figure out how to pay for it. We're talking five hundred thousand to a million."

"Insurance?" Otto's breathing quickened.

"Have you checked into this question with your insurance rep? You should."

"No. I haven't told anyone about this. It's driving me nuts. I can't sleep. Shit, for all I know, Kathy might leave me if she finds out. She's not happy with the way things are right now."

Jarek stiffened, and he suspected Otto's fear was well-founded. "Not to be too blunt. But her happiness is not the issue now. You want to live. I want to start our new business. Kathy will have to find other ways to satisfy her needs." Jarek thought he had the solution to that problem.

Otto swallowed hard. "That's a blunt assessment, Stephan."

"I'm sorry, Otto. It is what it is." Jarek didn't want to sugarcoat the severity of his patient's dilemma. Too much was at stake. He and Otto had planned their project for over a year. He saw it as a sure thing that would allow him to step up in financial status and move from the government pawn he had become to a successful business person. "What about your father's estate? That might ease the financial aspect of the operation."

"I don't know the details because my father likes to keep everything under his hat. But I'm assuming I will receive half of his estate. He's been a savvy investor. He also has some life insurance. So there's money there. But that can't be rushed. He has no idea about our business venture, and I don't want him to know about the need for a transplant. You don't understand my father. Until he dies, the business is his. He can call the shots. If he senses weakness, he will take over. Cancer or not..."

The doctor held his words as the waiter delivered their dinner, and neither man spoke until the waiter left. Jarek broke the silence. "That is it, Otto. The timing of the transplant is not in your hands. You're dealing with a bureaucracy that doesn't care about you. You cannot rush it. You cannot will it. It's not like one of your normal business problems. So don't think of it that way. You might have to think out of the box."

Otto poked at his food. Jarek's words caught hold. "What do you mean?"

Jarek leaned back. "I'm thinking off the cuff here. For sure, this is not medical advice. But you're aware I have contacts with medical people living here who had practices or worked in the former Eastern Bloc?"

"Of course. The new guys who will work for us in our venture."

Jarek took his time. He wanted Otto to believe that he concocted his new idea on the spur of the moment. "Just thinking here, Otto...not med-techs, but an actual medical team. Cardiothoracic surgeons, anesthesiologists, perfusionists, and nurses. And of course, you would have to secure a heart and lungs if those are required."

"Secure a heart. From where?"

Jarek started to dig into his dinner and took a bite. "It's a crazy idea. But they are available. Google it."

"You can buy a heart online?"

Jarek smiled and continued to eat. "Eat your dinner, Otto. We can talk and eat."

Otto picked at his food and nibbled.

"That's better. Relax. Yes. Organs are available online and delivered to your door. From God knows where. But we're just talking." Jarek sipped his wine. "It's illegal here to buy an organ...period. That approach is not possible. The only legal way to find a heart and have it transplanted is to follow through with the national organ donor process."

"I'm confused. You're just joking about buying a heart, getting a medical team together, and operating outside the normal system?"

"I wouldn't say joking," said Jarek, "just my way of making you aware of what you are up against. The medical system is unaccommodating, the supply of organs is limited, and even if you were the richest man in the world, you couldn't buy a heart for a transplant. You would be breaking the law. The system controls everything. It's a wonderful business, but only for a few lucky recipients. Worldwide, every year, a million patients need an organ, but only one hundred thousand succeed."

"And the others?"

Jarek shrugged. "They die."

Otto's eyes scanned the dining room, hoping something useful would pop into his head.

"Wait a minute. I thought the entire organ donation system was controlled by the medical community. They wouldn't allow me to bring my own donor heart to the hospital for installation by their teams. Everything is run through the national organ donation system, right?"

"Yes."

"I get it. I could go to another country and have the procedure done."

"No. I wouldn't suggest that. Every country plays the same game. You can't cheat or bribe your way to the front of the line. Your chances of having a transplant here are the same or better than in other countries. And there are many side issues. Like insurance and follow-up treatment."

"So, I'm fucked," Having said the word, Otto peeked around the room to make sure no one heard him. No one seemed to care about his expression of frustration. "Are you telling me that I could have Elon Musk money and still be unable to buy a new heart?"

"Not legally. Think, Otto. Back to reality. It sounds like you can solve the money problems, insurance questions aside. But we have no real control over the timing and delivery of a donor heart. It must be the right heart. The blood type and size must be compatible with your body."

"Blood type, I get...but size?"

"Well, you couldn't put a young boy's heart in your body. Or a small woman." Jarek smiled. "But opposite sex donors are more likely to fail. So, the heart would have to come from a male donor with a body similar to yours in size and weight."

"Exact?"

"No. Close is good enough."

"Would a donor of your size work? Or are you too big?

Jarek thought. "I think I'd be close enough, Otto, but I'm not offering." He chuckled.

"So there should be lots of hearts out there in guys about our height and build?"

"I agree." Jarek sensed that Otto was anxious to simplify all the factors involved. "It sounds easy. But there are other issues. There are delivery times and other practicalities. To avoid rejection, the old rule for a cold heart was four to six hours between point A and point B. Therefore, our male donor has to live...or die relatively close. I think it might be possible to extend the time limits with new procedures that allow for the delivery of a beating heart."

Otto stopped eating and leaned back. "So what are you suggesting with your team of rogue Eastern Bloc doctors?"

"I'm not suggesting anything, just thinking out of the box. A fascinating idea."

"The only box I want to stay out of is a casket. Think out of that box."

Jarek chuckled, then dabbed his mouth with a napkin. "Imagine we assemble the finest team of skilled foreigners, find the right heart, and set up shop in your new space that you just finished. Oh...and we buy or rent the right equipment. And we do the transplant on *your* schedule...not their schedule."

"Are you for real?"

"Otto, it's just an idea." He shook his head. "A fantasy. I hate to think of you watching the clock, waiting for some guy somewhere within two-hundred-fifty miles to die, leaving a heart to be donated to someone. And some computer algorithm runs the numbers and decides that you can continue living." He pursed his lips. "And I'm a doctor. But that is what the system offers. It's not much more than a hope and a prayer."

Otto took and released a deep breath. "Of course, you're trying to be helpful, Stephan. But we have to deal with reality."

Jarek appeared humbled. "You're right. Let's at least enjoy our meal. And I do recommend you sign up for the national organ donation list tomorrow. Time is running out."

"Sign up," Otto muttered the words, his eyes glazed over. Someone seeing him might guess he was about to walk to the gallows.

Chapter 10

B orrowing Kathy's blood-red Mini Cooper, I left before Otto came home and drove downtown to meet Terry Walker for drinks. The streets were still wet from the storm, but drying quickly in the trailing gentle breezes from the southwest. From what I could see and hear, the rain showers passing through had not dampened the festivities. I parked in a remote lot and drifted toward the noise, music, lights, and smoke; the area was jammed with people having fun.

Naperville's Oktoberfest was a make-believe version of a European village square. Big tents, small tents, and mobile food trucks filled an open grassy area. Smoke from broiling brats and frankfurters billowed out and drifted up past the party lights into the black sky. The visitors swelled and surged in their traditional green, grey, and brown Bavarian mountain hats, some sporting suspended lederhosen, multicolored hiking socks, and shoes with buckles. I spotted Terry Walker waiting beneath the entry sign of the largest tent: *Willkommen.*

"Hey, Walker, how's it hanging?"

"Like a ball python. Thanks for asking."

My buddy and I headed into the festivities. The sound of live music, traditional, rock, and even some reggae, pulsed through the canvas stretched over the wispy structural frame. Hanging banners and twinkly little lights filled the tent ceiling, and below a sea of long picnic tables with blue-checkered tablecloths provided seating for the noisy multitude of beer drinkers and sausage chewers. The enthusiastic patrons consumed the beer by the barrel with roving beer vendors ensuring no glass would ever go dry, while they devoured an inexhaustible torrent of Germanic junk food. A busy band of enterprising youngsters called 'schnitzel schleppers' refilled their plates and were rewarded by half-drunk parents and neighbors. Terry and I sat near the stage for a twenty-minute eternity, pummeled by pounding polka music as we ate our brats and fries with gusto and drank beer from glass mugs emblazoned with the town logo.

"Enough?" asked Terry.

"Enough to get the picture...ya, hey, der. Let's grab some air."

We walked away until the music faded. A few hundred feet from the fest, we found solitude in the linear park, appropriately named River Walk, the one feature of my hometown I offered as proof of civilization whenever an effete urbanite challenged my quasi-rural roots. Terry and I sat side by side on a bench overlooking a bend in the river. An animation of scattered mayflies, visible in the glow of a decorative street light, flittered above the black waters of the Du Page River as it flowed silently toward the Gulf of Mexico a thousand miles south.

"They'll be gone soon enough," mumbled Terry.

"What?"

"The bugs. Winter's coming."

"It's not even Halloween, Terry."

"I'm prepping my mind and body. I'm not ready," he said with some seriousness.

"You're thirty-two years old and still cringing at the thought of winter? You should visit me in Colorado. Lots of snow."

"Invite me, Alex. I'll be there."

"I will if..."

"If what?"

"If things work out. I'm in a bit of a bind, Terry."

"What's up?"

"Do you want the entire story or a quick wrap-up?" I asked.

Terry turned his body to face me. "Give me the abridged version. I'm a quick study."

I rolled my eyes as he responded. "OK. First, my job. You know what I do, right?"

Terry chuckled. "You travel around the world. Make a few notes. Take photographs. Write stories about places most people will never visit. And sell the packages to East Coast magazines and cable TV."

"I guess you could say that...it was a respectable gig...before the Internet. The web and AI have killed everything. The slicks are dying. The Sunday newspaper magazines are almost dead. TV is a confusing nightmare of stations, channels, videos, and devices. And everyone is doing my job. Not as well, maybe. But good enough to satisfy the demand for well-written, pithy tales of visits to foreign lands backed by full-color photos or AI-generated videos. Four or five keyboard clicks will deliver it to your door, and you're done."

"So that gig is over?"

I nodded. "I think so. I haven't made a deal in over a year." I squirmed. "Fact is, I'm broke, Terry."

"That sucks," Terry kept pushing. "OK. What's next?"

"Well, when I got the call from my brother. I was relieved. I thought the long train ride and the change of scenery would open my mind to new ideas."

"And..."

"You know I left here ten years ago to free myself from my father's business. I was out the door, but I asked him for an advance on my inheritance so I could start a new life. He was generous. He was sad I was leaving, but hoped I would find my way. He gave me quite a hunk of cash, which got me started and turned into a lifestyle business. I was happy, and I guess he was OK with the idea. After that, I never saw him or Otto until now. I'm set to visit with the old man tomorrow."

"Are you going to ask him for money?"

I leaned back. "That would be ballsy, but I wouldn't bother. My welcome was over forever when I refused to help run his business and took the early payoff. He's dying now. So they say. I talked to Otto, who doesn't know anything about my financial problems. Optimistically, he said my father would take care of me."

"Does Kathy?"

I didn't answer the question. Friend or no friend, the conversation deserved some thought. "I need a break, Terry. Give me a moment." I said as I got up and walked to the river railing.

"Take your time," he said as he sucked on his cigarette, "I'm not going anywhere."

A small boat, packed with partying people, lights ablaze, motored upstream. A couple of attractive women on the boat waved and taunted me. Not knowing what they were shouting, I nevertheless waved back. They laughed and disappeared into the darkness, the chugging of their outboard motor fading in the cool, clear night air. Settled now, I returned to the bench and sat next to my friend.

I was ready to talk. "Kathy...she doesn't know about my financial situation. And other things..."

"Jeez, you've been saving these up, haven't you?"

"Lucky you. You're the only one. I don't have a priest."

"Father Walker is here. Say three Hail Marys and kiss my ass in the morning," said Terry.

"Right. Bless you, Father."

"Spit the whole thing out, Alex. The suspense is killing me."

"OK. Back to Denver for a moment. I'd had some issues when I left. Not insignificant issues."

"More money problems?" He paused. "By the way, I can't help you. Margie and I are up to our ears in debt. But go ahead."

"Never entered my mind." I chuckled nervously. "I had a woman in Denver. We were close. I lived with her for over a year. She wanted to get married...I didn't."

"Did you love her?"

I waited. "Who can say? Again...I wasn't ready to commit. That's not one of my strong suits. Last month, we agreed to split up." I paused for a long count. "But then she...killed herself."

"What?"

I cleared my throat. "I came home one night, and she was hanging from the back porch...we lived in a three-story building. She strung a rope over a porch beam, made a noose of sorts, stepped over the railing, and killed herself."

"Jesus." Terry recoiled. "I would have freaked out."

"I was. I'm still shaking, thinking about it. But all I could do was cut her down. She was gone. They took her away. I notified her older sister. And that was that."

Terry shifted in his seat. "That was that? That's a bit callous, Alex."

"Well, what would you do? I didn't want it to happen. I didn't know she would fall apart."

"Forget it. I'm not blaming you. I just feel sorry for her. Did she leave anyone behind?"

"Only her sister. We talked for a while. She seemed nice."

"Any funeral?"

"No. The sister said she might have a memorial service, but nothing came of that."

"Were the police called in? They usually get involved in the case of suicide."

"That too. Just before I left to come here, the cops called on me. They said they were doing inquiries...whatever that means. I told them I had to come here. They took down my brother's details. And I left town."

Terry thought about it. "Just fishing?"

"I suppose they're doing their job, but..."

"What happened? With the woman?"

I pursed my lips. "That night...she and I argued. I left to take a walk. A long walk that ended in a bar. I had a drink or two. I was tired of the whole thing."

"Meaning?"

"I don't know. Living together...until when? I was getting a little too domesticated." She asked many questions. I didn't have answers. 'Where are you going to go?'" I just shook my head. "She had no idea I was out of cash. I couldn't tell her. She had some shit job. She tried...it paid for the groceries. But it wasn't working out. In the end, we were at each other's throats, always arguing about the bills. So, I called it off. I told her I was leaving. I didn't realize..."

"You know, Alex. Sometimes you're an ass. You only think about yourself."

"I think the cops thought the same thing. I couldn't spin a story that made me appear like anything but a bum. But it just happened, and she was gone."

"What was her name?"

"Her name?"

"Yes."

I paused to think. "Camilla...Mexican-American. Religious gal. I still can't believe she did it."

Terry stood. "Let's walk downriver. I parked in the lot at the end."

I got up. "I'm parked there, too."

We walked along the narrow path bordering the river, climbed some stairs, and continued walking toward the old covered bridge. When we reached the fountain anchoring one end of the bridge, we stopped and sat at the edge of the water feature. Terry lit another cigarette, inhaled deeply, and blew out the smoke like poisonous gas.

A moment passed, and he took another drag, leaving the cigarette in his mouth. He interlocked his fingers. "All right." As he talked, the Marlboro danced in his mouth. "You're broke. The cops are investigating the death of your lover in Denver. Your father is dying. Anything else?"

I gave him a look. "Don't be so flippant. I thought we could talk. I don't have anyone here to share my thoughts with. OK?"

Terry took another drag. "Right. Not to be morbid. But when your father goes, your problems will be solved. Right?"

I shrugged my shoulders. "I'm not rooting for that."

"How are things working out at Otto's?"

I cocked my head to one side.

"Could be better, eh?" Terry commented. "You can always stay at our place to get your bearings. We've got a room in the basement that's livable. You should think about it."

"Got cable? I like to watch that channel with the classic movies. Puts me to sleep."

"Sure. Cable, we got. Shower, toilet, you name it."

"And Margie?"

"I think I can convince Margie to put up with you for a while for an old friend like you. I imagine it's no picnic watching Otto with Kathy, considering..."

"Well..." I paused as Terry dropped his cigarette to the ground and crushed it.

"You can't kiss off those cancer sticks?"

"Don't worry about me. Two in the morning. One at lunch and one at night. Well...sort of. Margie is all over me about the smoking, so I don't need another supporting opinion."

"OK."

"You didn't tell me anything about your brother or Kathy. You still got the hots for her?"

I leaned back. "Leave it alone, Sherlock."

74

Terry smiled. "I thought so. You think you fucked up because you let her go? Now you regret it."

"I never was able to get her out of my head."

"Hey. She's not the same innocent girl you had a crush on. And you're not a kid anymore. People grow up. They change...and not always for the better."

"She's caught in my memories. One of those fond memories you keep on sugarcoating."

"Forget the sugar...add some lemon juice, Alex. She's married to your brother. Save yourself some grief. Give the situation a reality check."

I rolled my eyes. "It's a little late now."

Terry studied me, shook his head from side to side, and made a face that animated life into his woolly caterpillar of a mustache. "No...don't tell me."

"I didn't start it. She's...we..."

"Save it, Alex. There's nothing I don't get about Kathy. But it seems a little weird. She's coming on to you?"

I nodded. "I'm not surprised."

"What?"

"She's a tiger. I've heard stories."

"What stories?"

"Not one to spread gossip, but I'd stay away from that situation. Grab your inheritance and get out of town."

I shrugged my shoulders. "Too late."

Father Walker searched the heavens for help. "You did the deed already?"

I turned away. "Never said that." My words hung in the air.

He mumbled, "You rat bastard. No wonder Margie never liked you."

Chapter 11

The next day, I was hungover. Wine and women, beer and brats, and last night's boys' night out with old buddy Terry resulted in less shut-eye and more angst. I dragged my body downstairs to find my brother, dressed for the day, and Kathy in a blue and orange Chicago Bears sweatshirt; her legs were bare, and only God and Papa Bear could tell if anything was under the shirt. The couple sat across from each other at the kitchen island counter, and their noisy discussion was cut short when she spotted me.

"Well, you made it back to the living, sleepy-head." She smiled. "Coffee?"

I croaked out a greeting.

"Fun night?" asked Otto.

"Hey, we're both looking a tad worn."

Otto nodded. "I haven't been getting my beauty winks either, and I've got a business to run. I feel like shit most of the time."

"Your meds aren't working?"

"I wish it were that simple," he said.

I stood next to Kathy. She touched my hand intentionally as she rose from the chair toward the prep area behind Otto. Not visible to her husband, this little gesture was no doubt intended to remind me of yesterday. "Cream in your coffee?" She turned the simple question into a sultry proposition.

For a dazed moment, I froze and unfroze. "Ah, no. Black."

"Sure. Hot and black," she said. "Just like my men." She wore a wicked smile, quite pleased with her attempt at humor.

I looked up at her, thinking what a strange couple they were.

"What's good for the gander is good for the goose? Right?" she said.

"You got us there, Babe." Otto rolled his eyes. "She's stealing our best material, Alex," said Otto, looking more bemused than amused.

Kathy placed a steaming cup of coffee in front of me. "Hot. No cream or sugar because you're sweet enough, Alex."

"Ain't she something?" asked Otto. Kathy stood beside him and put her hand on his shoulder. He glanced up at her, wearing a stupid smile.

I sipped my coffee, then nodded. "That she is. One of a kind."

"So, I take it you secured your medical passport from Jarek?"

"Squared away," I said. "More extensive than I thought. But I assume he's up to date on what's required to get beyond Father's nurse."

"Believe me. The old man is getting a bit goofy. Can't blame him. The whole world was frightened by the pandemic. Excellent for business, though."

"Otto..." Kathy gave him a disapproving glance.

"What? That's what we do," Otto said. "Hey, I don't kill them. I move them off the stage to find eternity. Last year was our best ever."

Kathy wasn't buying it. "Cold-hearted, Otto," she said.

"Hey. This week we're going downtown, and I'm going to buy you a new and expensive bauble. So don't complain."

I listened, one coffee sip at a time, waking up. "Otto's got a point...on the top of his head."

"Put it in gear...dear," said Otto. "Alex and I need a little man-talk time."

Kathy left, smiling at me as she sashayed away. Her tan, shoeless feet padded the white tile floor, her long legs animated, and her loose breasts bounced.

"Gotcha."

"What?"

"Taking a peek." Otto laughed. "Lookie. Lookie. No touchie."

I shrugged my shoulders, smiled, and remembering yesterday, I swallowed any response I might attempt.

Otto nodded and pursed his lips. "She likes you. You're lucky. She's got a cold shoulder most of the time. So...let's talk about your meeting with Father. OK?"

"Sure."

"I'm certain he's going to tell you our firm is in trouble. Or that I'm unsure about what I'm doing. That his mind would be put at ease if you joined the company. But that doesn't interest you, right?"

"I told you. I don't have the slightest..."

Otto interrupted. "That's fine. But I see him in action every day. He'll try his best to make you believe the business is on a razor edge, ready to slip away. That's where his head is. I think he's conflating his physical condition with the strength of the business. You should understand that everything is going fine. As I mentioned, it's been a strong year."

"I'm happy for you, Otto, but..."

"He may try to convince you my health is an issue."

"Is it?"

"No. Dr. Jarek and I have it under control."

"So why the concern?"

Otto paused. "He's getting old. Dying. Like many people nearing the end, he needs to leave his mark on the world. Our business is the most important thing in his life. He spent his whole life building the business, sometimes at the expense of other things and people."

"Like Mother..."

Otto looked into his coffee cup. "Exactly," he said.

"He's also driving me nuts about having an heir."

"I'm not following you," I said.

"He's disappointed because Kathy and I are childless. We've been married for five years, and it hasn't happened. I won't dive into the details, but we're working with other doctors to solve the problem. You would think it would be like falling off a horse, but...I guess not. No matter, we'll find a way. Kathy would like a kid. So would I."

The inside information made me uneasy. My phone dinged. I stood and checked the message, relieved I had an excuse to leave.

"That's my ride. I'm gone, Bro. Thanks for the info. I'll try to quiet his mind. Got to go. You know he's not one for tardiness."

Chapter 12

Frederick Reinhart, my father, had his own mansion, not as large as his son's, but Frederick's was located in the Historic District. The 1890s farmhouse, which had been built by my great-grandfather, had been modified many times but retained its rural roots. The original Reinhart had three children, two boys, and a girl. One of the boys died in the First World War, the girl got married and moved to Boston, and the last son was my grandfather. He inherited the home. He and his wife had three children, Frederick, and two girls. The family funeral business was started post-war by the grandfather. By the 1980s, my father had taken over the business and his father's house, which became my home for the first two decades of my life.

The old white house looked stunning in the morning sunlight; the leaves of the awakened ancient trees surrounding it glowed bright yellow, a picture postcard of an autumn dream. Its sturdy appearance, welcoming porches, and simple traditional detailing were emblematic of Old Naperville. As I stood on the curb facing the house, for the first time in a decade, a flurry of memories returned, some bad, some pleasant. My childhood remembrances were graced with my mother's tender kindness, which dulled the memories of my father's cold, old-school, harsh Germanic personality.

As I entered the home on time, apprehensive and a bit nervous, I was greeted by a male nurse. While the young man was somewhat deferential, he didn't hesitate to deal with the need for a physician's report. As we talked in the entrance hall, I handed him the envelope. The nurse asked me to sit in the living room. I sat on the same sofa that Otto and I used as a trampoline as kids. I scanned the room.

Nothing had changed. The same furniture and pictures, the same Oriental carpet, the same gold-framed decorative mirror over the white wooden fireplace mantle, and the original white wooden slat blinds on the windows. As the late morning sun sliced through the double-hung fenestration at the end of the room, it landed on the antique carpet, warming it and releasing the residual faint odor of formaldehyde. For decades, my father had carried the chemical into the house on the soles of his shoes, always connecting the mortuary's embalming area with our family's home. It was a smell that my mother attempted to remove, mask over, or ignore. The odor found me again. It would never go away.

The nurse returned and walked me to the back of the house, leading to a room that years ago, my mother had mentioned, pre-war, she said, served as a billiard room and gathering place for cigar-smoking men. It was narrow, but long. It connected to a porch that ran the width of the house. Before I was born, the porch had been enclosed with a wall of windows that overlooked a Japanese garden complete with a koi pond and decorative lighting. When Otto and I were young, this room was used as a television room and study. The porch was our indoor playground, and the koi pond was a location of constant boyhood mischief. The nurse commented that in the last few months, this area had been converted to a combined bedroom and office. I peeked into the room. The old man's new hide-out was all business. A hospital-type bed and the bathroom beyond were discreetly semi-concealed by a decorative screen, and the front half of the room, his office, had a desk, an overstuffed chair, an ottoman, and a small sofa.

As I entered, he sat at his desk in a wooden swivel chair. For someone who was supposed to be at death's door, Frederick Reinhart looked pretty good. His crisp pressed slacks, white silk shirt, and navy blue smoking jacket raised the bar for hospice attire. Only his mocassins betrayed an otherwise perfect image of money and power.

He glanced over and smiled, then he stood and took a few steps forward. I moved in to him, and we shook hands businesslike. I was surprised that my father, while thinner, was able to maintain his bearing. And save for his skin color and eyes, which in the dim light of the room appeared yellowish, and his hair, now white, he remained an impressive man, tall, angular, and wearing his classic not-to-be-messed-with look.

"My son," he said. "You have returned."

"Hello, Father."

I adjusted our handshake to assume a two-handed politician grip, grasping his forearm from below. This was as close as he would ever get to a man-hug. I looked into his yellow eyes and detected tears. I couldn't know if they arose from our reunion or were caused by the pain of his illness.

"Please close the door, Alex."

I did as requested and watched the old man in his painful retreat to his stuffed leather chair. I sat before him on the ottoman.

"Just in time, if you listen to my doctors."

"How are you feeling?"

He nodded. "Not bad. A bit of pain." His hand touched his midsection. "I get tired fast, and I itch. But Richard, my 'assistant,' scratches what itches...on command." He chuckled. "Kathy showed me your travel writings in one of those fancy magazines. Very impressive. Well written. And your photography is spot on. Great stuff." He paused. "You've carved a place for yourself in the world. Does a father proud."

My mind flashed back to the last time I saw him ten years ago. There was no talk of pride then. Nor were many pleasantries exchanged. Father promised to deposit an agreed sum of money into my checking account. At that moment, we shook hands, and almost wordlessly, I left carrying a duffle bag over my shoulder, drifted into a waiting cab, and away from the Reinhart world of bodies, embalming equipment, hearses, flower cars, caskets, urns, and crematoria. We had never exchanged written or verbal words in the intervening period.

"That's very kind of you. I'm surprised you followed my work."

The old man held a handkerchief to his mouth, coughed, and wiped the spittle away before replying. He swallowed. "Well. I wouldn't put it in those words. But I was glad to see you were enjoying the world and gainfully employed. I suppose an occasional letter or note would have been nice. But, of course, that's a two-way street, isn't it?"

I looked up at the ceiling, took a quiet cleansing breath, and replied: "I guess that's water over the proverbial dam. I'm here now, and I'm happy to see you."

My father rubbed his hands together and nodded. "So it is, Alex. And so am I."

Like two old army buddies remembering better times, we had a lively conversation for the next half hour. I shared stories of my travels, and my father dredged up memories of our family vacation car trips around the Great Lakes. He seemed pleased to be able to recall memories of my mother and happier times. Strangely, there was no talk about Otto or the mortuary business, almost as if I had never left. It was no secret that I had always been my father's favorite. Unlike my younger brother, I was good at sports and showed some talent as a photographer, artist, and writer. I was fit and reasonably good-looking, the presumed heir to the family business.

Before I left home, I knew this was my destiny, a pre-programmed future not of my choosing. That schism, my father's unwelcome presumptions, my denial of his plans, and the residual pain of my mother's death summed up the reasons I left Naperville. My departure left my father with no choice but to induct Otto into the business. In the undertow of these dark swirling waters, without much thought, I also left my steady girlfriend, Kathy Price. I had to get away from everyone and everything to avoid drowning. But then and now, I regretted the abruptness of the termination of my relationship with Kathy.

The conversation turned as we felt the pressure of time. The old man was tired; he rubbed his yellowing eyes with two balled fists more than once. Sometimes, it almost seemed like his weary orbs were tearing, but I was convinced that this was unlikely. Frederick Reinhart never cried, not even at my mother's wake and funeral. I cried, less and less each year, but I remembered.

My father sipped water from a tumbler and, with some effort, returned it to the table. Then he seemed to gain strength. "We have to talk," he said as if the past hour's conversation was separate from the actual business of the reunion.

I sensed it was time to change position, equalize the body language, and re-establish a level playing field. I stood and stretched my legs and arms. Then I added a little distance by sitting on the sofa adjacent to my father's chair. "As you used to tell me when I was young, new to the world and filled with stories to tell you and questions to ask...I'm all ears." I smiled. "I was at least five before I realized this was just a figure of speech."

He nodded, dropped a hint of a smile, and moved on. "We'll listen up, my son." The tone of his voice had changed as he straightened up in his chair. He was no longer the mellow, proud parent gushing over fond memories of the past. He was Frederick Reinhart, sole owner and C.E.O of Reinhart Funeral Home, a prominent family business serving Naperville for almost eight decades. "I have quite a list of items on my agenda. First, about your brother. I assume you know?"

The conversation paused.

"He mentioned he had some issues with his heart."

"That's an understatement. He is weak. I don't like the way he looks. He's never been a strong person. Never. But for the last few months, he seems to be struggling against himself. And that Jarek. I don't trust him at all. My spies tell me he's a regular visitor at the mortuary. Spends a lot of time with Otto." Frederick looked distant. "I'm concerned. In my condition, I haven't been able to oversee daily operations at the business. But I can read the financial reports."

I interjected, "Otto told me this year was going to be very good."

"Could be. I agree with that on the income side. But something's happening on the expense side. For the past six months, profits have been flat. Expenses are up. I'm concerned about the bottom line. Maybe you can help?

"I don't see how I could. Otto and I talked. And I agreed with him that I would stay out of the family business no matter what happens."

"Like me...moving on?" Frederick chuckled.

"Sorry. I didn't mean to be so blunt."

"Forget it, Alex. They say I have months. I know the score, and I understand you have no interest in working in the business. But you haven't abandoned the family...have you?"

I contemplated my father's words. "I have not. I realize that the family that built this business and the Reinhart name are special. I wouldn't do anything to damage our family's reputation and history. I'm certain Otto would not either for many good reasons, including the fact...I'm assuming...that it will be his business in the future."

Frederick smiled. "You will have to wait for the reading of my will to confirm your assumptions, but the answer is 'yes'. Otto will inherit the business, and you will not. Consider the lump sum I gave you ten years ago as the sale price of your half of the business."

"Always did."

"Good. Then that's nice and clean. Nevertheless, you will receive a generous portion of the remainder of my estate, and I have also made you my executor. Do you have a problem with that?"

I mulled it over. "Well..." I nodded. "I think I can handle that."

"OK. So consider it a favor to your dying old man. I'll have my accountant in soon enough. We'll go over the books. I'm sure everything will make sense, and I can rest in peace. I just need you to be my eyes and ears. I need a snoop who I can trust. And you're that guy."

"Snoop?"

Frederick Reinhart was enjoying the conversation. "How long are you going to remain in town?"

"I'm not sure. I got the call from Otto, and I guess in a way I misinterpreted it. I sort of dropped everything and hopped a train."

"No loose ends back there?"

"None."

The old man smiled. "That's touching, Alex. I mean it. In any event...can you stay awhile?"

I shrugged. "I closed out my affairs in Denver. And it was always my intention to spend some time here. Renew friendships. See the family. And then move on. I'm thinking of Florida. Maybe the Keys. Who knows?"

"A regular Hemingway." Frederick smiled. "Sounds like fun. It's your life. Go for it." He shifted in his chair and ran his fingers through his hair. "But can you stay until..."

I cut him off. "Sure. I will. And I'll be the best executor you ever had," I said with a smile.

"Very droll." The old man chuckled. "Fine. You can see. I'm stuck here in this house. I clean up well, but I'm afraid my energy levels are very low. So, it's up to you to check things out at the business. Otto doesn't have time or interest to keep me apprised, but you look pretty hearty. While you're here. Just keep your eyes open. Something's bothering me in my gut, but I'm not sure what. Maybe it's my damn pancreas. That thing is shot. But after you spend fifty years watching over something like a mother hen, you tend to worry."

"I get you. What do you suggest?"

"Just visit. Get Otto to have Jan Gorger show you around. See if the paper towel dispensers in the washrooms are filled and that everything is clean and neat. That kind of stuff. Pretend you're a customer. Use that critical eye of yours. And dig a little into that Jarek guy. I think he and Otto are up to something. Get your buddy Terry to help you. He's a professional snoop. Right? If you need some funds. Just ask."

"OK. I can do that."

"And don't mention our conversation today with anyone."

"Terry?"

"Yes, of course. But remind him this is all strictly confidential."

"Another thing. I think Otto is living beyond his means. I pay him a decent salary, but you've been to his house. That place is expensive. The wife is expensive. And he's a sucker for her. He'll do anything to keep her happy."

Now I felt something crawling inside me. The elder Reinhart was back in his old form, making plans and setting things in motion.

"Are you suggesting that Otto is using business funds for his own needs?"

I hit a nerve. He tensed. "I'm not suggesting anything. That's why I'm asking you to look. You're family." He flipped the conversation. "I know it's been years since you visited the place."

I recalled. "Not since..."

"Right." He nodded. "But you need to look at it with fresh eyes. You're the sensitive one in the family. See what you think. I'll entertain any thoughts you may have. Any changes you would make. Think toward the future. I trust you, Alex. You know the business, you understand people, and you always see the big picture. Look ahead. See what has to be done. In the past, I only questioned your commitment...nothing else. I know when you make your mind up...like the last time...when you decided to ride into the sunset...that will be that. So this will be our last chance to make sure we maintain the good name of Reinhart."

I nodded and smiled. "Everyone rides into the sunset sooner or later."

"So true. But I still own it. Reinhart Funeral Home. You know, at this point, within reason, I can do whatever I want. Fifty years from now, I want my image in a gold frame in the lobby along with the history of the Reinhart family."

"Sounds like a plan, Father. I'm on it."

"Come back soon, Alex. Time waits for no man."

Frederick appeared to relax in his chair as if he removed a weight from his chest. By the time I left the room, he was nodding off. I was pleased with the meeting. It was weird but very civilized. I was left with the feeling the old man had been expecting me to arrive on the scene and fix things that he could not. The ten years of separation between us disappeared in one late-morning hour. Although my coming home experience was less painful and in some ways more pleasant than I had imagined, it had become far more complicated.

Chapter 13

Otto and I drove to the family funeral home the next morning in his Mercedes.

I asked: "How much did this little slice of German engineering cost?"

My brother glanced at me. "Nobody buys company cars anymore, Alex. Business lease. Makes it easy for the IRS. It's a no-questions-asked business expense. At least by the IRS. Father asks a lot of questions, but he doesn't understand how important image is. This...is an S-Class. They start at about a hundred twenty.

"That's a fair chunk of change. The undertaking business must be...bury-bury good."

Otto chuckled. "Funny man...Alex Reinhart."

Given my general dislike of the funeral world, Otto questioned the purpose of the tour of facilities. I told him that our father suggested it. About to ask 'Why?', Otto had an 'aha' moment: Frederick was a proud man. Otto suggested the old man wanted to remind his eldest son of what could be created through hard work and dedication, two attributes Otto presumed were not evident in his oldest son. Although I knew our father's concerns had nothing to do with Otto's perception of family relations, I agreed with my brother's analysis. It fit everyone's worldview of the Frederick-Alex father-son relationship.

"Can the business support your exquisite taste in automobiles?"

Otto smiled. "As I mentioned, the death business is on an upward trajectory this year. We may gross about three million."

"I guess it covers it."

"Hey, I've got to keep Kathy comfortable." He chuckled.

"She appeared to like the bracelet you bought her yesterday."

"Almost a thousand bucks. She should like it."

"A small price to pay for marital happiness, right?" I said.

Otto ignored my quip and went silent while I recalled last night's dinner for three, in many ways a painful experience. She teased me by playing footsie under the table, and after dinner, she found ways to steal a kiss or grab my butt when Otto left the room. This dangerous game must end.

"I'm working on methods to bring up the gross without increasing expenses."

I put thoughts of Kathy to bed and responded. "How so?"

He cleared his throat and shook his head. "Bad Juju to get ahead of oneself. But you'll see. We're moving on some major improvements which should enhance the bottom line."

"You and Father..."

Otto stretched his neck and squeezed the nascent wattle under his chin with a finger and thumb like a rope tightening around it. "You know. He hasn't been to work for several months, and he's part-time for the last year. Life goes on. Right?"

"You da' boss, Otto."

"Technically," said Otto, "he's still the boss, but things will soon change. We have different styles. He and I. He's a traditionalist like Grandfather. I'm more of a realist. Our industry is changing fast...everything. We're swimming in a riptide of unrelenting novelty. You can't fight it. You don't go the way you started...you swim away from the pull of the status quo and into new but safer, more profitable waters. Right?"

"Father knew that," I said. "I understand he fought with Grandfather about moving the funeral home from downtown up north. But he knew a business that can't grow will have to go. It's like a fish in a fishbowl. Can't grow. Needs a fish tank. Reinhart Funeral Homes and Crematory would have died decades ago or been bought out if Father didn't find the northside site. He and Grandfather were stuck in a small building with bad auto access. Unable to expand. But he predicted an exciting future. Do you know what the population of Naperville was in the mid-seventies?"

"Nope." Grunted Otto.

"About 25,000. And today it's approaching 150,000. Five times growth in fifty years. He saw that coming. The old man took a lot of heat for leaving downtown. Quite a risk. That took balls."

"But now they've shriveled," said Otto, smiling.

"He's got cancer," I reminded him. "A little slack, please."

Otto lowered his head. "You're right. I'm an ass. But I'm an ass with big balls." He laughed.

We arrived at the funeral home. When built the low-slung masonry building with limestone accents, Wrightian roofs, and cantilevered entrance canopy was acclaimed by the local papers as something new in mortuary design, but as I viewed it for the first time in over a decade, it was a little tired. Maybe Frederick did fall behind the times, and Otto was correct in suggesting changes were necessary. For the moment, I was a reporter, not a critic, so I made a mental note. The parking lot appeared somewhat worn, and the landscape was doing its own thing. But these are routine items, rote repairs, and other deferred maintenance. Customer first impressions are all-important. No one in Naperville wanted to sing a second-rate swan song. All this was obvious, and I wondered about it but said nothing.

Otto pulled into a six-car garage in the back. The Mercedes shared space with a hearse, a flower car, a limo, and some motorized maintenance vehicles. The garage connected to the building with an expansive, high-ceilinged covered drive-thru lane. As we walked from one building to the other, I tensed. We entered the man door adjacent to the pair of doors reserved for departing caskets. Already, I sensed today's visit might be a painful trip into my past. The last time

I entered this building was to attend my mother's wake and funeral. Otto held the door open. As I entered, the faint smell of embalming fluid hit me. Like my mother, it reeked of death. Others working in the backroom space may become acclimated, but I couldn't stand that smell. We came in through the back end of the building and the business, a place no customer visited. Otto moved through a coat room for employees that also served as a staging room for the movement of bodies to a waiting hearse on their way to the cemetery.

After making an internal call from a wall-mounted phone, he turned to me. "I spoke with Gorger. He's on his way down..." We made eye contact. "Hey. Are you lost? This is all new to you, right?"

I nodded. "I was in this area once."

"We'll do the front too, but we'll start our tour here in the back. This should be enlightening for you. Doesn't take long to get into the swing of things. You're not squeamish, are you?"

"What?"

"You know. Bodies, body fluids...dead folk." He smiled as he teased.

"Not my everyday activity, but I'll power through."

Otto gave me a wry smile. "This back section is the processing and preparation section. Embalming rooms, cold storage, crematorium, delivery areas, staff break room, and this departure area. The public spaces in front may be what you remember and are familiar with. Admin and sales areas, merchandise display, visitation rooms, chapel."

"My memories are vague. It was a long time ago."

Just then, a tall, thin, fiftyish man entered the room. Gorger had recessed cheekbones, a strong chin, a pockmarked face, and a head full of dirty dog hair. His eyes were black pebbles set into the bony recesses of his skull. Dressed in an olive green jumpsuit, his open-collar black shirt peeked through the zippered front, revealing an aggressive matte of grey-black chest hair that lay below. He wore the sour expression of a man who spends his days talking to the dead. I tried to ignore his somewhat grotesque appearance.

"So you're Mr. Reinhart's other son, Alex. A pleasure to meet you. I've been working with Frederick for years."

We shook hands. Upon release, there was a residual stickiness.

"Jan Gorger."

I nodded. "My father speaks well of you," I said.

"Jan is the number one man in the back end. Chief embalmer. A total of four," said Otto.

"We're a competent team," said Gorger, "working together under a couple of strong leaders."

"Thanks for the paid endorsement, Jan. Keep an eye out for that Christmas bonus."

Gorger laughed a bit too loudly. "Well, should we begin the tour?"

"Let's go. Lead the way, Jan."

The first stop on their tour was the embalming room, a simple, well-lighted space with lots of stainless steel, seamless black counters, and white wall cabinets. Two places on the counter were equipped with what appeared to be electronic devices with hoses out the side. When I posed the question. Otto explained these were pumps designed to force the embalming fluids into the circulation system of the deceased while flushing out the blood. In addition, other single-function sinks were mounted on walls. Above the two embalming tables, lengths of flexible exhaust piping, intended to suck out chemical fumes, hung from the ceiling like serpents dangling from a jungle tree.

I focused on the current crop of dead bodies being processed, about to have their bodies embalmed. Three lay on stainless steel embalming tables. The two mortuary professionals didn't focus on the obvious. The dead 'elephant in the room', a mass of grey, dead flesh, was ignored. One was almost finished with the process, only a tie and pocket square short of being display-ready, and the other two waited for Gorger under white sheets with their arms resting on their abdomens, hands one atop the other. I tried not to stare. The young woman in her early twenties could have qualified for a movie part in a fairy tale. I couldn't help but think she would have liked a little more privacy.

"You OK, Alex?" asked my brother.

I snapped out of my gaze and focused on Otto. "OK...a little disturbed, but OK."

"You know all of our embalmers must attend many classes and pass state licensing. Medical or surgical skills are not required, but this work involves similar skills. The point is they are professionals." Otto cued Jan Gorger. "And Jan here is the most experienced of our team. He manages the embalming and the operation of the crematory. He also has the distinction of having worked for many years as an assistant in the morgue of a major hospital in Milwaukee. So he has a way with a scalpel. Right, Jan?"

Gorger's chest appeared to rise as he internalized the praise from his employer. "That was a long time ago, Otto. But it's kind of like riding a bicycle. When you've cut up as many corpses as I have...well, let's put it this way...it's all muscle memory."

I nodded with false appreciation and felt compelled to join in the conversation. "I heard that President Lincoln is a kind of folk hero in the world of embalming. Well, not Old Abe, but the embalmers who did the work on his body in Washington and then sent it across the country to be buried in Springfield."

"You're right, Alex. Thousands of mourners saw the body as it traveled north. People appreciated Lincoln's appearance, and the funeral industry has been chugging along ever since."

I glanced around the room. "This equipment appears new to me. Is it?

"We're always improving. We replaced a lot of older equipment. Demand was way up. It was a perfect time. It's my job to determine where the money should flow. I like to put it where it generates the most income. The faster we can process, the faster we can service the public, and the more income we see."

"So this new equipment pays for itself?"

Otto nodded. "Saves time. It pays for itself in less than a year. Plus, we keep our competition at bay. You know we're not the only funeral home in the area."

I nodded.

"If that's it, we'll move on," said Gorger.

We exited and walked down the corridor heading for the crematory, passing a door with a *No Admittance* temporary sign attached. I stopped cold. "What's this?"

Otto swung his head back. "Oh. That's an area under construction. More improvements. Nothing to see yet."

"Adding to the embalming area?" I wasn't concerned about becoming a pest, and I was curious.

Otto paused, then said, "Open the door, Jan." Gorger complied.

"Take a quick gander, Alex, but don't step on the floor. Just been laid."

Gorger reached in and switched on the lights, and I peeked in. The room flooded with light and smelled of fresh adhesive. There was an entry hall, with a toilet room to the right and an open area to the left. Eight feet distant, a half-open sliding door led to the larger space. I took a look at the room, walls painted light green, square in plan, with seamless flooring and bright ceiling lighting arranged in a ring. No equipment had been installed in either space.

"Impressive. Is it going to connect to the embalming room?"

"I don't think so. This may be a stand-alone facility. New technology. We may want to feature it. Haven't decided yet, but it could have a connecting door."

Jan locked it down, and we proceeded ahead, passing a room Otto identified as the cooler. He suggested not visiting that room as the corpses within were not embalmed, awaited cremation, and might be disfigured.

"I'll pass," I said, now weary of body viewing.

"One more facility and we'll show you the public area." With a wave of his hand over a motion-sensor lock, Otto opened the last door at the end of the corridor and presented the crematory. "Here it is. Our pride and joy."

I stepped into the chamber, the air was warm and fresh, and the space immaculately clean with white, smooth walls, the floor a light grey terrazzo, and the ceiling white plaster. A massive stainless steel shed-like structure about ten feet high, seven feet across, and fifteen feet deep overwhelmed the space. A casket-sized rectangular vertically sliding door with a metal feeder track attached served as the path into the heart of the cooker. The small door to Hell was closed. I was curious to see the guts of the machine. Gorger got the nod from Otto and pushed a button. Slowly, the door opened, revealing the interior, which was lined with a rather cozy buff-colored fire brick. In the back of my mind, I compared the overall feel of this with the chamber-of-death vibe I got from visiting the embalming room. This area reminded me of a food-processing plant, all stainless steel, round corners, and smooth surfaces, versus the embalming room, which, even though very clean, bore a resemblance to a football stadium's public washroom. Of course, the lack of bodies in the crematory automatically gave it a homier atmosphere.

"You know we are lucky to be able to operate this wonder of wonders. I'm not certain we could have one now. From a zoning standpoint. The environmentalists are quite active in this community."

Gorger chimed in, "The strange thing is that many of the same people prefer this method of disposing of the dead. No land use issues. More efficient. No dangerous chemicals.

"The whole thing is automatic," said Otto. "You just push a button and off you go."

Gorger continued his tour speech. "These bodies are not embalmed. They are bathed, cleaned, dressed, and ready for transport from the cooler in a burnable box. Sometimes wood. Sometimes cardboard. We just remove all foreign objects like jewelry, watches, and prosthetics...whatever. We place a metal I.D. tag on the wrist. And process them in the retort at 1800 degrees for two hours. All that's left are bones and dust, which are mechanically pulverized, and the metal I.D. The entire procedure is computerized...neat and clean. And I think it does less harm to the environment overall." Gorger glanced over to Otto after making the last statement.

Otto jumped in. "I wouldn't make an argument one way or the other. The choice is determined by the family and the deceased. It's their choice. We're in the funeral business. We're not futurists. Here in the Naperville area, the traditional method is still pulling more than sixty percent of the business. But every year more are choosing cremation."

"Which is more profitable?" I asked.

Otto smiled. "Profit is all about offering choices and markup. The traditional 'final resting place' shopping choices we can offer are limited to caskets. But the days of buying fancy caskets may be ending. It's a lot of money for something that's only seen for a few days and then buried underground forever. When money is involved, the need for impressive presentation often falls by the wayside, tempered by the pocketbook. But the cremains or ashes, if you prefer, can be buried in simple solid containers or be parceled out as keepsakes in many ways. We've got an exceptional line of urns, including some beautiful wood-turned vessels. We also offer a vast choice of jewelry keepsakes. Crosses, rings, bracelets, tiny silver tubes, and hearts. Even golden rifle cartridges hung on 18-karat gold chains, loaded with small portions of the beloved's remains. Very personal. It's a profitable area of the business now. Something the old man never thought much of."

I smiled. "Old school thinking."

"You are correct," he agreed, "ya snooze ya lose, right? The one thing we can count on is change. We are adapting to a changing marketplace. Who knows in twenty years traditional cemeteries may be as outdated as dial phones and 8-track tapes." He chuckled.

"The public parks of the future...wooded...ponds and swans." I speculated.

"Whatever. We are ready here at Reinhart Funeral Home and Crematory. Right, Jan?"

I looked at Gorger. For a moment, I thought he was going to click his heels together and salute my brother, but he restrained himself and nodded with his eyes looking up for divine affirmation. Otto dismissed him, and the embalmer padded down the corridor to his embalming room.

We left the non-public part of the building and toured the public areas. I was familiar with these spaces. Compared to the clean finishes and lines of the cremation machine, the viewing rooms, chapels, offices, and sales rooms were traditional and felt old-fashioned. Otto mentioned he would like to update the interiors with a more contemporary look. This made sense, and I made a mental note, suspecting these traditional interior designs of American funeral homes were intended to mimic nearby homes. Gorger had explained that before embalming techniques became commonplace, the deceased person would be laid out in the parlor of his own home for a day or two. I assume funeral homes maintained the tradition by continuing the residential 'living room' feel for their viewing and visitation rooms. I agreed with Otto that more families were choosing cremation, and more were celebrating the life rather than mourning the loss. Otto might be thinking ahead of their father, just as Frederick had done when he convinced his father to move away from the center of town into a new facility, surrounded by access roadways with abundant parking spaces, and plenty of room for funeral staging areas. Otto was right, life goes on, and so does death.

Other than reporting, I completed my first task for my father, now to move on to phase two of snooping, as requested by my father, the employment of my good friend Terry.

Chapter 14

L ate morning, I left the mortuary, stood outside below its front door canopy, cell phone in hand, and called Terry Walker, telling him I was heading his way. My old friend's office was about a mile west. The sun warmed my face, and a crisp light breeze carried the smells I had almost forgotten, burning leaves mixed with distant farm odors that perfumed the autumn air. The late October day was perfect for a walk, and walking let me think. I decided against taking a noisy route along the highway and chose a zigzag path, which let me drift along under the trees on the sidewalks of residential areas.

My thoughts floated in a sea of fall colors. I walked past the tidy white houses filled with tidy white people, happy to live their mundane, yet meaningful lives. Work, school, local sports, neighborhood events, church on Sunday, rinse and repeat. Ten years ago, I left the coziness of this small-town life to take on the big, bad world and removed myself from the family business that consumed the lives of my father and brother. I was a man free to express my creativity, becoming somewhat famous and soon having a decent-sized bank account. Although my current sources of income were drying up, and I'd have to find another way to write for a living, I had no reservations about my choices.

But thoughts of Kathy filled my mind. She was here. And I wished somehow I had never left her behind. Walking along and thinking of my life ten years earlier, I played a game of What If? But these self-arguments caused me to think in circles. One can't live their life backward. This sage advice was delivered to Kathy by me, as if I knew something, but now I had doubts. Her words confirm the mistake also. I didn't assign too much weight to our recent sexual adventure, except that I believed Kathy and I were two lost souls who, with the passage of time, gained a new perspective, found each other, connected, and loved.

But she might be playing some kind of game. It was in her nature to be dangerously playful, or she was bored because Otto couldn't satisfy her. This thought drove me into an ethical corner I couldn't escape, and there was no way to spin my actions in a positive direction. Guilt intervened. The thought of adultery with my brother's wife told me my old-fashioned morality was returning; I knew I was on a path leading to an unpleasant ending. As I crossed a side street without looking, the driver of an oncoming car hit the brakes and honked the horn. I snapped back to the present, to a world that included my brother.

My walk had turned south, and after a few more minutes, I returned to the highway lined with fast-food joints, auto repair shops, car washes, and small shopping centers. With the increase of discordant noise, I started searching. A half-block ahead, I spotted a place fitting Terry's description, a little strip center built of painted concrete block, a one-story building adjacent to a paved alley. I checked the address numbers; Terry's office faced the alley and was without show-window exposure. At least the door was glazed. It wore greyed, stick-on vinyl letters reading: *T. WALKER, Confidential Invest gations*. I pulled the handle, but it was locked. I pushed my face nearer to the glass in vain, but I couldn't see inside. I waited. Then I heard a buzzer signaling the release of the lock, and I eased open the door.

"Alex Reinhart...my man," announced Terry from the darkened corner of the fifteen-by-twenty room. He sat behind a massive, worn oak desk. A single gooseneck lamp lit up the detective-limo driver's face. Terry Walker looked like he crawled out of a 1950s men's magazine crime story. He smoked a cigarette, releasing the smoke dramatically.

"I noticed the private 'I' in your sign on the door has been stolen."

"It's a cruel world," he replied. "When business picks up, I'm going to buy some new letters. I don't have much foot traffic. Come on and join me." Terry's office furniture, a desk, a couple of chairs, a bookcase, a rectangular banquet room table with four stacking chairs, and a few file cabinets floated in the space. The muffled but intelligible voices from a radio broadcasting in an adjacent tenant space wormed into the detective's private office, mocking any thoughts of confidentiality.

"It's dark in here." I sniffed the air. "Smoking again?"

Terry chuckled and blew smoke rings into the air. "My clients...if they ever visit...are impressed by the Chandleresque style."

"I'll bet. But can we have a bit more light? Sunlight blinded me. In this darkness, I might trip and fall."

Terry reached behind and flipped a light switch.

I checked out the room. "Jesus. Now I understand why you keep it 'lights out'. You need a cleaning lady, Terry."

"Nobody comes here, and I like the atmosphere. It energizes me."

I dusted off the guest chair in a dramatic manner and sat.

"You walked here?"

"Yes," I said. "I pretended I was fifteen again, wandering around town."

Terry snubbed out the Marlboro in a dirty brown glass ashtray half-filled with crushed butts and dead ashes. It continued to smoke itself. "How was your tour of Reinhartland?"

"You're still cooking, Marlowe." I pointed to the smoking ashtray. After rolling his eyes, he fixed the problem.

I leaned back in the chair and told my story. "I learned somethings. And confirmed others. I learned all about the embalming and cremation business. Spent some time with some satisfied pre-cemetery customers. Got my hands dirty and filled my nose with chemicals. I also confirmed my need to get the fuck out of Dodge." I shook my head. "I have no interest in that business."

"Necessary though..."

"So is garbage collection. Doesn't make me want to make it a career."

"Picky, picky, picky. As they say: 'Someone's got to do it.' And Otto and your old man are making a decent living shuffling stiffs along the Green Mile. Could have been all yours, Alex. You only needed to suck it up and join the rest of us." Terry lit up another cigarette.

"Must you?" I asked without any real concern.

He blew out the smoke. "Margie won't let me smoke at home. My customers won't let me smoke in the limo. And my kids think I'm some kind of anti-environmental freak." His eyes darted left, and he made a comedic face. "So if you don't mind..."

"Suit yourself." I'm used to it. "The Paris *Métros* reek of cigarette smoke, cheap cologne, and dog breath. Doesn't bother me. I'm thinking of your lungs."

"We're all going to die sometime. Death is inevitable."

"Yes...let's talk about the death business." I leaned into the desk while Terry fell back into his swivel chair, his cigarette dangling between his lips.

"I'm all ears."

"Right. I met with my father yesterday about the business. His illness kept him away for many months, so now he's got a bug up his butt thinking something is amiss. According to him, the income is OK, but the cash flow is weak. He intimated Otto can't always be trusted."

The springs in Terry's vintage chair squeaked as he leaned forward. "Why doesn't he ask his son?"

"That's not how he works. When he goes to war, he wants a loaded weapon and plenty of ammo. And he never asks an incriminating question unless he already has the answer."

"A regular Perry Mason." Terry nodded and stroked his massive mustache with his thumb and forefinger. "I think this issue came up in the past."

I smiled. "You are a detective. The answer is 'yes'. Otto got involved. Hooked on. Addicted. Whatever. To cocaine."

"And his habit was supported by the business profits?"

"I guess so. We didn't talk too much about it, but I got that impression. I didn't want to go for the juggler, since the monkey is off Otto's back now."

"So what did you learn on your visit to the funeral home?"

"Well, I didn't find any strange white powder," I answered. "But Otto is making physical improvements to the backroom areas. There's new construction adjacent to the embalming room. Otto poo-pooed it, but it's money spent. He suggested it's something new that might provide more income. He's always looking ahead, away from our father's traditional outlook. I don't know what this might involve. It is isolated from other uses. Otto is hot on the jewelry angle of cremation. There must be plenty of profit in baubles."

"I don't follow."

"Putting human ashes, they call cremains, in jewelry like rings and necklaces and selling them to the family members of the deceased."

"That's weird."

"Not so, Romeo. I guess it's popular now. Could be he's thinking of making his own line of trinkets. The mark-ups on jewelry are steep."

"So he's worried about Otto stuffing coke up his nose, and instead Otto is stuffing human remains into over-priced junk jewelry and selling it for a profit to emotionally compromised customers."

"It's all legit." I gestured with my open palms in frustration. "Fact is, I don't know. But you're the detective. He's building something in the back area. Expenditures my father is unaware of, and the old man is willing to pay you to find out what is going on. So it's a real job."

"Super. That I like. What else?"

I paused to recall. "Father made a point of talking about this Dr. Stephan Jarek guy. He doesn't like him at all. I got the feeling he had reasons, but he didn't explain. Jarek is Otto's personal doctor. Yesterday he gave me a physical exam."

"What?... Why?"

"That's a long story. The old man is somewhat paranoid about germs. So he won't allow anyone in unless they're germ-free."

"Are you?"

"Who is?" I shower every morning, "It's stupid...but old people do go stupid."

"So long as he doesn't forget to pay my bill. No cut-rates for old friends."

"Don't worry. Father is straight-arrow. 100 per cent. He's got his family's reputation to protect. You'll be paid in full."

"When can I start?" He maintained a straight face and said, "I've got a little lull in business at the moment."

I smiled. "Lucky day for the Reinharts. You're hired. Do your thing and report back to me. The sooner the better. And we can deliver it to my father. For that, you would need a physical." I glanced around and made a face, "But your hygiene is poor. You might not pass muster."

"Screw you. I'm parasite-free and sweet-smelling. Just ask Margie."

I feigned sniffing the air like a bomb-squad canine. "I may do that."

"OK." Alex stood. "I'm out of here. Give me a lift back?"

Walker didn't rise from his chair. He snubbed out his cigarette. "Sit down, Alex. We have to talk."

With no idea of what Terry wanted to discuss, he appeared intent, so I kept my ass in the chair. My job was done. I leaned back and relaxed. "What's up?"

He looked into my eyes with determination. "Alex. This is one of those moments between friends. I'm concerned about you. I think you're losing your judgment. Strange because you wouldn't be where you are in life without excellent judgment. I mean, I would never wander around some of those remote jungle areas or mountain passes. I've seen your work. You like taking risks, but now you must control your urges."

"What the hell are you talking about?"

Terry shook his head and made a face like a priest counseling a wayward kid. "You're messing with fire. I don't want anyone getting hurt. And I've seen enough 'domestics' to sense trouble.

I drew a blank.

"I'm talking about Kathy, you dork."

He tweaked my anger. Friend or no friend, Terry entered a sensitive area. "I could say this is none of your business."

Terry looked me in the eye. "And I could say you are living in a fantasy world. You've been in there for the last ten years. And in Denver, you experienced a traumatic experience involving another woman. Someone you may have loved or whatever. And now you're sleeping in a bed a mere thirty feet away from your long-lost love. Your brother's wife. And you're dreaming of having sex with her again. We don't know what she is thinking, except we all know Kathy...she's a walking time bomb of sensuality."

"That's a good one. You've been watching too many cable shows, Terry. We slipped up once. But it won't happen again."

"That's what they all say. Until they smell each other again, and Mother Nature takes over. I don't want a newspaper report of you two found in bed by Otto." He raised his voice, "*Two lovers shotgunned to death while engaged in a sex act. Services at Reinhart Funeral Home.* Got it?...this is serious stuff, Alex."

I thought he might leap across the desk to make his point; I waited, ready to defend myself.

For twenty seconds, we stewed in our thoughts of brotherly love. Terry had always been a confidant. In many ways, he was more of a brother than Otto, more truthful and trustworthy, and not subject to my father's intrusive parental nature. And it worked both ways. I had straightened him out when we were young bucks. Terry was prone to bar fights almost without provocation. One Saturday night in a noisy biker bar just outside town, I intervened, and everyone's teeth remained in their heads. While Terry was a fighter, I was a lover who often followed my dick into dangerous situations, and Terry never forgot.

"Remember when I saved your butt in Wisconsin," he said. "You got suckered into taking that beautiful young lass home to her cottage on the lake. What was her name? Ah, yes...Kitty. No one was home. You went to work on her, and then her three brothers returned from a fun night's partying. I told you. Didn't I? Thankfully for you, I hung around, and when you figured it out and busted out of her bedroom window, ran to my car, carrying your pants, we drove non-stop back to Naperville. Remember?"

I smiled. "Fun times. Another exciting experience, Terry. Life is full of them."

"You're full of shit, Reinhart. Fun my ass. We could have both been killed."

I paused. "Yep. You're right. So you think I should behave myself? You think I'm looking for trouble because the woman I love is my brother's wife. You're suggesting that's a problem?"

"Duh..."

Terry settled down. "I'll talk to Margie tonight, and by tomorrow night, you will be staying with us in our house. That is, if you can keep your dick in your pants for one night."

"So crude."

"So stupid. Don't be a sucker or a dead fucker."

"OK. Deal."

Chapter 15

I put up with an additional barrage of unrequested, but good-hearted, advice during the drive to my brother's house. As I exited the car, he said, "I'll pick you up tomorrow morning at ten. Sweet dreams and no..." He pointed to his crotch, shook his head, and looked at me. His phone beeped. Not waiting for me to respond, he took off to service another limo client.

Assuming Otto was still at work, I pushed the bell button, waited, and rang again with no result. Perhaps Kathy was in her studio. I walked around the house and down the path leading to the little artist studio in the meadow. With no response to my knocking, I tried the handle and pushed the door open halfway. "Kathy? There was no sound. I called out again, but louder.

About to leave, I looked around the room and spotted a new canvas resting on the easel in the center of the studio space. As I neared it, I focused on the pencil-lined sketch; her next move would be to apply paint. The image, although faint, was quite clear. For a long moment, I stared at it in disbelief, tingling inside, realizing Otto might wander to the back looking for his wife and discover this cozy headshot of a man and a woman, me and Kathy. While in reality, the tiny gold bell necklace she wore would hardly attract attention, this future painting had turned the shiny birthday bell into a focal point like a pearl earring in a Vermeer. I could only imagine the human emotions she might add to the painting. Terry's snapshot was on its way to becoming a painted portrait that would immediately attract attention and many questions simply because it was different from all of Kathy's other artwork. Standing in our little love nest, in my brother's backyard, I was stunned, and I reacted. Without thinking, I looked around, grabbed the canvas, and hid it behind another larger painting leaning against the studio wall. My panic subsided.

Kathy was drifting into dangerous waters, and for many good reasons, she had to be restrained. Maybe subconsciously, she wanted Otto to find the painting, and the discovery would become the catalyst for ending their marriage. I did not want that to happen. If there were a place in the future for Kathy and me to reclaim our past, that would be great. But at this moment, my family was already overflowing with emotion, tension, and pain. She would have to realize now was not the time to create more confusion and angst. For Otto, who was battling his disease, for our father who was dying, and for me, still trying to erase the indelible memory of Camilla dangling from a rope, no additional emotional trauma was needed.

Returning to the front porch of the house, I sat for about a half-hour worrying and wondering what to tell her when she arrived. Terry's demands were on point. I needed to create some space. I waited. The soothing sounds of the female fountain lady pouring out her troubles quieted me. Head down, eyes closed, lost in thought, I jumped as Kathy's car pulled up, jammed on the brakes, and slid to a stop. She rolled down the passenger side window and offered a pickup line and a smile. "Looking for a ride, stranger?"

Ignoring the innuendo, I got up and entered her car. She reached over and grabbed high up on my left thigh. "A pleasant surprise to find you sitting on my front porch. How was your funeral home tour?"

"It went well. No problems. I stopped by Terry's office, and he dropped me here." For a while, I stared out the windshield, gathering my thoughts.

"Yes. What's up? You look weird," she said.

"I rang the bell, thinking you were out back."

She smiled. "You devil, you."

"No. That's not it. I went back and didn't find you. I opened the door, and I saw your new painting. You and I hugging as young lovers reunited."

"Oh. Nosy...aren't you?" She retracted her hand and leaned back into the car seat. "It was supposed to be a surprise."

"Sure." I shook my head. "Are you losing it? What happened when I arrived..."

"Yes..." she smiled.

"Well...it's not going to happen again. Not here. And you can't be presenting us as a couple. Don't you have any sense?"

"Are you ashamed again, Alex?"

"Nothing to do with shame. I'm concerned about lust, lost love, broken hearts, and broken marriages. I'm not sure where you and I are going, but..."

"But you want to control things. You think I'm reckless and foolish," she continued.

"No. I'm the foolish one. We can't play games. My brother is struggling with his health. My father is dying. And you and I are acting like teenagers in love. When I thought about coming back, I put everything in perspective. I thought I would return...visit my brother and meet you again. But I figured by this time you would be fat, ugly, and boring...not the girl I gave up, and it would be simple. I could leave you without a second thought."

"And then..." she said with a wicked gleam in her eyes.

"And I came back, and I fell under your spell. You were...are...beautiful, talented, intelligent and..."

"Sexy?"

"Yes. All of the above. Face it. I'm a fool."

Her face reflected her confusion. "Is this your strange way of getting rid of me? Alex, you are a nutcase. Listen to yourself. You might learn something." She smiled. "Did you like the sketch?"

We were communicating on a different wavelength. I tried to make her understand. "I hid it behind another painting. It looks fine. You and I together. But what are you thinking? Otto will freak out."

"He never comes into my studio. He's been told to stay out. But who cares? How is it any different than Terry's photo of the two of us? I used his shot to set it up."

"The photo took two seconds. And I could erase it with one click. That's one difference. This one's a labor of love."

She lowered her head and talked into her chest. "I wanted to hold on to you. That's all. I can't guess what's ahead. I just wanted something permanent. You want me to burn it?"

"No. Whitewash it. Put it on the shelf. Please."

"OK," she said. "But you're a Debbie-Downer, Mr. Reinhart. Trifling with my love."

I sat without commenting, gathering my thoughts, and then spoke. "Tomorrow morning, I'm moving to Terry's place. I need space. Can we also agree to put whatever we are as a couple on the shelf for a while? You understand how I feel about you. How I've always felt. That's not going away. I hope we are on the same wavelength. But if this is going anywhere, we have to give it time to develop. Time to..."

"Time to what, Alex?" She pouted. "Time to turn and run away in fright. Never see each other again?"

We held hands and looked at each other. "No. No running away. But, I don't want this place...Otto's place. To be an incubator for our relationship. Something else...anything else...but not that."

"OK. I get it, Alex," she said, "but I want you to understand. I'm finished with Otto. Whether you're around or not, it's going to end."

"Oh." This was news to me. I wasn't quite sure if it was good news or bad. Her comment started me thinking about ropes and endings. I paused. "Maybe in your mind, I'm slinking away like a beaten man. Maybe you think blowing up our world would permit us to pick up the pieces and build something new and better. That's the stuff of cheap novels and bad movies. If you want to preserve something for us in the future, you have to be willing to resolve everything with care."

She took a deep breath, released it with a head shake, and smiled. This unnerved me.

"This is not a joke," I said, "Please think about what I am saying. We're on dangerous ground. Someone could get hurt."

"All right, Mr. Gloom, I'm thinking I'm going into the house. I will begin preparing dinner for the three of us...that should be fun. And since Otto said he would be home early, you might want to take my car...drive around, and come back about five-thirty...maybe a few minutes later. Go sightseeing. Think about war and famine. However, you amuse yourself. Come back. He will be home by then, and we can have a nice family dinner. I will make Otto's favorite meal, you guys can do manly things, and tomorrow morning you can leave and move in with your good buddy."

I returned her hand. "OK. Thanks. I'll do that. But I need to use your facilities first. OK?"

"No," she said with a frown which became a smile. "Just kidding. Don't forget to put the seat down."

Chapter 16

Terry and Margie Walker lived a few blocks north of Terry's office. Their house was a typical two-story vinyl-siding-clad shoe box with three bedrooms up and everything else squeezed into the first floor; only the full basement below made the house livable. We approached, and I viewed my new temporary home. The neighborhood was kid-friendly and a great location for growing up. Trees, sidewalks, a short walk to the school, and a ten-minute drive to work for my friend. He and Margie had started their family early; I didn't realize it then, but she was pregnant with little Charlie when she grabbed her high school diploma. They had the rarest of all forms of love affairs: two high school sweethearts who married and managed to stay together. Their two boys shared the same age spread as Otto and me. According to Terry, the kids, Charlie and Eddie, were thrilled with my visit. I wasn't excited, but I was relieved. As Terry pulled the car into the driveway, two big orange pumpkins on the front porch, waiting to be carved, popped into view. I imagined these might become fearsome night monsters after the two junior surgeons did their best, but now the bulbous pumpkins looked deceptively docile.

"I see the boys are anxious," I said.

"Huh."

"The pumpkins are out...still a while to Halloween."

"Kids...they can't wait."

He pushed the door opener button, and the Lincoln eased into the semi-darkness of the garage.

"This way, Alex. She's expecting us."

Thinking ahead, I left my bag in the car in case we needed to make a quick getaway; Terry left the garage door open. Maybe he had the same thought. He got out, opened the door leading to the kitchen area, and took one step past the threshold. As soon as his left foot landed on wet vinyl, a distant voice, powerful and shrill, shouted, "Stop. Terry Walker, I always tell you to check before you walk on my floors. I just finished."

"Sorry, Dear," he said, his body frozen in time waiting for some direction from the little woman. "Should we come in the front door?"

"No point to that now. Come on in. I'll just do it again."

I took a quick look as I entered, walking behind Terry like a troublesome puppy. Margie Walker, 'five feet two and eyes are blue' according to Terry, stood hands on hips, wearing blue jeans with rolled pant legs and a pink sweatshirt embossed with white letters that spoke the truth: *BOSSY WOMEN RULE.* She had packed on about twenty-five extra pounds since high school, but otherwise, she was the same pie-faced, red-haired, spitfire of a woman.

"Hello, Margie. It's been a while." Tip-toeing gingerly on the sacred floor, I closed the distance, stood towering before her, owned a big smile, and hugged her like a living ragdoll. "Missed you guys." As I released her, I said, "Can you blame me?"

She blushed and took on her husband, commanding: "Terry. I'll show your friend the accommodations. Get his bags." Her attention returned to me. "Mind you...this isn't a historic mansion on the river."

"I am in your debt," I said.

She made a face and nodded. "Someone stepped into the frying pan, I understand. Don't feel bad. From what I hear, you're not the first."

That sign on the door of Walker's office: *Confidential Invest gations.* My ass. With or without the 'I', it was false advertising. He must have revealed everything about Kathy to his wife.

"Margie. Please..." said Terry as he headed out the door.

"I'll get your bag, Alex." The rattle of the garage door closing shook the house. I guess Terry determined that he and I wouldn't have to escape.

Margie and I descended the stairs. She mumbled to herself. "He thinks he's conning me. He reeks of cigarette smoke."

"How's that?"

"Nothin'...you men are all the same," she said, her voice trailing.

We negotiated the stairs carefully. I ducked my head at the last stair riser to avoid hitting the header and entered the rec room. Dropped acoustical tile ceiling, lay-in light fixtures, simulated-grained brown faux-wood paneling, and tan-mush vinyl tile flooring created a perfect rendition of 1960s suburban basement remodeling. Since this was my home for a while, I was glad the Walkers had installed a full bathroom. Things might work if they could keep the two boys upstairs.

"I brought this rack out of storage so you can hang up clothes on it." She rolled the tubular closet into a neutral corner of the basement. The sofa's a pull-out. All your bedding is on that chair."

My eyes followed her directions. I nodded.

"Towels and such are in the bath. And the washer-dryer is in there." Margie pointed to a door separating the finished world from the unfinished. "Don't forget to clean out the dryer filter after each use. We don't want any fires. I tuned in to FOX the other day. Did you know that over 15,000 home fires every year are caused by dirty clothes dryer filters?"

"Sounds bad," I said with a thoughtful look.

She made a face, a red one. "Are you making fun of me, Alex Reinhart?"

I shook my head, looking like a cookie-jar kid. "Ah. No. Not at all. Fire is a serious thing. I don't want us to end up dead in the Reinhart Funeral Home."

"Well, I'll leave you alone. Consider this your home away from home. The kids have been warned to stay out of here." She smiled. "Oh. And no food down here. Drinks are OK, but no food. This is mouse season. Those little bastards will be lining up outside come the first cold spell. I can't say how they get in here. Terry says they can crawl through a quarter-inch hole. But..." she screwed up her face, "he may be exaggerating a bit." As she climbed the stairs, she made a final pronouncement: "I'll send him down. And don't always hang around down here. Come upstairs, and we'll treat you like family."

I smiled, not certain if that was a good thing or not. I heard the door close at the top of the stairs, looked around, and checked out the bath. Pretty grim, but after all, it was a basement. At least I won't have to look Otto in the eye at dinner while Kathy plays footsie with me.

The door opened at the top of the stairs, and Terry made his way down carrying my bag. He dropped it onto the floor.

"Thanks, friend. Sit down. Let's talk a little."

"OK," he said, welcoming a brief respite. We sat at opposite ends of the sofa and leaned in to face each other. "The Mrs. treating you well?"

I smiled. "Like one of the family."

Terry gave me a warped grin. "That's a good sign. Most of my other friends never make it past the garage. Sometimes we all watch TV in there. Even in winter. Four or five neighborhood guys bundled up like we're sitting in the stands. Drinking beer. We'll do the Bears games in the regular season, and I like Green Bay or Steelers post-season."

"Bears still stink?"

"Do they shit in the woods? Watching them is always painful. We drink our way through the games."

I sized up my old friend. "Lucky you. Nice wife. Nice kids. You're good, man. I always thought you made a mistake getting married early and having kids. But now I'm not so sure. Life buzzes along, and pretty soon we're all old and grey. Like my father."

Terry shrugged. "You thinking about your brother and his wife?"

"I guess so. I did a lot of thinking since I arrived."

"About your woman in Denver?"

"Yep. She and Kathy." I paused. "I'm bad luck. I stumble in and wander out. Leaving a mess behind."

He laughed. "Well, not everyone can have all of this." He stretched his arms out. "Look at me. I'm losing my hair, overweight, and I'm just past thirty. My dick still works for taking a piss, but it's almost always 'on-call' for any other duty. I don't know. Becoming my father at an early age makes me feel old. I envy you. A man of the world. Unleashed. No rings. No strings. Not so bad, Jocko."

"I suppose. That's me...but you guys are the prototypical sitcom family. *'Here they are...The Walkers: Terry, Margie, Charlie, and Eddie.* All you need is a crotchety old-guy neighbor."

"Got one of those. I'll introduce you. Hey, it is what it is. What about you?" He asked. "Did you take care of Kathy?"

"Done for now. Things cooled down when I told her I was moving in with you."

"That would do it." He chuckled. "You're like a mob informant going into a witness protection program. You're now officially a suburbanite...and a rat. But at least Otto is none the wiser. You'll soon be gone for another ten years. Maybe we can visit you in Florida."

"Sure." I cocked my head. "Any luck with your investigations?"

"Uh. I've got some irons in the fire. I'll check public records. And I found the contractor who's working on the backroom improvements at the mortuary. He's a friend of a friend. I'm going to quiz him."

"Anything on Dr. Jarek?"

Terry nodded. "Jarek...that was easier. "He seems on the up and up. Comes out of Milwaukee. No money behind him. Just a regular guy who worked himself up from lower-middle-class roots. Served in the Army. Went to school on the government's dime. Got his sheepskin and interned in a Milwaukee hospital. After that, he came to Illinois. He worked for several years in a family medical practice in Berwyn. Five or six years ago, he opened his own office in Aurora."

"OK," I said, "but he seemed a little weird to me."

"How so?"

"He's tall, but it's like he has a Napoleon complex. Wants to impress. Tries too hard to be the 'go-to guy', the best little doctor in Aurora. That kind of thing."

"Maybe. So far, he's come up clean. Both you and your father don't like this guy."

"Well, I guess he can't be all bad. He is treating my brother."

"Think about it. He's treating, and you're cheating. Who's the bad guy here?"

I was stunned by his comment for a moment. "I don't blame you for being judgmental. I'm a rat. Through and through. But this thing with Kathy smoldered for a whole decade. Spontaneous combustion. It just happened. We didn't plan it."

Terry appeared to digest his excuse. "Alex, you had a rough month. I can't imagine how it felt to find your woman hanging herself. She ended her life, but she also drove a knife into your heart. There are many ways to end a relationship, but...that was a brutal choice. My advice: cut yourself some slack. Be nice-nice to your brother. And forget the whole thing. If that's all it is...that's it. It's over. Right?"

The question sunk in. "I hope so, Terry." For me, this conversation was over, too painful to contemplate. I rose and walked a few feet, looked around the basement, and turned back to face him. "Staying here is the best place for me now. A cold shower of reality.

Thanks." The sofa found my butt again, and I leaned back, talking into the air. "And I'm going to see my father tomorrow. Can I tell him you'll have something soon?"

The detective rubbed his mustache before replying. "I need another day or two."

"Good. I'd like to put an end to this whole thing. Spying for the old man is at least as disgusting as cheating with my brother's wife, without the fun part. Once you and I settle his concerns, they can make a smooth transition to put Otto in charge before the current boss dies. Then...I'm on my way."

Chapter 17

I returned to my father's house to bring him up to date. This time, the nurse allowed me to enter without any health screenings. I stepped into his office and sensed this meeting would be different. The old man remained seated. Unlike last time, he looked tired. I shook hands with him, and at his request, located a bottle of Scotch and poured a drink for each of us. I sat, and we began our session with a toast.

"Cheers," he said, "happy to see you." His voice got caught somewhere, and he cleared his throat gently. He took his time drinking the Scotch, savoring every sip, allowing a level of comfort and satisfaction to build inside his deteriorated body. "I got a call from Gorger. Dedicated guy that Jan. He's been the biggest supporter of Reinhart. Gave you the full tour. I gather?"

"He and Otto. Top to bottom. Impressive. Including the new cremation unit."

Frederick nodded. "I'm not surprised you like it. Nothing sentimental about that device. All business."

"I guess it's the way of the future," I said.

He rested his elbow on the arm of the chair with his drink in hand, jutted his chin upward, and was deep in thought for a moment. He mused. "People today don't have time to die and be remembered with respect. Everyone is in a hurry. Fast cars, fast food, and fast transitions to the other side. I guess Reinhart Funeral Home is not bucking the trend. I tried to maintain dignity and remembrance, but the business moved from bronze caskets and granite mausoleums to an era of irreverent keepsakes and gizmos."

I remember something engraved on a gravestone on my cemetery visit. "*Time marches on and change is certain*."

"So true," he said, "so true." He regrouped. "What about it? What did you think about our situation?"

I scanned my memory. "Keep in mind, I've been away so long, these are almost first impressions."

"Go ahead, Alex...you won't hurt my feelings."

"OK. The outside." I shook my head. "It looks somewhat neglected. The parking lot is tired. Some areas need to be replaced and sealed. Others just sealed. The landscape has a mind of its own. Not a major issue, but it makes the place somewhat shabby."

The old man remained stoic.

"The sign at the corner. A new one is required. You have to find the right blend of tradition and contemporary. I think your growth market is younger people. The older residents already have the Reinhart name established in their memory, but others, newbies to funeral services, may drive by the building, and without thinking, formulate an impression. Only to be recalled later, when a grandparent dies, and the time arrives to become a customer of your services. That initial drive-by must make the correct statement. At the moment...not so much."

"You're doing fine." He smiled. "I was certain asking you to do this would be useful. What about the inside?"

I paused. "Well...it's a little traditional for me. Dated. Sure, it costs money to change, but you might consider a facelift. Something more contemporary. You wouldn't have to spend a fortune. Some paint, lighting, carpeting, and accessories. The place is functional, but it feels like Granny's brocade purse."

Frederick nodded. "Is that it?" He waited.

I recalled my tour. "The casket viewing room."

"Yes..."

I made a face. "It's depressing. All those empty caskets. An unorganized array of empty caskets on wheels. People will think of them as they would when buying a car. Except no one wants to take a test drive. I checked online, and I found that other funeral homes are using quarter-sized wall-mounted displays. With the right display lighting, it can create an exciting floor-to-ceiling wall of funereal cockpits."

"Is that all?"

I chuckled. "You asked for it, Father."

"I did...and you delivered. Thank you. You have given me something to keep me busy as I shuffle off this mortal coil. A fresh pair of eyes. Necessary. Otto and I have been blinded by time, illness...mine, and his...and familiarity. We're too close to see the overall picture. And you are the artist." He leaned back. "That's excellent. Anything else?"

"No. Except...and keep in mind...I don't claim knowledge of your enterprise, but Otto gave me the impression he might be working on something new. Possibly on the jewelry side of cremation. He's been doing a little remodeling in the backroom area. He has something in mind."

"What?" he asked. "I'm not aware of anything."

"I have no real idea. Some improvements in the space next to the embalming room have been completed."

My father looked like he was remembering a mental picture of the back area. "I've been away for a while," he said, "I'll have to ask him. It could be buried in the financials. What else?"

"What else? I've got Terry snooping. I explained your concerns. He deals with family matters all the time. Often divorce stuff. So he's familiar with the ins and outs of money misappropriation. It's a common element. So he's going through his routine with discretion, of course. I should have his report soon. A couple of days."

"Fine. I appreciate this, Alex. I hate to sit here guessing. I need to know. But I want to keep it close to the chest."

At this point in our conversation, no one spoke for at least a minute. The clock on the mantle clicked away the seconds. We each sipped our Scotch, and for me, it was pleasant. I was pleased to spend time with my father after all these years. Our quiet moment was broken when the old man drifted into a story his father had told him when he was young about a group of German-American soldiers in World War I in a water-filled trench somewhere in France. One of the soldiers was my grandfather's relative. This cousin wrote a letter from the trenches saying they did not fear the sniper rifles of the German army, nor their screaming artillery shells, nor the poison gas, but what he feared most were the cooties, rats, and trench foot. The other fears might kill or wound a soldier and send him to the rear or into a grave. It was the cooties, rats, and diseased feet that were part of the daily grind, offering no relief, sympathy, or hope." His words trailed off. By the time he finished the long story, he had forgotten the punch line.

"Sorry, Alex. I'm certain this tale held special meaning for my father, but for the life of me, I can't remember what."

I wanted to help my father, but he was at a loss for words. This led to another awkward moment of silence.

My father appeared to be dozing; then he brightened, mumbled, and found his voice. "It's all about family, Alex. All about tradition. I will tell you something interesting. About Kathy. Beautiful gal. You've always maintained a soft spot in your heart for her. Right?"

Kathy again, I thought. "We dated for quite a while. But that was before Otto met her."

"Yes...yes. So it was. Well...she is important for the Reinhart legacy. I've talked to her about this subject. I have no grandchildren. No one to carry on the family name. Unless you have someone."

I shook my head. "No. No wife. No children. Trust me, I would have mentioned it." I smiled.

He chuckled. "Of course. I always suspected you would never commit to any marital relationship. That's you. But Kathy. She is the key. You are aware that your brother is firing blanks. He has a low sperm count. So low that no child will ever be conceived bearing the Reinhart name. It's not Kathy's problem. They have tried. They have been to doctors and consultants. They've worked on it for years, but regrettably, for them and me, it is not going to happen. Well, of course, it could happen." He was wide-eyed now, catching the flow of his story. "This may all be new to you. I would think so. Did you know much about her?"

I chuckled. "I only knew what I liked. She was eighteen, innocent-looking, and very attractive. I was twenty-one and full of hormones."

"Well...he paused as if working on an approach, his eyes glanced up and to the right, before returning to mine. "She comes from common stock. I met them at the wedding. Her father was a city bus driver, and her mother worked downtown in the dimestore selling goldfish. Nice people, I guess. Salt of the earth. Both are dead now. But Kathy has always been a bit adventurous...like you. Always looking for a little excitement. Except that her world of adventure is a world of bodily pleasures. Are you following me?" His lips curled up at the corners into a half-smile. "I'm sure this doesn't shock you because you dated her."

I shook my head. "We were kids when we dated. It was all pretty tame."

"Well, at some point, and this is before she and Otto were married...she was impregnated by another man. A black man. Of course, there was no thought of marriage. She never saw him again."

I listened to his story with discernment.

"Don't get me wrong. But in this town, if you have a black baby, you'd better be prepared to leave town. Right?"

"Did she have the baby?"

"Of course not. By this time, Otto was smitten with her. She used to be Dr. Jarek's office manager."

"I didn't realize Otto and Jarek knew each other," I commented.

"I assume that's where Otto was introduced to Kathy. Jarek was his doctor. In any event, Otto came to me and begged me to arrange an abortion in another state; it was done, and all went well. I think that cemented Otto's marriage proposal. After that, Kathy and Otto were married. I mention this as a matter of background. So Kathy and I understand each other. And she understands how dedicated I am to having an heir. I talked with her a few weeks ago. Alone. Otto was not involved in our conversation. I explained to her that my estate would pass to you and Otto alone. She is not a beneficiary. That if any of the estate is shared with her from Otto, it was all his choice. Are you with me?"

I understood, but after his war story, I wondered where this was leading, if anywhere. I only nodded.

"This may seem somewhat outrageous," he said, "but if you think about it...it's sensible for everyone. I told her if she could carry my grandchild...if there was an heir...and I emphasized 'my grandchild'. She would get one-quarter of the estate. You and Otto would split the remainder. A sacrifice for you two brothers, but it is my estate, and it is a family matter. And I'm sure you agree my intentions are honorable and in the best interest of the family." He smiled. "Generous on my part, which demonstrates how important this is to me."

"And what did she say?" I asked the question without emotion in my voice, and I didn't know where he was leading. However, I had my suspicions.

"Wait...because this involves you. The baby must be *my* heir. So Otto informed me you were returning home, and I had an idea." He paused.

"The idea?"

"Yes. Coming to that...so to speak." He smiled. "Kathy and you could get together and...well, you know...create an heir for me."

His words crawled into my alcohol-dulled brain. I put down my drink, stood, and began circling the room. I didn't speak. I viewed my father out of the corners of my eyes. I would guess my look was not kind.

Frederick's old age and illness hadn't quieted his need for control. "I'm sure this appears somewhat crude to you." He smiled.

"It's a strange request. I'm curious. What was her response?" My father could not guess the intensity of my interest in his bizarre scheme.

"Well, I was hoping she might consider it. She didn't reject the idea, and that was enough for me. I only wanted to plant the seed. She's capable of executing the plan, and this way she'll never have to beg Otto for money. She's a strong, independent woman with a good head on her shoulders. What do you think, Alex?"

"I think...it's all presumptuous," I took a deep breath and cocked my head to one side as I spoke. "I have been thinking kind thoughts about you, Father. I didn't come here out of pity, nor to collect part of your estate. I came to bid you farewell. But then you asked me for my advice on your business. And you wanted me to snoop on my brother. Now, you're asking me to bed your daughter-in-law so that you can have an heir."

My father smiled. "Come on, Alex. Drop the little boy attitude. A roll in the hay or two with Kathy isn't exactly a torture chamber. I'm not suggesting you force her, and I'm sure she wouldn't mind reuniting with you. I planted a seed, and you could also...for the sake of the family. Tell me, has she approached you?"

I didn't respond, but I may have become flushed.

"Aha," he chortled, "It looks like a dying old man's fantasy might be a possibility. Just think about it, Alex. Have fun...but be discreet. We don't want to upset Otto. He's got a bad heart. You would be doing her and me a substantial favor. Just think it over."

"Think it over," without intention, I raised my voice, "how can I not?" I screwed up my face and shook my head. "I think your mind may be drifting. You can't just manipulate Otto and me. We're not your puppets, Father."

His face was without emotion, almost quizzical. I looked at him knowing, and not caring, I ruffled the feathers of the peacock patriarch of the Reinhart family. "I'm sorry. I don't want to talk about this. Honestly, I think you have stepped across the line with this Kathy idea." I have to go now. Thanks for the drink, Father, and good night." I left him holding his almost empty glass of Scotch, looking bewildered.

The two-mile walk to Terry's house allowed me to bathe my mind in the fresh, chilly evening air. I walked through the quiet neighborhoods, lighted only by occasional streetlamps and early bird Halloween decorations. Overwhelmed with thoughts of my father, I remembered my mother. No wonder she couldn't last. She hated his business, but she was trapped in a loveless marriage to a strange man who harbored dangerous ideas. Coming home to Naperville was a mistake. I had been drawn into my father's web of intrigue and deceit, and now the too-good-to-be-true magical moment of my reconnection with Kathy had been tainted by a dying, delusional, dictatorial old man. I would rather live with an impossible romantic dream than be suckered into a contrived scheme intended to continue the Reinhart family name while providing financial gain for my lost love.

By the time I reached Terry's house, the black October darkness and a creeping depression had enveloped me.

Chapter 18

I spent the next morning in Terry's basement, a recluse, so quiet, the hard-hearted Margie opened the upstairs door and yelled down a wellness check. After assuring her I hadn't fallen victim to ravenous mice, I quit sulking, showered, dressed, and tried to improve my standing as a grateful guest. She took one look at me, and somehow her motherly instinct sensed I was a wounded bird. She offered, and I accepted the all-purpose remedy for morose kids, a peanut butter and jelly sandwich, and a glass of milk. Her medicine worked, and I tried to make her day better by offering to be of some use. She accepted my offer. Vacuuming the carpeting throughout the house was my penance. It was a good workout, and I had a better feel for the rigors of suburban domestic life. After I worked off my penance and a walk around the neighborhood, I returned feeling less like a victim and more in control. I had evolved a new game plan which only required me to do the right thing.

By late afternoon, I heard the family Walker assembling above me. The kids, Terry and Margie, were upstairs jawing about issues unknown to me. I climbed up to the arena, and as I appeared, things quieted down. When Margie left the room, I convinced Terry to take everyone out for a decent dinner on Uncle Alex. He grabbed my eighty-dollar bribe, rounded up the family, and headed to an upscale burger joint.

The house was empty, and my skin crawled, my blood boiled, and my heart pounded. It was time for a showdown. With little or no self-control, I telephoned Kathy and asked her to stop by for a visit; my invitation no doubt sounded more like an order. Regardless, she agreed and arrived twenty minutes later. To avoid any hint of impropriety, our meeting was held outdoors in the Walker backyard. Side by side, we drifted to and fro on the ancient swinging bench. A gentle breeze deposited her delicious scent upon me, almost stealing my resolve.

"I'm happy to be with you, Alex. You'll have to tell me what's going on. But it's good to be here. I knew you couldn't live without me." She reached down to take my hand. I must have reacted in some way. She pulled her hand away. "OK. My mistake. Sometimes I can misread situations. I tend to fantasize. In a good way."

My eyes met hers, and she stole my soul again. "Kathy..." I looked around. Clouds gathered as a light breeze fluttered the fringed canopy above. Somewhere down the street, little kids played in the park, making the high-pitched kid noises only they can generate. "I wanted to see you because I'm lost. Maybe I was lost before I returned home, but now I am deep in the woods."

"Let me guess. You are upset because of the sex. I'm married to your brother. And we had sex. Is that a good guess?"

I shifted my weight, and Terry's lawn swing moved back a little, let it return, and stopped cold in mid-swing. "There's that. Yes."

"And..."

"And...I visited my father yesterday afternoon. We had a very interesting talk."

"About what?"

"About my ideas for improvements to the funeral home...and other things."

She chuckled. "Well, is that the cause of an emergency meeting? Is that why you won't hold my hand?"

I made a face. "He told me something I didn't want to hear. He said he discussed his desire to have a grandchild to pass down the Reinhart name. He said he talked to you."

She looked out across the Walkers' backyard, surveying the scattering of flotsam and jetsam left behind by Terry's two boys: a soccer ball, a toy dart gun, a plastic bat, and a two-wheel bike lying on the ground. "Frederick and kids. That's a laugh. If he were here now, he would order Terry's boys to pick up their stuff and file it away in appropriate storage containers, each one labeled and color-coded. Yes, he and I talked about grandkids. What about it?"

"He said Otto couldn't deliver the goods. To use his words: 'Otto was firing blanks.'"

She chuckled. "How colorful. I didn't think he could be that poetic." She shook her head as if to dismiss the thought. "Alex, I didn't come here to talk about Otto's shortcomings."

"OK. The old man told me he made you an offer. If you could get pregnant with what I'll call a 'Reinhart baby', he would cut you in on his inheritance. Do you remember that?"

She gave me a hard look. "Oh. Yes...hard to forget that one. I can't believe he discussed that with you."

"Not a discussion. A sales presentation."

"What was he selling?"

"You. Or at least the possibility of family-approved sex with you."

This time she laughed. "So you ran this through the massive personal-relationship computer sitting on your shoulders and connected the dots. Two days ago, I lured you into a compromising...let's say moral dilemma...where I'm a honey pot, but you, maybe even with some reluctance, could satisfy your latent lust without a tinge of guilt. Because everyone, including my father-in-law. Is, at least in spirit, in on the game. Is that what's bothering you?"

I cleared my throat. "I suppose that's one way of putting it." I pushed the swing back, and we began rocking again. I kept it rocking while I formulated my response. The swing squeaked like two lovers getting it off on an old bed until I stopped it. "Coming out of Father's mouth...he was hopeful and expectant. I assume he didn't know we already put the operation into action."

She snapped back. "You're a prick, Alex. A dumb prick. Maybe the goofy old man offered you a bigger cut of the pie if you succeeded? That's possible too...right?"

All sounds in the yard went dead: no birds chirping, no happy kids, no beating hearts, only dead quiet. I swallowed. "Maybe I am. Maybe I'm stupid."

Kathy chuckled. "You were pitiful enough ten years ago when you avoided having sex with me because of your 'Madonna-whore complex'. Now you've evolved that to be a 'Madonna-grifting-whore' complex. Your growth as an enlightened human is astounding."

Out on a limb and sawing it off, I suspected one more word would drop me to the ground. I didn't speak.

"And to think, I enjoyed your company. I felt like a kid again. I thought you were different than the other Reinhart men. But you are as calculating, abusive, and rude as the other two."

We didn't rock, and we didn't talk for a painful moment. She began to sob. "I hoped...stupid of me. I thought we found something. Something that fell by the wayside, but somehow we retrieved it and brought it back to life. But..." She turned her head and knuckled away a tear. I reached over and wiped off her other cheek with the flat of my hand. "Don't try to be nice, Alex. You're right. I want you for your sperm. It's as simple as that. Nothing else. A good time and a few ounces of 'vital bodily fluid'. You nailed it."

"I'm sorry, Kathy."

"Sorry? Do you think I like being married to a Frederick clone? Do you think I like being associated with the death business? Is that what you think?" She waited. Then, in the quiet voice of a person suffering, she said: "I hoped you, and I would be kindred spirits...soul mates...reunited. Two people who appreciate life and don't profit from death. Two creative forces who could help each other express the life given to them."

We sat rocking again and not talking. Until she spoke: "In a way, Otto and his father rescued me. They saved me from a life you know nothing about."

"I got some idea," I mumbled.

She scoffed. "Got it. Old Frederick gave you the cook's tour of a confused young woman's life of lust and pleasure. Only to be saved by the Teutonic Knights of Naperville. So he told you everything?" She waited without response. " Well, this was the reality. My childhood was a total nightmare. My father was an oversexed drunk who constantly abused my mother like she was a blow-up sex doll. And when she got pregnant again, he kicked her in the belly. A cheap abortion. She would never have sex with him again. So he started pawing me. I couldn't take it. I had to get out. You wouldn't have me. You left town, and I looked elsewhere for solutions. All bad decisions."

"I didn't know."

We stopped talking and sat together, lost in our thoughts. I thought about our relationship ten years ago. We were both desperate then.

She broke the silence. "That's the point. I couldn't tell you, and if I did...would you have saved me? I don't think so. I would just be another millstone around your neck. Like your father and his mortuary business. You wanted out of your situation."

I shrugged my shoulders and shook my head.

"Later, Otto offered me a way out of my troubles. But, now I have a joyless, loveless, sexless marriage... like your mother. I am wounded, Alex. With or without you, I will make changes. You inspired me. I'm a big girl. I'll find my way. Are you disgusted now? Disappointed? What?"

I thought. "Lost. I didn't want to..."

"What...break up a lovely family. The big house, the cars, and the respectable business...all irreparably damaged by you. Squash an old, dying man and destroy a prematurely aging husband suffering from a weak heart? Does that sum it up?"

I lowered my head to my chest, a beaten man now. "I was looking for love. I'll admit it. I thought for a moment I found it. But I am not the asshole you might think. I came here at the wrong time. I had the stuffing beat out of me in Denver. I didn't tell you because our little fling was too much fun. I didn't want to pour cold water on it. But my discussions with my father, my funeral home tour, and the cemetery." I pursed my lips. "I know now why I left Naperville. I should have never come back home. You are not the problem. The problem is me. I create situations that become painful for other people. Just like this one."

"What are you talking about, Alex?"

I looked around and became self-conscious. "Can we go for a walk? It's almost time for the family to come home, and I don't want them to ask a lot of questions."

She grabbed my hand, and this time I didn't resist as we walked around the side of the house along the driveway and headed down the tree-lined sidewalk. Instinctively, we dropped the hand-holding to eliminate the possibility of neighborhood gossip. As we walked, leaves fell off the trees, like brightly-colored petals from dying flowers. A growing breeze swirled the kaleidoscope of fallen leaves at our feet. A storm was coming.

"So..."

"I left Denver in a hurry. Otto called me, I dropped everything, and a few days later I was on a train headed home." She listened and appeared to be thinking.

She said, "I told Otto it was too soon. He made it sound as if your father was on death's door. As you know, the old geezer is not about to depart early."

"That was my impression when I saw him. I took off from Denver in a hurry. I was living with someone. A nice girl named Camilla. And I had to tell her I was leaving, not just to visit family, but most likely for good. From my point of view, it was the right time to end our relationship. So I did."

"Your girlfriend?" she asked.

"Yes. We lived together for about a year. Our lease was up, and so too was our time together."

"The usual for you."

I nodded. "The night I explained the situation here, I was going home, my father was dying, and I would be seeing Otto and you for the first time in many years...I also told her I might not be returning. We argued, and I left to walk it off. I had a couple of drinks and returned later that evening, and she was...she had committed suicide."

"No."

"Yes. It was terrible. Just awful. Trust me."

We stopped walking, faced each other, and embraced. I broke down, and she let me cry on her shoulder for a long time. A cool wind shot down from the north and stirred up thousands of dead leaves into a maelstrom. The sky darkened. We ran back along the walk, and rain fell in sheets, pelting our faces. Kathy's car was parked nearby. We were cold and wet when we reached it, entered, and slammed the doors to keep out the rain. Faces dripping, we sat breathing hard. The windows fogged. Rain pounded on the roof and bounced off the windshield. I used my handkerchief to wipe her face and mine.

She spoke: "I'm sorry, Alex. I didn't know. I only thought about myself. You must have been crushed."

I shook my head in pain, and drips flew from my head. "I was...still am. It's made a mess of me. And then you..." I scoffed. "You enter my life again. And guilt runs rampant."

"I get it now," she said as she brushed my hair back and pulled me close. "I get it."

We kissed and released, leaned back, and stared out, watching and listening to the rainfall. Our words drifted out and steamed the windshield.

"What will we do?"

She looked at me for a few long seconds. "A few days ago, you had a good idea. Put everything on hold...things were getting out of hand. And after, I was doing fine until you called me today."

I remained quiet as I took in her words. "So...we go back to sitting in our neutral corners pretending we're just in-laws, ignoring my father's stupid comments, and allowing the future to happen?"

"Yes. I think that's it. For sure. In light of your recent trauma. I'm not that hardhearted, Alex. No matter what good old Frederick believes, I'm not a crazed woman lusting for money and sex. Let's put it in a box and tie a ribbon around it for now. OK?"

"In a box." I half-smiled. "Got it."

We sat without talking as if we had solved everything. The rain slowed and finally stopped. We looked at each other. I squeezed her hand and got out. I closed the door and put my hand against the window glass, leaving a fading imprint. She started the car and drove off. I watched her little red car disappear down the road as I walked a half-block back to my friend's house. It's hopeless, I thought. My arrival in town had only intensified my love for her. I knew my longing for her would never be satisfied, but she was right. Our relationship belonged in a box, like one of those hope chests, only my hope chest was filled with nothing, not even hope.

As I neared the Walker driveway, the rattling sounds of the garage door opening filled the late October air, causing unknown dogs to bark at each other. The big Lincoln carrying Terry, Margie, and the two boys pulled into their suburban dream. I gave them a wave of my fingers as they passed. No one saw the lonely figure in the wet darkness. The car proceeded on, and the big door closed with a thud.

The ball, in a box and tied with a pretty blue ribbon, was in my court now.

Chapter 19

The following day, I met Otto for a man-to-man talk. "Thanks for meeting me here. Terry's basement wouldn't work," said Otto, shaking his head. "I still don't quite understand why you moved out of our place."

"No offense intended, Otto. It's where I am right now. OK?"

My brother nodded, and he cocked his head, appearing to accept my non-answer. We sat on a bench in the shadow of the Millennium Carillon in a park in the center of town, a 160-foot-high monument, and sometimes called a boondoggle by residents. "I remember lots of talk about tearing this thing down," I said. "I envisioned the headlines: *Enormous Musical Phallus Declared Impotent.*" As the words left my mouth, I regretted saying them, remembering my recent conversation with Kathy about male potency, yet Otto didn't blink.

"The townspeople spent millions on repairs, but I think it's fixed now. Seventy-two bells and six octaves. The whole enchilada. Father donated to the original construction...dropped ten thousand in the pot. But this baby was a black hole of donation money, with the concrete cracking and the steel rusting. Popping apart piece by piece. The city gave up on demolition. Guess they couldn't face failure."

"So it's here to stay now?"

"Who can say? Nothing is forever." Otto ran one hand through his thinning hair, exposing his scalp glistening in the bright sunlight. "I think the bells are working. But I'm not a bell guy. Are you?"

"Nope. For certain...no wedding bells."

Otto chuckled.

"And after climbing the Great Pyramid in Egypt, this attempt at eternal greatness looks puny," I said as I stared at the tower, spotting something incongruous. "Are those cell phone transmitters tucked in between the panels at the top?"

Otto nodded. "Yep, it's got to earn its keep. Like everything and everybody in life. As the old man always says: There's no free lunch."

"He's all business, all the time."

"Guess that's what put Mother in an early grave."

"We'll never understand why she took her life," I suggested. "People are complicated."

"That they are." He paused. "I wanted to thank you for getting Kathy out of her funk."

Otto sounded sincere, but I shrugged my shoulders all the while thinking I had the actual answer.

He continued: "I've been busy keeping a lot of balls in the air. The business, my health, Father's health. Everyone is sucking gas. But since you came, things improved. Kathy's happier. And thanks to you, Father is thinking about dressing up the public areas of the building."

"He asked my opinion, so I bounced some ideas off him. I couldn't tell whether they pissed him off or pleased."

"That's the way he is," said Otto. "You should try working for him." He took a deep breath and exhaled.

"No thanks, brother. I leave that to you. I came back to visit Father and you and Kathy." I gazed out across the park, thinking. "They say you can't go home again. No man ever steps in the same river twice. Not the same river, and he's not the same man. All those adages aside...some places never change."

"You got that right."

"Naperville is one of them. And I haven't changed either, Otto." I shook my head and smiled. "I leave all this to you. This is your world."

"Thanks…" he said without conviction as he began to perspire. "I get what you're saying. But…"

"Are you all right?"

Otto thought for a moment. "The answer is no. That's why I dragged you out of Terry's basement." He swallowed hard. His face screwed up; something was wrong.

"I've got serious health issues, Alex. My heart is shot."

"I thought it was all under control."

Otto opened his eyes and took a deep breath. "So did I. But last week I found out I need a heart transplant."

This news stunned me. I was a man of words, but I stumbled in response. "Jeez. No other options…"

"I've asked…but I haven't heard one. I'm on a list now."

"For a transplant?"

"Right. You have to wait in line, and they have to select you."

"Who's they?"

Otto made a face. "The medical system. Once you're on the list waiting…you can only pray…I guess."

My mind fell into thoughts of prayer. Otto might push the right buttons and receive divine assistance. I hoped so, but it never worked for me. In the distance, something caught my eye: two little boys chased each other up and down the grassy hill at the base of the carillon, screaming happy sounds in the joy of youth. Those two boys now sat on this bench, and at least one of them was dying. I shook myself out of my reverie.

"Does Kathy know?"

"Yeah. I told her this morning. It was time."

"How did she take it?"

"Handled it well. But you know her. She has a way of staying calm. She's quite the optimist."

"Always sees the bright side," I agreed.

Otto tilted his head. "Better than her having a breakdown. She didn't like my explanation of what was involved, so I said, "Give my doctor a call. Not wanting to go through the whole drill again."

"Sounds reasonable. And Father? Did you tell him?"

"No. Not yet. By the time it happens. If it happens. He'll be gone. And I'll be next."

"Why do you say that?" I reacted. "Aren't these transplants commonplace now?"

"You bet. Everybody wants a new heart. That's the problem. People are living longer now. So there are fewer healthy hearts available. Supply and demand. There aren't enough to go around, so they ration them."

"Is it a matter of money?"

"No. That would be too simple..." replied Otto, his voice trailing off.

"Well. I'm here for you, Otto." I put my arm around my brother's shoulder.

"Thanks." Otto buried his head in his chest as if he were going to cry. He mumbled, "Can you stay a while? In town...until I get a handle on things."

I contemplated his question, but I didn't want to make any promises I couldn't keep. "We'll see. I have issues to take care of in Denver."

He nodded. "I understand. Everyone has problems. And I haven't asked you once about anything in your life."

"Understandable, Otto. Totally. Let's take it day by day for now. You've been walloped. But you're a fighter."

Otto brightened. "That I am. Remember when the two of us were young, I had my heart operation. Mother and Father were in the hospital with me outside my room. I overheard them talking. She sounded crazy with fear. She told him I might die on the operating table, but the old man didn't encourage her negativity. He said everything would work out." He paused. "And he was right, but I guess she couldn't handle it."

"You were always her favorite, Otto. She worried about you."

"And you?" he asked. "Did she worry about you?"

I thought about it. "She liked to remind me that I was her little man, whatever that meant."

"Nothing's changed, Alex, I'm still in trouble and..."

"You'll be fine. Father was correct. At least about you. I'm certain everything will work out."

Chapter 20

D r. Stephan Jarek warily approached the Cozy Hours, a one-story, flat-roofed, twelve-unit motel located a few miles north of Naperville. He followed his usual routine, which was to drive past the building to ensure no one was following his intended victim. His slow pass allowed him to spot the red Mini Cooper and convinced him the parking lot was free of followers, watchers, or other troublemakers. He pulled in and parked as far as possible from his destination. Except for his white shirt and red tie, the tall doctor was dressed in black from head to toe, including his leather boots. He straightened his tie in the rearview mirror before exiting the car. His eyes focused on his goal. The heavy drapes of the motel room were pushed apart by someone whose face was revealed and disappeared quickly. She was waiting.

Jarek crossed the parking lot to the building. He strutted along the narrow sidewalk in front, the metal cleats on his boots clicking with every step. When he reached the door marked "6", he paused to center his mind on his character, and he pounded on the door.

"Hello...who's there?" A cautious female voice inquired.

Jarek responded in a commanding voice. "I am the landlord. Open this door."

The lock rattled, and the door opened, revealing a sweet-looking but frightened teenage girl. She wore a simple pink gingham cotton dress with a soft white belt cinching her middle. White trim ringed the top and the bottom of the dress. Her auburn hair was set in pigtails, and a fuzzy white collar with a small, round pink puff in the middle graced her long neck. "My mother and father have gone to town," she said. "So I'm all alone. Can you come back later...mister?"

He stepped into the room, swinging the door closed behind him. It slammed shut, shaking the walls of the old building. "That's too bad because your old man owes me plenty." He scanned her from top to bottom. "We could even things out somehow." He chuckled and removed his black bolero cowboy hat, tossing it on an easy chair in the corner. "Don't be frightened, little one. I'm only here to collect the rent."

Kathy Reinhart panted and wore a face full of terror. Her eyes were wild, and her mouth was agape. She backed away from the stranger inch by inch until the back of her bare legs bumped up against the bed.

Jarek stepped boldly toward her, pinning her. She pushed on his chest, forcing him back to no avail. He took one step forward, and they stood face to face. Her breasts, straining the cotton fabric of the dress, squeezed against him as he pulled her close. With open palms, she slapped his face, hard enough to get a rise out of him. Voice breathless, her face reddened, she acted her part. "No...no. Leave me alone."

"Wildcat, you are. I like that." He held her at the waist with one arm and reached up to remove his tie with the other. In seconds, it was off. He spun her around, his hands found her wrists, and he brought them together behind her back. He used his tie to bind them. In no hurry now, he held her in place, gripping the binding with one hand and reaching under her dress with the other.

She shivered as his fingers probed. She pretended to struggle, but his grip remained unforgiving.

"Stop, mister. I won't fight. Please."

He released his pressure and slid his hand down her wet thighs. She turned to face him, arms behind her back.

"Untie me. You won't regret it," she said with a little smile.

"No funny stuff, bitch." Still standing, he reached around to loosen the tie, which he tossed on the bed, all the while his body pushed up into hers. He took his time, and this simple chore led to a rhythmic dance for both. His hands grabbed her backside, and he drew her toward him. Her hands were free now. She brought them up to the top button of his white shirt, and she started a slow process of unbuttoning it until his bare chest was exposed. The fingers of both her hands danced across his hairy chest, stopping on occasion to pinch his nipples. Too much for him, he pulled off his jacket and tossed it onto the chair. They kissed passionately. She teased his crotch with her raised knee, working it around and making him groan. He pushed her away but maintained a tight grip on the neck of her dress. In one slashing motion, he ripped the gingham off her body, leaving her naked except for the little white collar with the pink puff in the middle.

Kathy pretended to be shocked by his behavior, bringing her hands up to contain and conceal her unleashed breasts. She adopted a schoolgirl pose, changing her posture to a demure crouch while he stripped off all his clothes. Rough and careless, he grabbed her, tossed her onto the bed, and lay atop her writhing body. He held her arms over her head. His hands found the red tie, and he bound her wrists. As he forced himself into her, she kept her arms over her head, pretending they were tied to an imaginary bedpost. She struggled and moaned. This was comfortable territory for both, and soon they forgot the story and their roles and became animalisticly lost in lust.

In submission, excited, she reached over his head and pulled down hard. Their two heads came together in pain. She cried out as his forehead met hers above her right eye. None of this rough behavior made any difference. The animals would have their way.

A half-hour later, they lay next to each other, cooling down under a sheet. Her only post-sex lover talk sounded more medicinal than sexual. "I needed that," she said. "Sometimes I have nowhere to go, and I want to get it all out. Release all the tension."

"I am always ready for you, Kathy. Of course, you know that," he said. "Anytime."

"We're a couple of alley cats, Jarek," she said. "Nothing to brag about."

"You're my favorite pussy."

She shook her head and changed the conversation to current events. Their banal observations bounced from one newsworthy topic to the next. He was concerned about the financial markets, and she talked about the political scene. This continued until Jarek casually asked if she and Otto had discussed his medical condition.

"We talked this morning. He gave me the sad news," she said. "Sounds pretty bad. He didn't like the way you handled things. He was quite upset with you. Have you forgotten your bedside manner?"

He chuckled. "You should talk. You're the one who banged our heads together, making me bleed."

"I said I was sorry. Do you want me to kiss it?" She asked.

"No thanks. I think I've had enough for the day." He leaned back into his pillow and exhaled into the air. "But I'm not complaining."

"I didn't think you would, Mister Landlord. You stole my virginity," she said in her schoolgirl voice.

He rolled his eyes. "Ah...I wondered what it was. Come on, Kathy. You're a cat on a hot tin roof. I didn't steal anything. You delivered the way you always do."

"I'll take that as a compliment."

"But what of it? That was it. He was upset with me?" asked Jarek.

"He's upset with the whole thing. And I can't blame him. He's got nowhere to go. That medical system, of which you are so proud, is totally fucked up."

Jarek was miffed. "The system has rules for the betterment of everyone. It's rigid but fair."

She reached over and laid her right hand on the sheet covering his crotch. "Just like you, Black Bart."

"Stop it, Kathy. I can't stand your heartless banter."

"So now you have scruples?"

He looked up at the ceiling. "I'm a physician. Sworn to uphold the principles of non-maleficence, beneficence, autonomy, veracity, social justice, and..."

"You're forgetting one."

"I got it...confidentiality." He lifted his head off the pillow. "OK, so I drift away from that one on occasion. But I'm not married to the guy. I'm just his doctor."

"Lucky you."

"I made that mistake once. Not to be repeated."

"Marriage?"

"Right. I'm still paying for that. I feel sorry for him, and I'm pulling for him ninety-nine percent."

"Not a hundred?"

"I'm deducting one percent because he has you all the time instead of me." He smiled.

"It's nice to know I'm wanted. Are you concerned because of your business dealings?"

"Of course, but I am human. He's in trouble, and I would help him no matter what."

"The way he explained it," she said, "the whole thing is a giant crapshoot. Only the medical system has a sure thing. I think it's all set up to provide a constant cash flow and profits for you medical guys."

"You are so cynical."

"Otto says you might have other ideas...some kind of workaround."

Jarek made a face. "I wish. You know I'm inventive, Kathy. But any alternatives to staying within the system are illegal as a matter of law. I might have suggested some possibilities to him, but I wasn't trying to give him hope. I was simply pointing out our collective limitations by suggesting creative examples of illegal opportunities."

"There's nothing you would do to save him, and whatever business deals you may share?"

"Everything is on the table if the payoff is enough. But I'm not a criminal."

She laughed. "Come on, Stephan Jarek. You would sell your own mother's heart..."

"Stop it. My mother...rest her soul...is long gone and in Heaven." He paused. "Tell me. What happens if Otto dies before his father?"

"You mean his estate?"

"Well. Most likely, his brother will end up with all of it," she admitted.

"I don't like that," he said. "Not at all. Is that why you're so sweet on Alex?" His tone was sarcastic, and his follow-up smile was phony.

"Don't be crude. Alex and I have a relationship that still survives. Being with him reminds me of simpler times. I forgot how cute and innocent he is. Are you jealous?" She chuckled.

"Well, I'll never be cute and cuddly."

"I have a lot of names for you, Jarek..."

"I'll bet," he said. "I hate sharing you with anyone."

"Get over it," she said flatly.

He made a humming sound like he was thinking. "Maybe if Otto dies, you could marry Alex, and the three of us could share the old man's estate."

"That's the way you men think." She frowned. "Everything is about money."

"Well...try living without it sometime. I have, and it sucks. You'll have to watch the older brother. If he gets everything. That isn't fair to Otto, you, or me."

Kathy lifted herself, supporting her body on her elbow. She peered into Jarek's eyes. "How are you involved in Frederick's estate?"

"I'm not. But Otto and I have business plans. Plans that could make both of us rich. And you also, assuming you can stay married...and I can keep him alive."

"That's your job, Doctor. Your mission. Right?"

"You know he is an essential partner. One of a kind. I wouldn't want to lose that opportunity by losing him."

"How touching. If I were you, I wouldn't depend on good luck to solve your problems. I suggest you start looking for another partner or get ready to break the law to get him a new heart."

"Those are not attractive options."

"That's reality," she said. "Get Otto a new heart, and everyone will benefit."

He got up and began putting on his clothes. As he did, he studied Kathy lying on the bed naked, her legs apart, like she was airing it out. Unpredictable, wild, and calculating, she made for interesting times in an otherwise boring world. But maintaining some distance from her was a survival tactic he never forgot.

She eyed him with concern. "I don't want to be involved with any of your plans, Jarek. I've got my own plans." She spoke with confidence like someone holding a winning hand. He wondered what was on her mind, but not enough to inquire.

"That's what makes the world go around, sweet cheeks," he chuckled. They dropped the subject of the transplant, but he couldn't shake the problem. Of course, Kathy was correct. Something had to be done. The wheels of his mind began to spin.

Chapter 21

Late in the afternoon, I sat on the sofa in the Walkers' basement watching a cable TV cooking show when I received a phone call from my man.

"Alex. Terry here. I've got something for you."

"It's about time," I said.

"Don't pressure me." He paused. "Fine wine and all that."

"OK. What do you have?"

"About Otto and his business. Checking data on the State of Illinois Business Entity search site. I found something weird.

"What?"

"Are you at my house?" he asked.

"Yeah. Right now, I'm learning how to cook up a peach flambé. Don't worry, I won't burn down the place."

Terry paused. "Have you been drinking?"

"No...I'm just bored."

"Listen, my research struck gold. But I don't want to go into it on the phone. I'm in my office. Can you come over here and we can talk?" he asked.

"Gold? Now you're talking. I'll tell Margie what I'm up to, and I'll meet you in a few minutes."

"This is good stuff, Alex. You're going to like it."

"Well, don't pee in your pants. Be right over."

I slipped on a light jacket, bounded up the stairs, and found Margie kneeling; she was hard at work as usual, cleaning the first-floor powder room. Her butt, wrapped tight in grey stretch pants, greeted my face when I popped my head into the tiny space. "Margie..." I must have startled her.

"Hey, Alex. Don't sneak up on me like that. I'm not used to having another useless man busting into my business. What's up?"

"I'm walking over to Terry's office. He called, and we've got some of our own business to discuss."

She went back to work. Without even glancing up at me, she continued to brush around the inside of the toilet bowl. "That's exciting. I hope you and Philip Marlowe have fun. Make sure you two get back here for dinner. On time."

"Got it. Will do."

Escaping the basement brought a smile to my face. A few minutes later, as I neared Terry's office, I wondered what my detective buddy had found. It must be important. That eased my mind. I didn't want to have to negotiate with my dying father about the value of the services of T. Walker, Confidential Investigations. The old man would bitch and moan if my friend drew a blank and had the gall to bill for services rendered. I arrived. Terry spotted me through the glass and buzzed me into the office.

Shouting over the loud music pumping out of a boom box somewhere, I announced: "Terry Walker...I presume."

"*C'est moi.*" Walker sat behind his oak fortress, looking mysterious, desk lamp ablaze, his cigarette smoke wafting through the heavy air and darkness, like a scene from an old Philippe Noiret flick. "Can you turn that shit down?"

"Shit? That's Fishbone. *Party at Ground Zero*, man. Vintage ska."

I wore an if-you-don't-mind face and mimed the motion of flipping a light switch. Terry got the idea and killed the music. The room went dead.

"Are you smoking dope?"

"*Iimbécile.* I slid over into *Gauloises* today. *Pas bien?*"

I sat down facing the detective and adopted a pose. Shrugging my shoulders, I admitted, "I'm never certain which character you will be on any given day."

"I like to keep them guessing. You've seen our house. Not much mystery there. But here...in my little world," he spread his arms as if to gather in all the stale air, smoke, and harsh lights, "I can be anyone."

"Does Margie realize you lead this double life?"

He smiled. "She's never been here. Not once."

"Smart woman." I paused. "Now tell me. What's the story?"

"Yes..."

I waited.

He rolled out a name. "Biovatex, LLC"

I cocked my head. "Is that supposed to mean something?"

"It's a body broker business. Or I should say it's the name of a fledgling body broker business registered in the State of Illinois and owned by..."

"Terry...spit it out."

"Owned by Otto E. Reinhart and Stephan T. Jarek. Same address as the Reinhart Funeral Home and Crematory."

"What the hell is a body broker business?"

Terry took his time enjoying his presentation. "Simple, Alex. Body brokers are in the business of acquiring deceased human bodies, butchering them, and selling the parts and pieces to interested parties."

I rolled my eyes as his words stunned me. "Who...who buys the parts?"

"Universities, medical schools, testing labs for medical procedures and implants." Terry took a breath, exhaled, dragged on his French cigarette, and blasted out the smoke." It's a real business. And a quiet one. Those non-transplant tissue banks, as they call them, are making millions for the owners."

"Is this legal?"

"As far as I can tell. Many of these companies say they are not selling the body parts. According to them, the bodies are donated, and the brokers charge for the preparation and delivery of the item."

"More donations. Kind of like the organ transplant business," I suggested.

"Yes, but non-transplant tissues...let's say body parts which are not organs, may be sold or the services related to them. Processing, packaging, and delivery. That is legal. Your brother and his doctor buddy set up a Limited Liability Company...an LLC which identifies them as a *tissue bank*."

"What kind of parts?

"Well, not human organs. But bone marrow, arteries, hands, feet, legs, arms, torsos without organs, heads." Terry scratched the back of his head. "I'm not sure about brains. An organ or not? Heads for sure."

"Price?"

"It's not like selling organs where you can pawn off a beating heart for a half-million, but it's not chump change either. And it's all legal."

"How much is a head?" I joked, but the answer wasn't funny.

"Maybe $3,000. Come to think of it. I read it does come with a brain, tissues, and a face. But, I'll bet the eyes are a separate deal. Hey, I'm no expert."

"Gross."

"They've got package deals. A full body for ten grand. Anything goes. Except for organs."

I put my hand to my chin. "So this is Otto's new business. Papa's not going to like this."

"Doubt it." He chuckled.

"How do they acquire the bodies?"

"Donations. People donate through organizations or through funeral homes offering free cremation and other services if they hand over Uncle Louie's body to science or whoever."

"The old man will not want to hear that."

Terry inhaled and blew the smoke into the air with a flourish. "That's what he's paying me the big bucks for. B.T.W., when are we going to visit him and pass on the news?"

I mulled over my answer. "Not together. For a couple of reasons. One, this is family business, and that's nasty information. He might not want to admit that anyone can find out this ugly family secret."

"It takes a real shamus."

"I'm sure." I smiled. "Don't forget you would need a doctor's clearance to get in the door. We don't have time."

"What about my fee?" Terry gestured, holding his cigarette in the air.

"Wait for it. OK? Your detecting work for the family Reinhart may not be completed."

"How about a down payment...say a hundred bucks?"

"Maybe. Can you give me some proof of your work?"

"Sure, I've got copies of the LLC paperwork. I've got articles about the body broker business."

I took out my wallet. "Here's a hundred bucks. Take the family out for dinner again. Tell Margie the detective business is paying off." I chuckled. "By the way, I get the impression she's not a believer."

"Well. She'll whistle a new tune when I start getting corporate clients. Working on that."

Terry printed out the documents and placed them in a brown envelope. "Here you go." He looked at his watch. "Are you headed home? I can give you a lift. No extra charge."

"Busting my balls again." I quipped.

Walker cupped his hand over his burly mustache and slid it down, holding his chin. "My deluxe basement guest suite, limo rides,

Margie's cooking, and discount investigative services. And I'm busting...your balls?"

"Wait..." I punched in my father's phone number, and a raspy voice answered. "Hello, Father. I just finished a meeting with Terry Walker. I've got some important information for you." The old man rambled on and then responded. "Make it late afternoon tomorrow. See you." He disconnected.

"Hey, did you tell him what a wonderful job I'm doing? It couldn't hurt," said Terry with a smile.

"Don't worry, you'll be a hero. He said something about appreciating the quick service." With this little fib in place, I got up from my chair. "Let's get going. Margie's invited us for dinner."

Chapter 22

Today was a poor day to visit my father, but I had no choice in the timing of the message; Frederick Reinhart had to be told what Terry Walker had discovered. As I entered the room, the nurse was exiting. We exchanged glances and polite head nods. The setting now was different. My father was in bed, in a raised position, atop the blanket and clothed as if he were ready to take a walk around the house. However, reality denied him. His health worsened; his breathing was difficult. His skin had taken a deeper shade of yellow, and he appeared to have lost some fullness in his face. In my hand, I held the brown envelope Walker had given me. As I neared the bed, my father tried to reposition his body. His beleaguered face told the story of an old man caught in the grip of a deadly cancer, creating pain with even the slightest movement. This was the first time in my life that I felt pity for my father.

"Hard day, Father?"

The old man started to speak, cleared his throat, and responded. "Every day...especially today," he shook his head, "is not so good. But it is good to see you. I don't get many visitors."

I went fishing. "How about Otto?"

Father scowled. "He's a no-show. Same for his wife. If not for you and Gorger, I wouldn't have any. It's a shame you're not keen on the business. I could trust the two of you to run it well. I'm losing my faith in Otto."

I sat on the edge of the bed and countered his comments. "Otto is in bad shape. Like you, he's facing some difficult health challenges. Maybe he should be cut a little slack." I said.

"As you are aware, I'm not much of a slack-cutter." The old man reflected for a moment. "You may be right, Alex. With my departure from the day-to-day operations, he took over the entire load. He has good people working with him, but he is running out of steam. He's a young man. No wonder his wife takes to wandering..." he cut himself short. "I suppose that's inappropriate to say. But if a man who is married to that Kathy can't get it up. Well, he's not much of a man."

"Maybe, but his health problems are grim. He may not have enlightened you because he doesn't want to weigh you down." I countered.

Frederick Reinhart offered a wry smile. "You are a kind person, Alex, like your mother. The world needs more like you." He looked into my eyes. "So tell me, what is my conscientious, loyal, over-worked son up to?"

I was tired of sitting side-saddle on the bed; I stood up, stretched, found a desk chair, and rolled it over to the bed. I sat with one leg crossed over the other and my elbow resting on the armrest, all the while formulating an approach. "Well, kind or not, I find this kind of digging into Otto's life painful."

"When you dig, the likely result is dirty, calloused hands. So?"

"I met with Terry Walker. He's been doing great work..."

"Yes. Yes. Enough of the commercial. Don't worry. He'll get paid."

"Right. Terry searched the business records of the State of Illinois. He found out Otto and Stephan Jarek created a business and filed the paperwork with the State. A business entity search." I held up the envelope and began to pull out the file inside.

"Forget that. I can't read now. What does it say?"

I held the sheet and read from it. "Name of business: Biovatex, LLC...the Name of the Agent is an attorney with a LaSalle street address. This information does not disclose the nature of the business or the owners. However, Terry did more digging and found the owners were Otto E. Reinhart and Stephan T. Jarek. And...the business will be operated as a non-transplant tissue bank. And the current address is the same as the Reinhart Funeral Home."

I glanced at him. My father's face was drained of life.

"I'm sorry, Father."

Frederick's color returned and moved past yellow into the territory of red. "Did he describe this business?"

"Terry gave me a rundown. He said it's a body broker business."

"Well, he nailed it." His father's voice strengthened as if the news renewed his will to fight. "Our family didn't put in decades of decent, dedicated work to build the name and reputation of the Reinhart Funeral Home to have it crushed out by one stupid move by one greedy family member."

"These tissue banks are not all bad, are they?" I asked.

The old man swallowed. "Let me put it this way. From the standpoint of our aware and loyal clients and neighbors, this is tantamount to an orphanage brokering babies. It's worse than that. It's like an orphanage selling dead baby parts."

"But they serve a..."

He cut me short. "I remember a magazine article about the tissue bank business from a few years ago. The reporter, as a test, ordered two heads and a spine from one of these operations. After answering a few perfunctory questions, the tissue bank shipped out the frozen body parts to the reporter. It turned out that the parents of one of the donors were too poor to afford a decent burial or cremation. In return, the family donated it to the body broker, who said the body would be used for medical research. That's the way those people operate."

"It's hard to put a pleasant spin on this kind of operation, but it is a legal, legitimate business," I suggested.

"It may be legal, but whether it's ethical or not depends on how the company is operated and who the owners are. As far as I know, the relatives of the deceased are offered free cremation services if they donate. And you understand who provides these generous offers? And who feeds the bodies to the body brokers?"

I gave it a shot. "Funeral homes?"

"That's correct. How long do you think it would take for my competitors to find out that a Reinhart-owned tissue bank company was feeding bodies incestuously into its own body broker business? This would destroy our reputation."

"Terry did say it's legal."

"Well...bully for Terry. Legal...maybe. Ethical no. Not in my book. It's the perception that counts. I'm certain Otto and his doctor buddy have run the numbers and realize there is a tremendous potential profit. That may be. But making money is only one-half of a business. Providing a reputable, reliable, ethical service is the other half. If this is where Otto intends to make his mark, so be it." He raised his voice. "I won't let him take me and our family down. I won't allow it."

I recognized my father was distraught. "Consider dropping it for the moment. You're getting excited. Try to relax. I can talk to Otto and tell him what you believe. He'll have to reconsider."

"You're right, Alex. However, this is my business and my battle. I'll deal with Otto...not you."

"How's that, Father?"

He smiled. "I own a solid family-owned business with an honest history built over decades by those who cared. I own one hundred percent of the business. Otto is my employee. Yes, he is my son. But I do not have to employ him. And I do not have to allow him to trade off my family's reputation to build his new business. I don't care how professionally he handles his new body part business. He can run the most respectful, decent, non-transplant tissue bank in the state. But he can't work for the Reinhart Funeral home while having ownership in a body broker business."

"This will kill him, Father."

He sat silent for seconds before responding. "Everyone dies."

"You're going to talk to him?"

"Yes. Soon."

"Are you going to mention your source for this information?"

My father smiled. "You don't want any part of this? Do you? It's too messy, right?"

"No. I don't want either of you to take unnecessary risks. As far as I'm aware, at this moment, this entire body broker business is just words on paper. Let me talk to Otto. I can talk some sense into him."

"No. I understand your concern, but I have the hammer. It's my estate and my will. My wishes will allow anything to happen, or nothing. Otto doesn't have a pot to piss in ...some nice toys...including Kathy, but he doesn't own anything. The car is mine. The house is owned by the bank, the business is mine, and my estate is mine. And if I know Kathy...she's only there so long as she desires."

"That's pretty harsh, Father."

"That's the way it is, Son. Leave it be. I thank you for bringing this to my attention. But I'll handle it. I'll have my nurse call Otto, and we'll have it out tonight. Don't worry. I'll straighten him out." He leaned his head back, appearing relaxed now. "You know what you should do?"

"What's that?"

His father cocked his head to one side, and he smiled. "You should get working on creating my heir. Things are getting interesting."

I could tell my father relished the last moments of power in his fading existence. "Let's not go there again...OK?"

"You know I did include that conditional provision in the will." He shook his head from side to side. "And I don't think that Otto will make it happen. He's too busy destroying my legacy. However, that will never happen. Think about that Kathy thing. You would be doing everyone a favor. She'll ensure her future prosperity. If Otto's a good boy, he will have the son or daughter he could never create on his own, and you will have saved the family business, shared in my wealth, helped create a little nephew or niece, and made a dying man happy."

I needed to avoid my father's delusions but deal with my concern about his relationship with Otto. "For me, Father, don't mention Terry or me as informants. I don't think you understand how delicate his health is."

"So be it, but business is business."

"And my concerns?"

"I never mention my sources. It's my rule."

I kept the envelope and the papers and shoved them under my arm. Then I took my father's hand and held it in both my hands. "Good night, Father. Don't do anything rash. Stay in peace. Remember...it's late in the game."

Frederick Reinhart shook his head and smiled at his eldest son. "Your mother would be proud of you, Alex. Thank you."

Chapter 23

Early evening, the younger son arrived after receiving a phone call from the nurse telling him that his father wanted to meet tonight. Less than ten minutes later, Otto would be in a fight for his life. The nurse walked him into his father's office and left them alone. Otto closed the window blinds, leaving the small Tiffany wall sconces on either side of the bed to dimly illuminate the room. The combatants, Frederick and his son, tensed in the shadows, anticipating a battle for survival. Otto Reinhart faced a man who was at least as dead as he was alive. But Frederick Reinhart always inspired fear and awe in those who crossed his path. Otto was no exception. He stood trembling inside while studying his father lying on the bed. With a day-old beard and his grey hair sweaty and matted, Frederick appeared weak, but his yellowing, determined visage offered little hope for compromise. Otto opened the discussion and found out quickly that there were no secrets in Naperville.

"I will not allow it. Not now. Not ever." Frederick's words were clear but quiet.

"You don't understand, Father. I'm stuck now. Waiting for a donor heart, which may never arrive. If it does, I have to be ready. I need a lot of money. If I don't have the money, I'm a dead man. I must have a heart transplant. If you don't believe me, talk to my heart specialist, Dr. Rickenbacker. We're talking a million dollars or more. It's almost criminal. The entire system is set up to benefit the doctors, hospitals, and insurance companies. I'm just a pawn in this game." He raised his voice. "I must have everything in place, or they won't even provide a new heart. And if I don't get a new heart, I'll be dead sometime in the next few months. Do you get it?"

The old man rolled his bloodshot eyes. "Well...doesn't your health insurance cover it? That's what it's for, right?" he demanded, his voice tired and raspy.

"They have been covering some of my bills from my heart doctor. Remember, I already had heart surgery when I was a kid. And coverage for a transplant is a whole different ballgame. So far, I haven't received any details on the insurance. But I'm pressing them," Otto explained as his exasperation increased.

Unimpressed, Frederick Reinhart responded: "Son. I must admit I had no idea your heart health had regressed this far. But you can't expect the business to cover such extraordinary expenses. You receive an above-average salary. You have decent medical insurance. If you die, Kathy will be well taken care of by the life insurance provided by the company. We have key-person insurance. Term life insurance and disability insurance. You have to admit I've tried to consider everything."

Otto got up from his chair and walked around the room. "Listen to yourself, Father. You're on your deathbed, and the only thing that matters to you is whether your business will survive. That's it."

Frederick adjusted the two pillows he rested upon. In distress, he coughed. The coughing became uncontrollable. Otto helped him sit up and offered him a glass of water. The old man sipped the water and appeared to become more composed. For a few moments, neither man spoke. Frederick motioned that he wanted to lean back into the pillows, and Otto eased him back into position.

"I'm OK now. Do we have to continue this conversation?" His head sank into the pillows. "I think you understand I do not approve of you and your doctor-friend running a body broker business that connects in any way to Reinhart Funeral Home and Crematory." He stared at his son. "Is that clear?"

"You don't care about me. Do you? It's all about that damned business." He paused. "I'm dying, Father."

Frederick smiled weakly. "I understand dying, Otto. Everybody does it." He chuckled and coughed. "You. Me. The entire population of the planet. Death is part of life. It's the foundation of our family business. The dead are our sponsors...our customers...our friends, neighbors...and family. That sacred relationship is our bond with the world, which is inviolable. It must not be soiled by your greed or personal issues."

Otto screwed up his face, now flushed and bloody pink. "Jesus, Father. It's me, Otto. And I need your help. How about a little understanding? How about a little concern?"

His father didn't comment. The old man relaxed into his pillows. "I'm disappointed in you, Otto. You're not a thinker. You're not a leader. You're not a visionary." The last few words slipped out and melted into the air.

Otto's head swung back and forth like the head of a broken puppet. "You're the one who can't see the future. The world is changing. The funeral business must adapt. My new project may just be the one thing that keeps the Reinhart name relevant, operational, viable, and current. A source of income for the Reinhart family for generations."

His father coughed out a laugh, struggled, and then eased. "That's a joke. You have failed in that department, too, Otto. You married the prettiest girl on the block, but you're unable to give me an heir. You're not half the man I used to be."

Otto swallowed hard and stood silent, staring at his father. "Can't you bend your rules a little to make this work? I promise I'll never solicit bodies from the clients of our funeral home. Isn't that enough? I promise. You have my word."

Frederick appeared to be contemplating until he stated his position. "You don't understand, Otto," he said, his voice much stronger now. "I'm still running this operation. Remember, I can change my will and bequeath my company to anyone or any group I desire. Don't worry. I'll make sure you won't starve, but you will not own the business. You will be a non-voting shareholder, eligible for dividends or profit shares, but that's it. Or it could be I'll even offer it all to Alex. He's an idea man. And he's family. Maybe he could take over everything, including providing me with an heir. I don't think he would have any problem impregnating Kathy after you pass on. He's always been soft on her." He chuckled. "I think you know that, above all, I am a businessman, Otto. Forget that body broker idea. Stick to your last, Son. Life is simpler for everyone that way."

Otto exhaled a deep breath. He stepped up to the bed. Their eyes met. The words sputtered out of his mouth. "You're a tough person to love, Father. Impossible. I can see why Mother took the easy way out. Is this the way you handled her? Did you tell her your work was more important than anything...including her?"

This comment enraged the old man. His yellowed jaundiced skin flushed with fresh angry blood. Frederick Reinhart stewed until he became an orange man. He reached out. His left hand touched Otto's body just above the beltline. His fingers dug behind his son's belt, and he pulled him over onto him. Heads together like two lovers face to face, they locked into a final embrace. Frederick's bad breath and spittle filled Otto with disgust. In a whisper, the old man released his final word into Otto's ear. "Never..."

With some effort, Otto broke free of his father's grip. He stepped back and stared down Frederick. "You selfish old bastard. You deserve to die." Dispassionately, he watched the old man struggle to stay alive. For several minutes, Otto stood over the patriarch, weakened by cancer and pushed to the breaking point by their argument, as he grimaced in pain and his body convulsed. Otto realized the gravity of the situation, but he did nothing but observe. Frederick continued his dance with death. The old man fought to breathe. He grabbed his chest with both hands. He looked at his son, his eyes pleading for help. He reached for a push button that would call the nurse, but Otto ripped it away from him. Then he moved away, dropped into a chair, and for anguishing moments watched his father's body twitch and toss. It was all too much for Otto. He reacted in anger and desperation. He stood, took one of the pillows from the bed, and placed it over Frederick's contorted face. Holding it tight, Otto stole the remaining life from his father until all movement ended. He pulled the pillow off. The body of his father released a long, drawn-out breath ending in a strange gurgle and then went limp.

Otto, the expert in dead bodies, had created another. He stood shaking before his father's body. His rage decomposed into shocked remorse, and the pillow he held in one hand dropped onto the floor. Sweat fell off his forehead onto the pillow. He sucked in air in deep, painful breaths. As his blood pressure topped out, his head felt like it would explode. His own broken heart, now a monster inside him pressured every rib in his chest. He tried to quiet himself, but he could not. He backed up one slow step after another, sat in the chair, stared at his father's body, and began to cry. Not since the death of his mother had he cried like this. Minutes passed, maybe ten or fifteen, and then he quieted, and something told him that everything was happening for a reason. Everything would be fine. The gods had provided his answer. He was saved.

Chapter 24

Most likely, Frederick Reinhart's greatest after-death fear was that of being forgotten. He was not. Naperville responded with newspaper articles announcing his demise and detailing his contributions to the community. His two-day wake, orchestrated by Otto, was well-attended and opulent. He was laid out in a top-of-the-line casket, surrounded by a garden of floral arrangements, lulled into eternal sleep by a talented but subdued choral group from his church, and today transported by his old employee-friend Jan Gorger to be placed next to his wife, sharing the double-wide red granite headstone. For sure, he was going to be buried with all his body parts; Father was not one to share one bit of himself on the way out. However, both his pancreas and his heart were well out of warranty, and in the end, both had failed.

As Otto related the story: "We were discussing our family business when he stopped talking and suffered a heart attack." I'm sure this was true, except I suspected there was more to it. I realized my father would take Otto to the woodshed and guessed they had an angry argument about the potential body parts business, which may have been capped by a final negative command. All that is forgotten now. Otto never accused me of spying on him, and once the will is settled and the distributions made, I will take care of Terry's bill for investigation. I'm looking forward to reading the will to determine if the old man was able to slip in his conditional bequest related to Kathy and her potential Reinhart baby.

I'm not certain if I will miss him. He was, in many ways, a narcissistic bully who loved controlling people. But unlike Otto, Father and I reached some sort of tacit acknowledgment of each other's right to exist unhampered and free to make our own choices. He may have even respected me for holding my ground and leaving home. Who knows? He may have had other dreams beyond being the son of a funeral home director, destined to become a funeral home director, and begetting another son who would become, and so on...ad infinitum. I'll never know because this concept was not part of his *Gospel According to Frederick*. However, ten years ago, he let me go and sent me on my way with some of his riches and without hard feelings. I am grateful for that.

Otto, sitting to the left of me on a cold metal folding chair in the middle of the old downtown cemetery, did not have that luxury. Upon our father's death, he became the sole owner of Reinhart Funeral Home and Crematory, and by default, his wife, Kathy, was tied down to the business. As we sat a few feet horizontally and vertically from my mother's bones, I believe she silently implored us all to run away and live our lives free of that strange business. It's déjà vu all over again. Otto is under a death sentence, listening to his failing heart beat out a sour tune, anxiously waiting for a gift from an unknown donor before his music dies. Kathy, like my mother, might be trying to punch her way out of the black bag of family tradition. And I remain as always uncommitted to this town, the business, and anything other than the freedom to be human, creative, and alive. While I have, in my mind, floated the idea of sharing that commitment with a possible fellow traveler named Kathy, such is unlikely. Father's casket was now suspended above an open grave. Otto, Kathy, and I had a birds-eye view into the eternal darkness that awaited all of us after the struggles of our lives passed. It was a sobering view.

Aside from the presiding minister, several mourners sat behind our family, Frederick's top employees, including Jan Gorger, other managers, and staff. The old man had no living relatives except for us, resulting in a modest gathering. One other, invited here by Otto, Dr.

Stephan Jarek, observed from the back row. While the minister went through his routine, my mind wandered; I gazed over the graves of the hundreds of Naperville residents who retired here. The grim, misty late-fall day draped over all the dearly beloved like an old, grey, water-soaked trenchcoat.

Otto stood to place a rose atop the casket, and I glanced at Kathy. Her eyes expressed a sadness beyond the loss of the family's leader. In this light, despite her attempt to hide it with makeup, everyone could see that her face was bruised above her right eye. I wondered about that. She appeared desperate, like a little lost black-eyed toddler searching for her mother. Soon she and I also stood at the abyss and deposited our red roses on the polished hardwood roof of his new eternal home. Farewell, Papa. Then the ceremony ended. The three of us drifted away from the grave. We walked beneath giant elms now reluctantly releasing the last of their jaundiced leaves, filling the air with depressing hints of winter approaching. In the background, the minister reminded everyone of a post-burial reception; the family invited all to join. We walked toward Otto's car. He and Kathy were hand in hand; I remained alone with hands unoccupied. I wished to hug her and tell her that everything was going to be all right; truthfully, I wanted to do more than that. I called out to Otto and Kathy. "You guys go ahead to the restaurant. I'm going to walk. I need a break."

Otto gave me a wave of the hand to signal he understood. His response was about what I expected. He was weakening. Of course, the shock of Father's death had affected everyone in the family and those in his business, but Otto was a beaten man, physically and mentally. His heart condition could not be hidden. He seemed short of breath, and his skin always bore a bluish cast. If I compared his appearance to my father's post-death image, I would give Papa the nod. But that was all Gorger, the most experienced embalmer-cosmetologist in town. He told me he worked into the

169

late hours making his boss the best that he could be...under the circumstances. My eyes followed Otto and Kathy as they walked to their car. She allowed him to hang on to her elbow for support. Time was running out for Otto. Would he continue on the road to happiness or reach a dead end? His fate would be determined by unknown bureaucrats, medical professionals, and lucky charms.

I heard someone approaching from behind me and saw Dr. Jarek, who wore an expensive black suit, white shirt, and royal blue tie, appearing like a stage actor playing the part of a saddened mourner. I was not convinced by his costume. I guessed he was pleased that the major obstacle to the success and even existence of their Biovatex body broker business was at this moment descending into oblivion. Jarek tucked in his tie as he approached me, like a man zipping up at a gas station urinal. He was done with my father, and it was time to offer his brand of condolences. "You know, Alex. I never had any issues with your father, but Otto had many. And of course, he has his own medical problems. I don't think your father ever considered the pain he and the suffering Otto faces." I wasn't sure what to make of his proclamation. I nodded a little but said nothing.

Quite without thinking and reacting to some distant movement, I glanced over Jarek's shoulder toward the burial site. Something caught my attention. The mourners had departed, but a new person arrived at the gravesite. "Sorry, Doctor. I forgot something. Have to go back. See you at the reception." I left him wondering. Then he turned and headed to the parking area while I walked back to my father's grave. I wasn't certain why I was drawn away from my conversation with Jarek, but the image of some unknown person watching two cemetery workers shoveling dirt into the grave was at least a curious event. As I got near enough to see the sweat dripping off the workers' faces, it became clear the watcher was a woman, small, bent over, and old.

I approached from behind and startled her when I stood at her side. Neither of us spoke. Then she turned, looked up at me, and studied my face as if trying to remember me. I didn't recognize her. Many decades of life had not been kind to this woman, now hunched over and clad in a dark grey rumpled sack of a dress. Wisps of wiry grey hair poked out from beneath her babushka. Her face was a mask of uneven, droopy, caked skin, the corners of her milky, bloodshot eyes tumored, and her nose covered with pores. Still, it was a kind face, well-earned, and worn in dignity.

"Are you Alex? Or the other one?" Her battered voice betrayed years of cigarette and alcohol abuse.

"I'm Alex Reinhart. Have we met before?" I asked.

"We have...but I doubt you remember," she said.

"Did you know my father?"

She smiled and spoke, revealing a jumble of dancing yellowed incisors. "I knew Fritz very well."

"You call him Fritz."

"We were close friends when you were a boy...or maybe you were a young man by that time." She glanced at the workers, and they returned her look. One man set down his shovel, and the other did the same. They moved away and sat under a tree, appearing befuddled by the arrival of the final two mourners and their lack of decorum, but ever ready to take an unscheduled cigarette break from their back-breaking work.

"I don't remember you. Sorry. What is your name?" I asked.

"I am Amanda." She crossed her bare arms. "I'm going now, Alex. I gave him his due. As much as he deserved." She turned and walked away.

Apologetically, I waved to the two diggers and followed her.

"Wait, Amanda. Wait." A cold mist filled the air as I caught up to her, the two of us alone in a soggy meadow full of headstones. She wore a worried look now with tears in her eyes.

"What do you want?" she asked.

I searched for a quick answer. "What was he to you?"

She dropped her head into her chest, and I waited.

Her words eased out. "You don't remember me. We met once when I worked at the funeral home. I was your father's assistant. You were visiting."

I thought about the only time I was there as a child, and I remembered her now. "You were a blonde then, right?"

She gave me a hint of a smile and nodded. "You remember me."

"Yes. My mother's wake." This seemed to be an important connection to her past.

"I'm sorry."

"It's been a while."

"I know, but…" Her words struggled to come out.

"But what?" I asked.

She gazed into the mist. "You should know."

"Know what?"

"About your father and me."

I said nothing and waited, sensing something gripped her mind.

"Fritz and I were more than co-workers. We were lovers." She said with some pride in her voice.

I nodded, and words popped out of my mouth. "Right. Even when I was a kid, I suspected he played around."

Her pained face reacted to my insensitive words. She took a deep breath. "Virginia suspected also. Not that this was something new. But I was different than the others. We were a couple…Fritz and I. He wanted out of his marriage. He wanted me, and I wanted him. We had plans. He committed to me."

Her story unnerved me, but I said nothing.

"You should know. I know you suffered because of me. That's my cross to bear, but you should never feel you had anything to do with her taking her life."

I heard her voice, thin and distant; my thoughts drifted. The image of my mother lying dead on the floor of the bedroom appeared for a moment. I dissolved it by asking a simple question. "Why?"

She thought, then spoke: "He decided to leave your mother. We were in love. He told me she might welcome the news. Their marriage was not happy. She didn't like his business and was always depressed. That, except for the potential scandal, life would be better for everyone. Including you boys. So he told her. That was his way. He said he was going on a vacation with you and your brother. She had a week alone to deal with it...so he said. You know how he was. His mind was made up, and she would have to live with it. But she didn't want to. She ended everything."

I tried to absorb the news like an adult, but I didn't want to; for a moment, I was thirteen again, and I dragged it all into my being. The old woman must have understood my pain.

"I'm sorry. I thought I would pay my respects and leave. Everyone had gone. But it could be for the best. You're not a kid anymore, and I have nothing to hide. That's life." She reached out to me, hugged my arm gently, and left me alone with the dead.

I walked away from the old cemetery having buried both my parents, along with all their human weaknesses, vanity, and desperation. The old ghosts of the past had risen from the grave, exposing family secrets. I didn't need any more memories of the dead. I had no desire to spend more time with family, friends, and hangers-on. Walking without a destination on the hometown streets of Naperville allowed me to unpack my mind. Not long ago, I was ripped out of my life in Denver by my inability to maintain an honest relationship with a lovely woman. And I had come here to close the door on what remained of the past. The final scene was not what I had anticipated, but also not unexpected. My brother and father battled to the end. Frederick was dead, and Otto was dying. Was I supposed to wait and let it all unfold with my brother disintegrating as he waited for a new heart that most likely would never arrive? That sucked. I had enough of my family, the mortuary, old love stories, and Naperville. Was I the ideal guy to hold Kathy's hand as her world disappeared heartbeat by heartbeat? Or was I like my father's Amanda? The word 'homewrecker' bubbled up like a drowning victim in a muddy river.

My wandering brought me near the restaurant. By this time, I had walked off most of my angst. I entered and saw them seated in the back. Kathy spotted me first. She leaned over and said something to Otto. Looking quizzical, he glanced my way and nodded as she headed for me.

"What happened to you? I began to get worried." She asked.

"Sorry. I just didn't feel like reminiscing. I met an old woman..."

"What?"

"I'll tell you about it later. It can wait."

She moved next to me and guided me out of the view of the mourners.

"What's the matter, Kathy?"

Breathing rapidly, she kept her voice subdued. "I don't have much time. But I want you to know. Jarek. He told me something. He said Otto is concerned about my relationship with you. He suggested I stay away from you. I don't know where this is coming from. Jarek's always had his eye on me. He may be jealous. He said things were going to change now that your father was dead."

"Well. He's right," I said. "Things are changing, but it's nothing to do with you or me. We'll have to talk...later. Let's go." I guided her toward the gathering.

Chapter 25

Cold blue light from a single fluorescent fixture barely filled Dr. Jarek's empty reception room with an atmosphere of despair. The blond was off for the day; the office was closed. Jarek's private office offered a slightly better atmosphere. The two body-broker partners faced each other from opposite sides of the doctor's office desk. Otto looked haggard. A half-full cup of coffee and an empty water bottle got them through the initial pleasantries.

"Down to business, Otto. OK?"

"Right."

"We are all saddened by your father's death, but I am sure it provides you with some comfort. Nothing stands in the way of your inheritance of the business and half of his estate. This paves the way for us to move ahead."

Otto cleared his throat before speaking. "I'm meeting with our attorney tomorrow, so I'll be able to verify the exact distribution of the will. I should be the executor of the estate, and I have been managing our company for almost two years. It's mine. My brother should get half of the net estate proceeds. And that's that."

"Do you know the size of the estate?" asked Jarek.

"Don't for sure. My father kept it all close to his chest, but the attorney says he has all the details. Of course, it will take a while to track everything down," said Otto.

"Any guesses on your part?"

"My guess, excluding the business...only a guess...but say a couple of million."

Jarek smiled. "That's a start."

"What about Alex? Is he leaving town soon?"

Otto cocked his head. "I don't see why he would stay here. Alex really doesn't like Naperville."

"I'd like to know when he is leaving. Can you find out? And call me as soon as possible?" asked Jarek.

"Yes."

"He's not going to stay here waiting for a payout...is he?"

"No. I doubt it." Otto smiled. "Except for his schoolboy fascination with my wife, and his friendship with Terry Walker, he's got nothing...no ties. We're not that close."

"That's excellent. I'd like him out of the way while we're executing our plan." Jarek sipped his coffee. "Let's talk about our future, Otto."

"Fine."

Jarek leaned back in his chair. "I like to be straightforward in my business dealings...sometimes to the point of appearing blunt. But I find it best to put all the cards on the table." He nodded.

"We're talking about my transplant, right?" asked Otto.

"Of course, we settled everything else related to Biovatex. The real estate deal is headed for the attorneys. Our deposit is in place. Thank you. That's done. Of course, you have to be alive and well. I think that's our only topic for the day."

Otto swallowed. "Let's get to it," he said, putting his hand on his forehead and pushing his hair back. "I'm running out of rope and hope. I can't sleep at night."

"Otto, you have to remain calm," said Jarek, worried about the strain on his partner. "Tough to do, but necessary. Until you have a new heart implanted in your chest, you must conserve your energy. Have you talked to Kathy yet about the possibility of having the operation done out of the country?"

"I wanted to understand the entire plan before dropping anything on her," said Otto.

"OK. I suppose that's a good idea. We want everything to be neat and tight...anything new regarding the national transplant waiting list?"

"Nada." Otto shook his head. "I'm following your advice. Forget about that BS. It's not happening. Why torture myself?"

"Why indeed?" said Jarek. "Every day we wait, the weaker you will become...and the less likely your surgery will have a positive outcome. You must take the initiative, Otto. Your life is in your hands. It's as simple as that." Jarek leaned back in his chair. "I wanted to say this out front..."

Otto waited.

Jarek continued. "I'm 100% with you regarding your health issues and business-wise too. I will accept the risks involved, and I will donate my time and energy to resolve your heart problem at no additional cost to you. Look at it as a bonus for selecting me as your partner in Biovatex. However, all the other expenses are yours at cost. Fair enough?"

Otto nodded. "No markup. Understood. That helps."

"OK. We're ready to go." Jarek stood, walked to the window, and looked out. The morning sun filled the room. He turned to face his partner. "I have everyone lined up for the surgery. I have found all the required equipment we will need to purchase or rent. And..." he smiled, "I have even found sources for your new heart. Matching your needs."

"Can you share something about the donor?"

Jarek made a face. "You're better off not knowing anything about any donor. And the truth is, the exact donor is unknown at this time. It's one of those wait-and-watch situations."

"Timetable?"

"Within the next three weeks. It could be any day. You will have to tell everyone you will be leaving town for a month. Can your people keep things afloat while you are away?"

"Yes. That's covered. I've got good people, and I've been away before on extended vacations."

"And the new facilities are in order?"

"The surgical area is complete except for whatever special equipment is required for the operation," said Otto with a bit of pride in his voice.

"Excellent. What do your people know about the new space?"

"Not much. Except for Gorger."

Jarek gazed out the window. "Gorger..." he talked into the air, "we're going to need his help with logistics for the plan to work. Someone must move the equipment into the surgical theater, and someone will have to transport our guests." He turned back to face Otto. "And after the surgery, someone will have to provide for your caretaker while you recover. That's about two weeks or so. Can he be trusted to handle that?"

"Obviously, he's going to have to have some idea of what we are up to."

"So be it," said Jarek. Can he be trusted?"

"Absolutely."

"You understand we're breaking the law?"

"I get it."

"And Gorger?"

"I can make it worth his while."

"Will he keep his mouth shut?"

"I'm his boss. In every way."

"OK." Jarek sat again facing Otto. He smiled and nodded. "I have a three-man surgical team lined up, ready to go. They will arrive at O'Hare at our direction. The new heart will come by special carrier, delivered to me. I will be responsible for getting it to your facility on time."

Otto sighed. "Jesus. This sounds real, Stephan. I might just make it."

"You'll make it, Otto. My doctors are good...not cheap but good."

"What's the price tag for saving my life?

"Get ready," said Jarek. "Medical team...$250,000 plus transportation, lodging, expenses, etcetera. Equipment rental...say $75,000. And the new heart...120 to $140,000, depending on the source. We need the backup heart for sure. That's why I've got two sources in place. Once the plan is in motion, the heart must be available. Two weeks of post-op tracking and maintenance are included. After two weeks, you can return home from a soul-searching vacation alone in Mexico. But you will tell Kathy you are having a secret transplant operation in Mexico. Some people will think you just needed the time off to recover from your father's death. Others will hear the rumor that I will spread, that you and Kathy just needed some space and time. And if I can't personally handle the medical services you might require to keep your new heart pumping, Rickenbacker may even have to be let in on the supposed secret Mexican operation. We will play it by ear. One thing at a time. But when you return home, you will have to convalesce. You'll need a nurse."

"You forget about Kathy. She'll be my nurse."

Jarek smiled. "No. I can never forget about her. Couldn't find a better or prettier one. You're a lucky man, Otto. And soon...once you put your new heart into it. You will be putting a permanent smile back on her pretty face."

Otto thought for a moment. He wore a silly grin. "That's about a half-million. And that's about half price. Sounds like a good deal. Plus, it's a deal...not a half-baked promise like Rickenbacker suggested."

"The medical industry is big business, Otto. You are simply another customer. They and the insurance companies own the world. They keep us going...for a profit."

Otto shook his head. "You're a cynic, Dr. Jarek. A turncoat."

"No, you're wrong there, Otto. I'm a realist and a participant, and you will join me when we start our little business." He chuckled. "You thought there was money in dead people. You were right, but the money comes from keeping them alive...not from putting them six feet under. Once we get you up and running again, you and I are going to make some real money."

"I like the way you think, Stephan. I do."

"So are you ready?" He paused. "When you're in, you're in. There's no more hope for the mythical donor heart. And if things go south, we will be on our own. It might be risky to go running to the local hospital for repair. I'll work up a contingency plan in case we need it. You understand?"

"I get it."

"When we put everything in motion with my surgical team, we're committed because you will have to put up a non-refundable fifty percent down payment."

Otto stood. He shook Jarek's hand. "I'm afraid there is no other choice. Is there?"

"Not for you, Otto," said Jarek. "It's now or never."

Chapter 26

Downtown Naperville was an attractive, but humble place, not at all like the imposing LaSalle Street in Chicago's Loop. Most of the attorneys in town maintained offices in both locations. The Chicago site provided convenience and authority to their firms, while a local office gave the natives a friendly, relaxing atmosphere. Our attorney's office was situated on the second floor of a narrow three-story red-brick building in the middle of the town center, immediately north of City Hall.

Erwin Watson, a bald, short man with a decent tan, adjusted his demeanor depending on the venue. Today, he was the folksy downhome old friend, wearing a dark grey suit with a white shirt and a quiet blue bowtie, who was not too different in his place of business than when socializing or playing golf at the local country club. He requested his assistant serve refreshments to his clients. A bright, female junior lawyer followed his direction, handled drink orders, and disappeared into the back offices.

Watson sat erect in his chair, looking cherubic, his hands folded in front of him, resting on a dark brown file folder that I presumed held my father's final commands. He smiled politely. "All right," he said, "we begin."

I imagined he opened all his potentially contentious conversations between contestants, as he did this one, with the phrase: "Since we're all get-along people...this should be a breeze." One by one, he eyed each person seated at the heavy oak conference table, pausing at me sitting across the table at the end, then continuing his survey, smiling and nodding at Kathy and Otto. Behind him, a set of three double-hung windows provided a view of the neighboring buildings on the narrow street, and the incoming sunlight glowed off his bare pate and framed him in glare, making it hard for those at the table to detect any emotion his eyes or face might evoke.

"Let me again extend my condolences for the loss of your father and father-in-law. He was a giant in our community, and we will miss him." He paused and pulled papers out of the folder. "I have made a copy of his will for each of you. I prepared the original myself, and as you will see, I stopped by Frederick's home a little more than a week ago to secure his signature after he had made some changes." He passed out the copies, and now getting settled, he arranged his pen and yellow legal pad before him. Kathy and I both stared at the face of the document, but Otto already shuffled through the pages.

Watson looked up at his guests. "If you wait a moment before reading ahead...things will proceed nicely. Thank you." Watson sounded like a schoolteacher who had been ignored by a pupil.

Otto returned his copy to the table. He glanced up, his face now bearing an unpleasant expression.

"Alex, you are the named executor of the will, which requires you to locate and define all of your father's assets," said the attorney.

Otto peered at Watson. It was evident he chaffed at being admonished by the attorney in the manner of our father. "One moment," said Otto. "Father and I had talked. He said I would be the executor."

Watson was nonplussed. "That was one of his recent modifications to the will. Will you accept responsibility, Alex?"

"Not a problem. I can remain in town as necessary, but I'd like to move things along and finish this as soon as possible."

I could tell my brother was perturbed. "I can't imagine why our father changed his mind, but it's not a difficult task," he said. "I'm sure you can handle it, Alex. Father was most meticulous, and he walked me through his files about a month ago. I know where the keys to his safe deposit box are and the location of his investment files. We'll work together, Alex. I think we all want to move this along."

"There you go. Wonderful," said Watson. "Now, assuming everything goes off without a hitch, I will be filing this will with the probate court on your behalf. You and the creditors will get an official notice that the will is being probated. There is a time for claims against the estate. Any claims made will be verified and ultimately paid, and distribution checks will be issued by the executor...Alex." He smiled. "A pretty straightforward process which might take four to six months. In the interim, Alex is authorized to make any payments necessary to keep the lights on, so to speak. However, no distributions can be made from the estate, and the estate cannot be encumbered or used as security for any loans. So everyone who is supposed to receive a share of the estate must wait until the court paperwork is settled. Any questions?"

Otto fidgeted in his chair. "Can we get to the bequests? I'm sure we can handle the legwork without further explanation." My brother, never one for surprises, appeared anxious, now seeking to control the conversation and find out who got what.

Watson tried to smile, but it wasn't convincing. "OK, I understand. Now, the will is not complicated, but it is a bit unusual. Please turn to the third page, and you will find the itemization of bequests. There are several specific bequests to local charities that need no explanation. There are three individuals listed who are not sitting at this table. A Richard Nelson, who I believe was your father's nurse at the end, is scheduled to receive a sum of $10,000. Jan Gorger, an employee of your funeral home business, is bequeathed a sum of $25,000. And...a person named Amanda Johansson is to receive a sum of $25,000. I have the current addresses for all of these people. Questions?"

"Who is this Amanda? Otto, do you know her?" asked Kathy.

Otto had read ahead into the specific bequests, then glanced up at the attorney. "No...I don't...Edwin?"

"I only have the address. Your father informed me she was alive. You'll note she lives west of here in Sycamore."

Otto and Kathy turned to me for answers, but I remained silent concerning the mysterious Amanda. Of course, she was my father's number-one squeeze back in the day, but I wasn't about to muddy Watson's presentation, and I didn't believe this was anyone's business. I sensed we were about to jump into the exciting part of this otherwise boring ceremony. The anticipation brought silence to the room except for the five-gallon water bottle standing behind Watson; it chose this moment to burp and bubble.

Watson smiled. "Next...the will specifies Otto will receive sole and total ownership of the funeral home business."

"Any questions?" There were none. Otto nodded and smiled. No doubt he was pleased their father had not changed his will in response to the revelation of the impending body broker business. I guessed Kathy was unaware of Otto and Jarek's new business and the controversy it had stirred. I knew she was not interested in the mortuary business. But when money is involved, people are often less discriminating regarding the source if they feel entitled. People change their minds.

Watson continued. "In any event, we have arrived at the part of the will that requires some explanation. As an introduction, I know Frederick was concerned that the Reinhart family name might be lost. I believe he was hopeful he would, albeit most likely after his death, have an heir...a grandchild. Like every man, I don't think he believed he would die so soon. He told me he was going to inform Kathy of this conditional bequest, hoping to encourage the outcome he desired."

Otto erupted. "Is this even legal?"

Watson smiled. "I can assure you it is legal. Your father had the right to dispose of his property in any manner and to whomever he desired. I won't comment on the sensibility of any of his bequests, including this conditional bequest."

Otto began to sweat and pant. He addressed Kathy: "Did you know about this?" He raised his voice. "Did you talk to him?"

"We did talk..." she said, shrugging her shoulders.

The attorney interrupted. "I'm sorry. That would be a topic best discussed in private. Let me explain...it was Frederick Reinhart's intention as you can see from the wording in the will that any time up to thirty days after his death, pregnancy tests could be administered to determine if the grandchild was in process, and if so, upon a live birth delivery Kathy would receive her inheritance equal to twenty-five percent of the net estate excluding the entirety of the funeral home business and the payments of other bequests. I'm not a family planner..." he smiled, "but, Kathy, you have the right to take it any time up to the thirty-day limit. It's up to you. If you don't want to take it, you can simply forget about it, and time will run out. And the proceeds will be distributed as if the condition never existed."

"Even if I am pregnant?" she asked.

"Yes. If you are pregnant and the test shows this, then the courts would await the birth of the child. If it is a live birth, you would receive the specified share. Otherwise, that share is split fifty-fifty between Otto and Alex." Watson steepled his hands, elbows resting on the table. "This is not legal advice, and I suggest you find your own attorney, but any inheritance received by Otto will be his and not considered marital property."

Otto studied the attorney with a cold eye. Watson looked like a man who had stepped in sidewalk dog shit and wanted to go home and hose down his shoes.

Kathy appeared to be grasping the nature of her father-in-law's gift that informed her of her place in life. "What about the funeral home business? Is that community property?"

"As I said, you need to secure domestic legal advice elsewhere. I can..."

"Forget all that. Hear this, Edwin," said Otto, his face now reddened, realizing his father, from the grave, still directed his world, "isn't there anything..." he stammered, "it seems like I should have some say in this matter."

"I am only an advisor here for Alex, as executor. Informing him how to perform the duties of the position. That's my job. I'm here to help. Of course, it would be best if the three of you worked together as a team. Being an executor can sometimes be a difficult job. It's not too late to have the court appoint an outside executor. But that would increase expenses and quite possibly delay the settlement of the estate."

Otto pulled out his folded handkerchief and ran it across his moist forehead. "I'm not a well man, Edwin. I have medical issues. And this...thing is not helping."

The attorney rolled his eyes as if seeking help from Kathy or me. I decided to jump into the fray. "Edwin. Are we required to pursue this issue? I mean, is it mandated for Kathy to have these tests run?"

Watson looked relieved to have a question posed that he could answer. "That's a reasonable question. Testing or not is Kathy's option. If she chooses to be tested, the bequest is conditional in three ways. One, is Kathy pregnant? If not, this bequest is nullified. Two, if so, will the fetus be the heir of Frederick? If not, this bequest is nullified. Three, if the fetus is an heir, the bequest is still conditional on the live birth of the heir, or the termination of the pregnancy."

"Therefore," I checked out Kathy, Otto, and Watson one by one, "if the test were administered tomorrow, and Kathy were not pregnant, this would be a moot issue. The will could be processed, and the financial outcome for each party would be known."

"That's correct. However, I cannot recommend any action."

"I understand," I said. "In the end, this is Kathy's decision. But is it possible that the test results could be incorrect?"

Watson seemed ready to reply. He smiled. "Another good question, but the bequest is written to exclude that possibility. Two independent labs will provide the testing. Assuming both results are in agreement, providing a negative outcome. Then the bequest is terminated. That was Frederick's intention. I understand these tests are accurate."

I tossed out another question. "And if they are not? If they come up negative. But Kathy is pregnant?"

"Well, Frederick would be pleased. His intent was to have an heir. But Kathy would not share in his estate."

"And if the fetus was aborted after testing positive?"

Watson pondered it for a moment. "That is Kathy's choice, but without a viable fetus, there will be no heir, and the distribution of the estate will not include anything for Kathy."

Otto and I both stared at Kathy, seeking a response.

She didn't appear pleased with the conversation. "Your father has the last laugh, Otto." She shook her head and made a face. "He's putting us through the wringer from the grave."

"I'm sorry he did this, Kathy. I knew nothing about it. It's unnecessary. What's done is done. You're not pregnant. So take the test as soon as possible, and we can move on. I can't wait, and I think Alex would also want to put this topic to bed." He glanced at me for affirmation.

"Bedtime. I agree."

Otto wore a furrowed brow. He turned to Kathy. "You don't think you're pregnant? Do you?"

She shook her head. "I think I would have mentioned it, Otto."

"So, let's do the tests. OK? It's the only way to end this."

"I guess so. But if I were pregnant..."

"But you're not."

"But if I were. It might make sense for the baby and me to have a financial cushion." She smiled.

"What?" asked Otto. "I don't think you understand, Kathy. If so, it would be our child, and he or she would benefit from the estate funding. The result would be almost the same. You get that, don't you?"

Kathy turned to me as if waiting for advice. I remained silent, wondering if she knew something that I didn't. My own thoughts started spinning. I realized the carnal moment Kathy and I shared might result in a positive test result, but I suspected the procedure could not identify which of the Reinhart brothers satisfied my father's quest for an heir. The whole concept was doubtful since mine was a one-time event, and Otto, at least according to Papa, was firing blanks. I studied the faces around the table, trying to keep a poker face while the two men waited for the woman's answer.

"I have to think about this," she replied. "Can I have some time, Edwin?"

"Take all the time you wish, but if you are going ahead with the tests, I would do it as soon as possible. But that's your choice," said the attorney, defining our work from his. "Consult me for any questions or details you do not understand. The contact info for the selected lab testing services is in the will. Please remember that delay might lead to an unwanted termination of your potential financial benefits."

As I thought about the reality of human reproduction, of sperm, ova, and untidy beginnings, one word slid out of my mouth like a warm brown egg exiting a big fat hen. "Interesting."

Otto smirked; Kathy appeared lost in thought, ignoring my pithy comment.

And as Edwin Watson assembled his papers into a neat pile, he quipped: "Yes. To say the least." He rose from his chair, binder in his hand, appearing as a shadow in the window glare. "Thank you, all," he said. "Enjoy the rest of your day."

Chapter 27

The Reinhart family dispersed in front of the attorney's office. Otto, still wearing a worried look, said he would drop off his wife at home and then return to work, while I chose to take a long walk to allow me to assess my situation. I was nearing the end of my trip. My father and I were squared away, the scope of my inheritance was established, and it would be more than enough, no matter what happened. I might have to share a portion with Kathy if somehow she were pregnant. As I said at the meeting with the attorney, it could be interesting. However, that was a bridge to be crossed only at the will of the gods. I considered it a remote possibility. The topic of my brother's health remains unnerving. Other than our brief discussion on the swing at Terry's house, Kathy never spoke of it. I would guess she was not aware of the speculative nature of heart transplants or the costs involved. I'm sure she doesn't have any idea that her husband is a partner with her former boss, Dr. Jarek, in a fledgling body broker business. I didn't like Otto's approach: keep the little woman, barefoot, unaware, and in the kitchen. It's not fair to her or sensible for him. I've decided to call Otto and give them all a nudge in the right direction.

I walked around town thinking less about Otto's problems and more about my future. My gig as an international traveler and storyteller for the slicks was over. I wanted to become a novelist. My inheritance would allow me to write without worrying about my next meal, but creating a novel and getting it published and promoted are two different ordeals. I'm the same as thousands of other potential debut authors; maybe my successful years of magazine writing might provide some contacts. Hard work and hope will become my byline. After an hour of zombie-like walking, I found myself in front of Terry and Margie's house, my home away from home. I entered, made and ate lunch, dropped down into my basement suite, flipped on the TV, and then called Otto at work. He also wanted to talk, and we agreed to meet near the bell tower.

A few hours later, we again sat on a bench in the park, without speaking, both of us admired the impressive view of the large pond at the base of the tower. Ducks and visitors were actively closing out the season. The ducks glided through the water one last time before it iced over, and a few stalwart visitors drifted about in paddleboats destined to soon be drydocked. Except for some reluctant oaks, the trees surrounding the little lake were bare, the sun was dimming, and a chill was in the air.

"Watson was all business," I tendered.

Otto raised his eyebrows. "He's used to dealing with Father. A moment of pleasantries and then straight to the point."

"Can't say I blame him. Money talk always gets everyone's attention. I imagine he's had a few domestic tussles while reading wills."

"Especially, if you get fucked," said Otto. The last word of his response sounded full of pain.

"Is that your take?"

He shrugged his shoulders. "Who knows? I've got ants in my pants. Anxious...helpless...afraid. That would cover it."

"I'm with you, Otto. What can I do to help?"

We stared at the ducks now approaching shore; a big duck with five ducklings trailing behind arrived at land, and the family waddled up the grade through the grass. "I've got to line them up. Money, doctors, but most important...a new heart."

"Take it one step at a time. Does this conditional bequest issue bother you?"

"Not really. I can't imagine that Kathy would be pregnant," he paused, "we haven't..." He stopped. "Well, it's very unlikely."

I stopped to think. "It's not her fault, and whatever is happening, it's her body. Remember that. Best to get the whole thing out of the way as soon as possible, right? No matter what, it would be exciting to have a child on the way?"

"Sure. She's on board with that, too. I did read her the riot act. Maybe I was too hard, but she's going in tomorrow for the test. The sooner the better." He winced. "Much as I would like to have a kid, I can't believe the old man went behind my back to manipulate our relationship. I'll never forgive him for that. Some things push beyond the boundaries of decency." His lengthy and intense answer strained his weakened lungs to their limit, and he coughed to ease the tightness.

"You, OK?"

My brother nodded.

He didn't look good. But I pretended his impending death didn't exist. "I'm with you. Resolve this thing, and it's out of the way. If her inheritance is eliminated, will you be able to cover the costs of the transplant?" I asked.

"Yeah. I can put together enough. Otherwise, Kathy and I would have some serious talking to do." A weak smile followed. "Anyway, I've been able to maintain a pretty decent-sized life insurance policy that would provide financial security for the medical mafia, in the event I die on the operating table. I'm afraid to disclose that information. They might just put me down like an old dog, and grab the money."

"Not much of a joke, Otto."

"I'm just getting tired of doctors."

"A necessary evil."

"They are, but they're a chronic pain. Anyway, I do have the policy. And some health insurance coverage. So I think I can make it."

"When the estate is closed, I'll have a pretty good chunk of money too," I said. "I can loan..." he cut me short.

"That won't be necessary. I don't want to screw up your life with my debts. Don't worry about that." Otto looked out over the water. "Father's estate will provide. Any timetable for leaving town? You can't stay in Terry's basement too long. Winter's coming. The mice will eat you alive, or you'll freeze to death down there." He chuckled.

"I'm going to move on. Maybe not waiting for Kathy's test results. I'll juggle my time with my executor chores while heading down to the Florida Keys. I may have to rely on you to be my assistant executor if I'm out of town."

"No problem. We'll do it."

"I'll go down and check out the market. I might be able to find something modest on the water. I'm just looking for a salty piece of land."

"Sounds like fun. And what do you intend to do?"

"I'm a writer. I've got a few good stories in me. I'm going to write."

"That's what they do. Go for it."

We smiled at each other. "All I need is a publisher, and all you need is a heart. I'm not sure which is more difficult to find. Any news on your end?"

Otto leaned against the back of the bench, put his hands together, and interlocked his fingers. "That's the soft spot, Alex. I've got no control over that. None. Zippo. Time is what I need. Something I don't have. I tick off many of the boxes for getting a heart, but it's still a crapshoot. I have to keep breathing, keep making money, and wait...and I'm not good at waiting."

"What else can you do?" I asked.

"I can be proactive. I'm looking at other ways to get one. Other places."

"Any luck?"

"I might have something. I found a place in Mexico. It's a broker, an intermediary. Middleman. Whatever. I think that's how it works down there. The Mexicans are more flexible than these pricks up here. Across the border...money talks."

"Do you trust them?"

"I've got Jarek helping me. And I trust him."

"When will you find out?"

"I may have an answer in no more than a week." He checked the time. "Look, I've got to go now. Kathy will have dinner for me, and I've got to get her some flowers on the way home."

"Good idea. Women like stuff like that, right?" I said, hoping to bond with him.

"Women....who the hell knows? Can't hurt."

As we stood and walked toward Otto's car in the parking lot, dusk hung heavy in the cool air of the early evening. Opening the door of the Mercedes, he turned and gave me a man-hug. "Thanks for the offer of a loan. If you cut and run, I wouldn't hold it against you. Glad you're on my side. It's been quite a while since I felt any support from my family."

"Stay centered, Otto. Good night." I headed home, and I dwelled on my role in this family drama. My hands were dirty. I could try to pawn off my betrayal of my brother on his wife, but I've been around the block. Some things just shouldn't happen, yet they do.

Chapter 28

Tonight was Beggars' Night, October 30th. Although Terry and Margie's two boys were getting older, they weren't too old to deny themselves the fun of goofy costumes and grabbing a month's supply of free candy. Margie served an early dinner in anticipation of the annual holiday test run. The concept of Beggars' Night was born in wilder days. I doubt that Naperville's teenage population was ever dangerous. However, the pre-holiday tradition, created by concerned parents, was intended for the younger kids to beg one day early to avoid the older pranksters who might employ the 'trick' option of the Halloween 'trick or treat' extortion demand. Charlie and Eddie didn't care. Two nights of free candy was a better idea.

We sat at the round kitchen table, which was a tight fit before I arrived as a guest, but now required the careful placement of five chairs to permit clear passage from table to kitchen and back. Margie and Terry were on kid-patrol sitting at either side of the two boys who sat across from me. Charlie, the older boy, was an appropriate pirate, *sans* sword and hook, and I guess Eddie was a generic red and black superhero with unspecified superpowers. Throughout dinner, the boys behaved as typical animated pre-teens, their boisterousness controlled or at least tempered by she who must be obeyed. Tonight they were more antsy than ever, ready to pop out of the house and begin the annual heist.

"Boys, slow down, eat your dinner in a civilized manner," commanded Margie. "Terry..." She gave my friend a look to reprimand his sons without result. Next, her face expressed disgust.

I became her backup enforcer. "Alex, I'm sure you have a story or two from your travels." She winked at me.

I played along. "I might. Let's see," I said, surveying the two boys, "we have a pirate and a super-hero at the table. Maybe you guys have heard about the Alligator Man...*El Hombre Caimán*?" I looked at Charlie and Eddie. Charlie, directly across from me, gave me a wiseguy look; soon, he would become a teenage pain in the ass. I remember that age. But Eddie, the scrawny red-haired boy, was younger and less wary. He was eager to hear Uncle Alex's tall tale.

"OK. Let me tell you." I smiled. "When I was down in the jungles of Colombia, South America, doing a unique magazine story about the Madalena River, I was told the story of a mysterious being. If I remember right, this river is the largest in the northern Andes Mountains. Almost a thousand miles it runs downhill in a rampage before dumping out into the Caribbean Sea at Barranquilla. The river is enormous. Like the Rio Grande of South America. My crew and I rode a flat-bottom boat through a land of wild animals, dangerous native tribes, and jungle fever. We're talking iguanas, manatees, crocodiles, giant turtles, even hippopotamususses."

"You mean, hippopotami, Uncle Alex?" said Charlie.

"You are correctamundo, matey... hippopotami." Looking at Margie, I said, "These kids are smart like their mother."

"What about the Alligator Man?" asked Eddie.

"It's a tall tale told by the native population of Colombia. All about a man named Saúl Montenegro. Old Saúl had one weakness."

"You want to guess?"

Little Eddie exclaimed, "Kryptonite?"

"No. He was only a human with human desires. He loved to watch the women in the town bathe in the river. But..."

"You mean taking baths? Naked?" Charlie asked with a smile.

Margie cleared her throat.

"Uh...I don't know. Maybe, but whatever...the women didn't like him watching them, and they threw bars of soap at him to make him go away. But Saul didn't give up. He was a determined man, and he checked and found an old witch nearby who had a magic red potion that could change him from a man into an alligator. It worked like a charm. Once he was covered with the magic potion, he looked just like a lazy alligator. So every day he floated around in the river watching the women bathe, and none of them ever suspected him."

"Until?..."

I eyed Charlie. "You know this story."

He shook his head. "No. But all the fairy tales say that."

I gave him a look and continued. "Until...one day, the alligator returned home and found a friend of the witch. This guy was an amateur magician. The witch was busy making trouble elsewhere, so she sent this junior magician the magic white potion that would transform the alligator back to Old Saúl. But the new magician was so frightened at being face to face with the mean-looking alligator that he tripped and fell...spilling the potion. He ended up pouring only a little bit of the white potion...the one that makes him a man again...on the alligator's head. Now Old Saúl had the head of a man and the body of an alligator."

"That's weird," said Charlie.

"After that, he was called the Alligator Man, and he couldn't hide anymore. Everyone in the town was afraid of him, and so the men in the town chased him all the way downriver to the city of Barranquilla, where he died all alone. He was an unwanted freak, both human and alligator. And today, every Halloween, the ghost of Alligator Man still haunts everyone in that town. The men might be frightened, but it's those beautiful gals who still bathe in the Magdalena River he scares the most."

"That's a good one, Uncle Alex," said Charlie.

"Yeah," said Eddie.

"One more thing. Some people claim they have seen the Alligator Man, or his ghost, swimming in the big pond downtown. Here in Naperville."

"They have?" asked Eddie, his big blue eyes expressing wonder and fear.

I laughed. "I'm kidding, Eddie. But be careful when you're out begging tonight. He might be floating in someone's swimming pool."

Margie got up, picked up her dishes, and scoffed. "This Alligator Man sounds like an old pervert. She looked at the boys. "You remember what I told you boys about perverts?" They nodded and adopted concerned looks. She walked to the kitchen. "Put your dishes in the sink, boys, and grab your goodie bags. Let's go out and beg."

"Woo-hoo!" shouted Eddie.

"Terry, you clean up, and I want those lights up tonight. Got it?"

Like the boys, Terry grunted obediently and followed orders. He loaded the dirty dishes into the dishwasher and waited until the sound of the front door closing signaled the exit of the trio. The two old friends stood at the counter. "A little peace and quiet," he said. "Wanna beer?"

I nodded. "So I'm Uncle Alex now."

"The boys like you." He smiled. "You ought to think about getting some of your own before your dick falls off."

I looked down at my crotch. "Not a problem."

Beers in hand, we moved to the garage. He opened the big door, and we sat on a couple of old vinyl-clad kitchen chairs, drinking beer and looking out into the autumn darkness.

A cool breeze drifted into the stuffy garage. "This is the life," said Terry. "So when are you leaving?"

I pretended to be offended. "That's gratitude for you. I get you a big investigation job, teach your boys about reptilian Peeping Toms, and now you want me gone."

Terry held his beer bottle in one hand and gave me the fisheye.

"I'm sorry I couldn't pay your fee for services," Terry. "But even though I'm the executor, I don't think it's practical to assume the estate will pay you for putting the body broker bee in my father's bonnet. Otto might not like that."

Terry rubbed his mustache. "Can't argue with you there. But you think I'll ever get paid?"

"All my stuff is packed up and now waiting in storage in Miami. Once I get down there, I'll straighten out my finances and get you paid. Worst case, we wait for the estate to pay me, and I pay you."

"Just busting your balls." He chuckled. "When are you leaving town?"

"A couple of days. I've got a few 'goodbyes' to make, and I'm gone."

"That might be painful..."

"Yes..." I thought for a moment, realizing how painful it might be. "I've got to close the door on Naperville forever."

"Kids will miss you, Uncle Alex." Terry smiled.

"And Margie?"

He smirked. "You know what they say about house guests and fish."

"Yep. I've got to thank you both. It's been rich. This trip hasn't been much fun, but I enjoyed my stay here. You guys have to visit me when I settle in the Keys."

"That's a done deal, friend." He downed the rest of his beer, stood, and tossed the brown bottle into the trash. "I need your help to put up those pumpkin lights in front of the house. OK?"

"I'm your man."

We moved onto the concrete driveway. He showed me an old cardboard box filled with strings of mini jack-o'-lantern lights and extension cords. "Hang these all the way across the front of the house from the end of the garage to the front porch. There are nails up there in the soffit. All you do is hook them along and plug them in." He pointed to the electrical outlet on the far side of the garage door opening.

I nodded. "Piece of cake."

"There's a small ladder hanging on the wall over there. Should be a snap. Be careful on the ladder."

"Sure. This isn't my first rodeo, Django."

"Margie's got me doing decorations in the backyard. For who? I don't know." Terry ambled out of the garage muttering to himself.

I thought I heard something outside. It sounded like someone running. Viewing through the garage door opening into the night, I saw nothing. However, the security light above the door shone, and whatever created the noise did not fall in its yellow glow, and beyond the glow, darkness ruled. I fumbled through the box of plastic pumpkin lights. I heard distant shouting from across the street. Kids working the houses on that side of the street created more noise than normal, enough sound to be considered raucous any other night, but tonight, in the spirit of the season, expected and harmless.

I assessed my task. I walked out to the penumbra of the floodlight and envisioned my finished product. The lights would hang from left to right, starting at the edge of the house, above the garage door, extending about three feet to the projecting roof of the entry porch, then following the porch fascia and ending wrapped around to meet the next wall. Since Terry previously pounded in a series of well-spaced galvanized 10-penny nails, the project appeared simple.

I also noticed the two pumpkins on the front porch, now jack-o'-lanterns carved with scary faces by Charlie and Eddie. Lighted candles inside revealed the ugliness of the glowing, menacing creatures of the night. I gazed up and down the street. Porch lights beamed, and some houses glowed with strings of plastic ghosts, goblins, and illuminated pumpkins; the delightful, cozy, smoky autumn, small-town scene was a classic image, but different than in my childhood days three decades past. Halloween is more like the flip side of Christmas, and Naperville now looks more like

Potterville than Bedford Falls. Uncertain of the sociological or psychological relevance, if any, I wondered if it was devil worship or a recognition of the dual nature of humanity; my guess is the latter. Everyone is always looking for an out, a devil to blame, and everyone can be dangerous.

Without a sound, someone approached me from behind. The only tell was the crinkling of dried leaves under their shoes as they walked on the lawn. Startled, I turned and faced a couple of well-built teenage monsters with painted faces, one all white and the other all black. At first, because I didn't sense their approach, and then because their appearance was bizarre, it was a lot to process in a moment. My travels sharpened my senses: jungles, deep forests, icy tundra, and hostile tribes were my world for almost a decade. I developed a sensible respect and awareness of unseen danger, but after my off-year in Denver, my well of survival awareness dried up, and the instant realization hit me hard in the gut.

"Trick or treat," they offered nonchalantly. White-face wore a Cubs cap and black-face, a Sox cap. The white-faced kid carried a Little League baseball bat, its end covered with a foam beer cozy; the black-faced kid wore a catcher's mitt on his left hand and held a baseball in his right. He stood looking at me, tossing the ball into the air and then catching it. Part of his act, I guess.

I composed myself. "Sorry, guys. I'm only a worker. The candy-givers are out now. Come back in an hour or so."

Without a word or nod, white and black drifted back to the sidewalk and headed up the street. They caused me to reassess my comfort level and awareness. Naperville or Nairobi, bad guys are always looking for victims. I waited until they were lost in the dark of the night, and I refocused on my assignment.

The ladder Terry provided was wooden and about four feet tall, with treads on one half and wooden rails on the other. The hinge in the middle made it perfect for painters to climb up two steps, hang the roller tray at the top, paint an arm's length section of the upper wall, and descend to repeat the process. The ladder and paint could easily be moved to the next wall section. I wasn't painting walls, but the up-and-down process worked as well for hanging plastic pumpkins. Up and down, my job was half-finished in five minutes. I was never standing more than two feet off the ground, so my task did not activate my normal ladder-safety cautiousness, ingrained in every red-blooded suburban American. I was breezing along oblivious, but thinking again about Kathy. This happened about twenty times a day. I couldn't shake it. She was with me on that ladder.

I had plugged in the lights to test them, and I left them illuminated as I hung them from Terry's well-spaced nails. I moved the ladder to the right again, making sure of stability. The bearing was solid concrete. It was pitched somewhat front to back but tended to make the ladder more stable. The tricky part, if there was one, would be positioning the ladder to the right of the concrete driveway on the soft grassy area between the driveway and the porch. I increased my ladder-safety awareness at this point. The only weakness in the design of a painter's ladder is its lack of stability for left-to-right movements. Movement front-to-back required little thought, but if one leaned too far to one side, reaching out further to achieve his goal, he ran the risk of the ladder tipping over. Of course, I was only two feet up, and I had no paint to spill.

I remained cautious as I reached up, extended the string of lights, and hung the double wire over the nails, twisting one of the leads around them wherever possible. I glanced to my left to admire my work. Twelve lighted pumpkins proclaimed the weird meaning of Halloween, a small but impressive sight. I was happy to help the Walkers appear as dutiful citizens of Naperville. Back to work, I reached to the right with a little bit of a stretch to hook the wire. My fingers inched to the right, and the wire slipped over the nail...done.

At the same moment, something brought up the hairs on my neck: someone breathing, the moving of a bush, the distant yell of trick-or-treaters, or the anticipation of falling. I couldn't say. Eternity froze time, place, and me. All my senses left me but for one last loud noise that banged into my head like the slam of a swinging door.

Chapter 29

Terry Walker had finished his chores and entered the house from the backyard when he heard the doorbell ring. Opening the front door, he was greeted by a small gang of pre-teen costumed rascals. They were polite, and each one thanked him as he offered candy from Margie's giant white plastic bowl. He was amazed to see their restraint, one piece of candy each. They turned away, and as Terry was about to close the door, the last in line, a junior Count Dracula, spun his head back and said: "You know the dead guy you got out here looks pretty real." The door continued to close until Terry remembered Alex. Stepping outside on the porch, he glanced to his right. Someone's feet extended from an area of low bushes. Three steps later, the entire body of his friend came into view.

Alex was moving now. By the time Terry knelt next to him, his body had assumed the fetal position. Although he appeared to have sight, Alex showed no sign of recognition. One glance at the ladder now folded and lying askew in front of the open garage door told him the story. Four pumpkin lights hung limply from the soffit, casting an eerie orange glow on Alex's dirty blank face. There was no visible blood. Terry guessed the ladder had collapsed with Alex on it, and he must have been knocked out for minutes. Terry remembered working in the backyard and hearing a strange noise in the otherwise quiet evening. At least ten minutes had passed. As he bent over his friend, he berated himself for not reacting faster. With care, he reached out to help Alex rise to a sitting position, all the while mentally kicking himself in the ass for putting his friend in this spot.

"Alex. Are you OK?" No response. "Can you stand?" His questions fell on deaf ears. Alex dumbly peered out into space, eyes open, appearing dazed. "Up you go, buddy." It was a difficult process. Alex was able to rise, and with Terry holding him, they moved into the house. It didn't appear that any bones were broken. The injured man walked without hesitation or apparent pain. They found their way through the living room, and he helped Alex sit on the sofa. Terry asked him more questions, but soon gave up. Next, he examined Alex's face and head. His cheek was covered in dirt, and his hair was clogged with dead grass and evergreen needles, while his friend, still fogged out, sat head down, his arms resting on his legs. Terry rushed to the kitchen, grabbed a handful of paper towels, wet some at the sink, filled a tumbler with water, and returned. He dabbed and rubbed the skin to remove dirt, and brushed his hair until Alex jerked in reaction to a sensitive spot on his skull. Terry got a flashlight and examined the back and right rear of his friend's head, the area behind and above his ear; a close inspection revealed a reddened scuff mark which was slightly raised, but the skin was not cut or bleeding, no doubt the contact point. Alex's head must have hit a hard, flat surface, maybe a half-buried stone.

Terry had some experience with head impact concussions. For one season, after his graduation, he worked the sidelines handling the yard marker for the high school football team, so he had seen a few, but he would soon find out none of those had resulted in anything like Alex's condition.

"Can you tell me your name?" He asked him this same question several times without any response.

In time, Alex spoke. "What happened?"

Terry explained, starting with the long version of the answer.

It appeared as Alex listened, but he only had one response: "What happened?"

This question-response routine went on for an agonizing fifteen minutes before Alex acknowledged Terry's repetitive answer. He responded with a simple, "OK."

For Terry, those two spoken letters eased his anxiety. Alex had returned to the living room. Terry offered him some water, and Alex sipped. Terry repositioned him deeper into the sofa, and he telephoned Otto. Although concerned, Otto explained he was not well; however, he would call Dr. Jarek and ask him to stop by the house. Soon after, he called back and told Terry the doctor would arrive within a half-hour. Terry was relieved. Maybe overkill, he thought, but he welcomed the idea of a medical professional taking over. Victims of concussions often appeared normal even if they suffered severe damage. In the meantime, he continued to converse with Alex, or at least he attempted to do this. Things got better. Alex, still in a daze, was starting to make sense of the world.

About five minutes later, with Terry sitting next to Alex on the sofa, Margie and the two boys returned. Charlie and Eddie excitedly recalled their candy accumulation adventure, chattering back and forth, each kid announcing a better story. But their father's demeanor, and one look at Alex, caused them to quiet down. They stared at the broken man, wondering. Alex did nod and smile a little, but his response was out of character for good old Uncle Alex. The boys fell into unusual silence.

Margie jumped in. "What happened?" she asked.

"He was putting up the lights, and he fell off the ladder."

"Why was he putting up the lights, Terry?"

"Because I asked him to...no big deal. It was an accident."

Margie closed in on Alex, who, amidst their bickering, remained in a trance. She studied his eyes and surveyed the damage to his head, shaking her head from side to side. "Terry...you should take him to the emergency room. Now."

"Otto's doctor is coming, Marge. I'm handling it."

"He's a house guest, Terry. For Pete's sake. You're responsible, Terry." She turned to gather up her chicks. The two boys clung to each other, staring in fear.

"Is Uncle Alex going to be all right, Mom?" asked Eddie.

"He'll be fine. Put your candy in the kitchen, say good night to Uncle Alex, and then upstairs you go."

Charlie and Eddie ran to and fro but stopped short in front of the wounded Alex. They gave him gentle hugs, resulting in mini-nods from him, and then they bounded up the stairs.

Terry reached out to hold Alex's hand. They sat next to each other without talking for about fifteen minutes until the doorbell announced the arrival of the cavalry.

Terry opened the door, and Doctor Jarek slipped into the house on cat feet, wearing a black jogging outfit with yellow reflective stripes on the legs and wrists and a pair of $200 sneakers. He had been playing a game of tennis at a downtown indoor court when he received the call from Otto. Although Terry Walker had researched the doctor and was aware of him at Frederick's wake, this was the first time the two men met. Jarek went into action.

"And you are?" he asked.

"Terry Walker. I'm one of Alex's old friends. High school."

"I'm Stephan Jarek. I'm his doctor." He looked across the room, found his quarry, and slid in next to him on the sofa. "Hello, Alex. It's Dr. Jarek. Do you remember me?"

Alex, lost somewhere in the fog, snapped to attention. "Sure. What's up?" he asked as if nothing was wrong.

"I understand you fell from a ladder and hit your head. May I examine you?"

"Yeah. I guess so."

"Does your head hurt?"

"I don't know. I don't think so."

"Do you feel dizzy?"

"No."

"Fine. Please turn slightly to your left?" Alex shifted as directed, and Jarek stood, pulled a penlight out of his jacket pocket, and examined his skull; carefully, he moved the hairs exposing the point of impact. "That's good, Alex. Now turn your body to face me.

He held his right hand up with his index finger pointed. "Look at my finger. I'm going to make a letter in the air. Please keep looking at the tip of my finger as I do so." Jarek moved his hand to make a bold 'X' pattern, all while watching his patient's eye movement. Taking his time, the doctor continued to peer into his patient's eyes, sometimes using the penlight.

"Fine. Now let's go through a few questions. "Can you tell me what day it is?"

Alex paused and said: "Halloween...no, the day before."

"OK. I'm going to give you a list of three words. And I want you to remember them. Ready?"

"Cloud...Garden...Bicycle."

Alex appeared to be thinking.

"And how old are you?"

His response was delayed. "Thirty-three."

"OK. Please count backward five years starting from your current age."

Slower yet, he responded correctly, pausing at 'thirty-one' and then finishing.

"A minute ago, I gave you three words to remember. Can you tell me what they were?"

This stumped him. He shook his head in response.

"Please spell the word 'world' backward."

"World..." he said quietly. Alex considered this one as if he were using all his brain power. "...D...O...no L..." He stopped. "I'm sorry. My thinking is not the best now."

"You were standing on a ladder outside, putting up some lights," said Jarek. "Do you remember your friend Terry helping you come back into the house?"

"No..."

"But you know Terry, right?"

Alex smiled. "We go way back." He made a face. "I think I'm going to be sick. Terry..."

"I got it," said his friend, as he moved in fast and helped Alex walk to the powder room. Alex, on his own, found the toilet and threw up. Afterward, Terry helped him up, flushed the toilet, wiped his face with a towel, and brought him back. He sat alone, expressionless.

"Relax, Alex. Just stay where you are," said Jarek.

The doctor walked toward the kitchen and motioned for Terry to follow. Jarek spoke in a soft voice. "Alex appears to have had a concussion. I would like to check him into my hospital for testing and oversight."

"Is it bad, Doctor?"

"Until we see a scan, I can't say. The wound itself has not cut the scalp. This reduces concern, but the damage from concussions is caused by whiplash, a rapid movement of the skull jarred to a stop. The brain might be bruised, resulting in bleeding. If so, internal pressure builds, requiring drainage surgery. The best thing we can do for Terry is to put him under professional observation while waiting for the test results. I'm afraid that if we leave him here, something might go unnoticed. Why take the risk?"

"You're the doctor, Doctor."

"Fine. Please help me get him into my car, and I will get him admitted tonight. He'll have a solid, safe night's sleep, and you and your family will not be responsible. Agreed?"

Terry couldn't hide his relief. "Thanks, Doc. Let's get him in."

Jarek explained the situation to Alex. He said he understood, but he only wanted to lie down. He would be fine, according to him. Terry intervened by kneeling before Alex and making a strong argument for moving him to the hospital, cementing this option by suggesting Margie, as usual, was pissed at them. Alex recognized he might be becoming a liability. So he agreed with the move. The two men waltzed Alex, his legs still somewhat rubbery, into Jarek's car. Once he sat, Terry patted Alex on the shoulder, worked the seatbelt over his limp body, shut the door, and tapped his fingers on the window. The car backed down the drive. Alex tossed out a little wave to Terry, and then he was gone. Terry Walker gazed at his house, the ladder on the ground, the dangling glowing pumpkin lights, and mumbled to himself, shaking his head, "Fuckin' painter ladder."

Chapter 30

I was in a bed, somewhere, sometime in the early morning. Sunlight cut into the room; some fell upon my face, forcing me awake. Reality persisted. My eyes scanned the room. Last night was a nightmare. I had a fall, that is a fact. But what happened? I sought a hook on which to hang my thoughts. I remembered the black and white baseball guys. For some reason, those two worried me. I climbed up two steps on the ladder to install those stupid pumpkin lights, hooking the lights on nails, one by one. It all seemed so simple. Yet something caused all this. I remembered a big bang, then nothing, and later conversations with Terry and others, stupid talk, flashlights in my eyes. In the background, people talked about me, like I didn't exist.

I listened for several minutes before I formed an impression, guessing I was in a hospital. A shift change might be happening outside my door, and sounds of staff coming and going. I spotted a call button hanging off the safety bar on my bed, and I decided to ring for room service. I waited a couple of minutes and rang again.

This time, a male nurse arrived. He had a nice smile.

"Happy Halloween, Mr. Reinhart. Rise and shine."

"Easy for you to say. I have a nasty headache."

"Yes."

"Got an aspirin?"

He smiled at me again, like I was a diabetic child asking for a candy bar, shaking his head in quick motions. "Sadly, that is *verboten*...because of your concussion. You took a tour of 'Hollywood' last night. Made a fine little video. Your doctor..." he checked his chart, "Doctor Jarek has to review the diagnostic images first. Then he'll tell us what you can handle."

I remembered the name Jarek and squinted as if that would clear my mind. "Concussion?" I mumbled. For certain, that was not a cheer-up device for someone lying in a hospital bed.

"I guess you fell off a ladder. Hit the back of your head." He nodded. "I'm not the doctor, but that's why you have a headache." He smiled.

Yes, I thought. OK. I rolled my head to the left, reached with my free hand, and touched the scalp on the back of my head. Gingerly, I probed. No pain in the bandaged area, only a dull headache. "Pain killer?"

"Nope. We covered that. It's a blood thinner. Not legit if you have bleeding on the brain."

"How about breakfast?" I asked. I was hungry now.

He smiled. "We've got some excellent water for sure. Right next to you. Would you like a drink?"

I nodded, and he poured some into a plastic cup and helped me take a couple of sips. Leaving the cup on the rolling cart, he turned and walked out. "I'll check on breakfast," he said as he moved out of my view.

I tried to catch him on his way out. "When can I escape?" I was talking to myself. Other than the headache, everything was fine. In the distant valley of my memory, I envisioned all the events leading up to my fall and concussion, but later memories are weird, as if viewed through a cardboard tube, lacking context, and not helpful for reconstruction. The audio recollections are not much better, again without context or sequence. Stupid questions, more questions, background babbling, then not much more. Now I'm in this hospital room. Someone must have removed my clothes, slapped a bare-assed gown on me, and inserted a needle in the back of my hand. A bottle of something hangs above, connected to my hand with clear flexible tubing. Sleep must have come and gone. And that's it. I looked out at a vast plain of bureaucratic medical nothingness. The nurse talked about a concussion, which is something new to me. Except for sleep, occasional drinking bouts, and a one-time bad drug episode, I've always retained a tight grip on reality. Now I'm up here in an unknown hospital room, my recent memories scattered, inaccessible, and lost in the darkness of Beggars' Night. It's not a comfortable place. I was tired of talking to myself.

I guess my best move was to fall asleep because when I awakened I was looking at the face of an angel named Kathy. I guessed she wondered if I would recognize her. She held my hand. She was the last piece of the puzzle. I got the picture. Tears welled up in my eyes, and I pretended to be stronger than I was. She kissed my cheek and sat on the edge of the bed, our two hands reconnected. We didn't speak for minutes, I guess. I was in a quiet, comfortable place. I dropped off again into sleep.

"Wake up, sleepy head," she said in a soft angelic voice.

"What time is it?"

"It's about eleven. I've been watching you snooze,"

"Pretty exciting."

She smiled. "It is for me. I was told you were here, and I was quite worried, but I spoke with Stephan this morning, and he assured me you will be fine. He's supposed to be here before noon."

"Who's Stephan?"

"Doctor Jarek."

"Oh...am I leaving soon?"

"I hope so, but that's up to him."

"What were you doing climbing a ladder in the dark?"

I made a face. "Helping a friend?"

"Ah, your buddy Terry. I spoke with him this morning. He's very concerned about you, but his wife is keeping him busy today."

"No loss. He's a troublemaker. I prefer pretty women."

She pulled her hand away and walked to the other side of the room. A misty halo of sun circled her head as she bent over to grab the guest chair. I was a wounded Halloween victim lying in a hospital bed, but my eyes didn't know it. I couldn't resist tracing the outline of her body as the thin pale gold cotton dress tightened around her curves and then eased back into place...something for me to remember. Returning, she brought the chair close to the bed, found another pillow, lifted my shoulders and head, and slid in the second pillow. A sense of comfort washed over me. She smiled at me. "I'm so happy you're getting better. Otto wanted me to pass on his regrets. He couldn't come by. He's got his own medical issues. You know he would be here if possible."

"He's worse?"

She thought for a moment, appearing to consider her words. "It's a long story."

"I'm not going anywhere." I smiled.

"I guess it's all right to tell you. Don't tell anyone."

I braced myself for the worst.

"Otto took a ride to O'Hare this morning. He's flying to Mexico."

"What? Why?"

"The heart transplant. He decided not to wait for something to open up here. I guess he found a hospital outside the USA. Somewhere outside Mexico City that can do a transplant now." She shook her head. "You don't understand. He put up a good front, but his health has been deteriorating over the last few days. I'm not sure how he found out about this possibility. He's been on the computer and phone all week. He was desperate."

"He gave up on his doctors here?"

"Yes. They couldn't help him. I think the whole thing is out of their hands and..."

Perplexed, I questioned her. "Did you talk to Otto? Reason with him?"

"Of course. You know Otto. He knows best. The only person he trusts is Dr. Jarek. Those two should get married."

I wanted to tell her what Terry found out about the strange couple. In fact, they are married, if you count an LLC as a business 'marriage'. "But you're his wife."

"Alex, you don't understand. Otto's become a younger version of your father. Not so much a man of the Twenty-First Century. My opinion, or for that matter, any woman's opinion, is not worth much. I gave up trying a long time ago. I think the whole idea of heading for Mexico to have his heart transplant is crazy. But he has no patience. I almost think he's flipped. He doesn't want to die."

"Who does?"

"That's true, but his clock is about to unwind. Stop ticking. Ending the world of Otto Reinhart. He understands death. That's his business. Otto thinks he can beat a system indifferent to him. He feels like a chalk number on the blackboard about to be erased and replaced with another. It's sad. Of course, I hope he succeeds, but he's on his own now. I can only wait for news."

I tried to work out her story in my muddy mind. "What's his plan?"

"I believe he shifted his...our finances around so he can pay for the whole thing. He said after the operation, it would take about two weeks until he would be well enough to fly again. When he returns, he intends to toss the ball back in the hands of his doctors. He'll be a healthy man making money and buying his future one day at a time...insurance or not. He believes it will be cheaper, and most important...possible in Mexico. What do I know? He wants me to sit tight and cover for him while he is gone. He'll call in the next couple of days to clear everything up."

"Don't worry," I said. "When I get out of here, I'll find out. I'll discuss it with Doctor Jarek."

She shook her head. "Not going to happen, Alex. I already tried. Jarek is familiar with Otto's plans, and though he didn't approve of it, he said it was Otto's decision to make. And Otto demanded I not reveal anything about his trip to Mexico and the transplant. So keep this under your hat...OK? It's important to him."

I nodded and rolled my eyes.

"The people at his business think he's just off on a vacation to clear his head and rest."

"Without you?" I asked.

"I don't know what they think about me. Or what he told them. In any case, it's just a story."

I stared at the ceiling, feeling like a dump truck had poured a load of misery on me. The craziness of the last two days was undigested by my mind or body. I reached out to ground myself. My last conversations with my brother and his wife, only a few days ago, were all about money.

"What about the will?" I asked.

"Well, for one thing, I took Watson's advice and got my own attorney."

"That's kind of drastic, isn't it?

"Watson didn't think so."

"Does Otto know?"

She shook her head. "A married woman has to protect herself, Alex. The world is not as simple as you might think."

I chuckled. "Are you suggesting I'm simple-minded?"

Her big green eyes interrogated me as she ran her fingers through my hair. "Not simple-minded, but you are somewhat naïve."

I absorbed her comment like a loveable thin-skinned pincushion. "You're right. That's your business," I said. "Did you move ahead with the testing?"

"I didn't have a choice. Did I?"

"I guess not. Any results?"

"Maybe today," she said, her voice full of exasperation. "Like it matters."

"Sorry. I'm starting to mix my stories. Otto needed as much financial firepower as he could muster to buy the new heart. That would explain his anger with the will, and you and the attorney. From his viewpoint, you're all trying to kill him," I said.

"Blame your father, not me. He created this mess."

"He did, one way or the other, alive or dead, he's driving us nuts."

We were talked out and faced each other without speaking for a minute, our sad eyes seeking connection, like two puppies in love. I sensed all her pain, and I believe she sensed mine. "It's a screwed-up world, Kathy. Nothing makes sense...except for one thing."

She appeared to be hanging onto my words as if I were ready to reveal the secret to all of life's mysteries. "What?"

My mind went blank, eyes sliding shut. I was running out of gas. "Alex..."

Her voice stumbled in my wilderness. Words from deep inside me clawed their way to the surface and weakly emerged. "Except...for my love for you." I got it out, and then I was gone.

In my unconsciousness, my awareness in that period was only tweaked by the regular PA announcements from the hall outside, which I ignored or turned into dreams. A voice sought access into my private pixie-dust world. "Mr. Reinhart. Wake up." I struggled back and opened my eyes. Dr. Jarek, in hospital whites, maintained an imposing military bearing as he stood next to my bed. "I'll bet you're getting hungry. I've authorized a light lunch for you, Alex."

With one hand, I tried to adjust my pillows. The other hand is connected to the drip bottle above. My neck, more than my head, issued pain commands clearly suggesting any physical movement would be trouble. "Hey, Doctor. I guess I should thank you for the ride here."

"Not a problem. Do you know where we are?"

I didn't.

"Arbor Vista. It's a small private hospital southwest of Aurora. I like it because the staff is concerned for the needs of the patient and my needs also."

"I asked the nurse about my departure time, but he wasn't helpful."

Jarek didn't respond, but he did check my chart, and his eyes ran over the beeping heart monitor on the other side of the bed. "You're a lucky man, Alex. You did suffer a concussion, but we are not seeing any deleterious side effects, like subdural bleeding. The CT imaging does indicate a slight movement of your brain, but not enough to cause secondary damage."

"Does that mean I can leave?"

"I'd like you to spend one more night with us. We can get you out of bed. Someone will walk you around the hall. Test out your 'sea legs' so to speak. Makes sense for your body to experience mild physical activity. This will also provide a different kind of evaluation. We'll keep an eye out for any muscle weakness, double-vision, dizziness, or other balance disorders. Things like that. If all is well, tomorrow you'll be out of here. So, enjoy your lunch, bore yourself with daytime TV, and take a walk with a nurse. They're not all like Darone. He's a quality guy, but I'm old-school when it comes to nurses. I prefer the softer sex." He smiled as he hooked my chart to the bottom of the bed. "Have an exceptional day, Alex. See you tomorrow."

As he walked out, I remembered I was going to ask him about Otto. But the window of opportunity closed. I didn't know what I could do about my brother's situation in any event, and I knew Jarek would button up if I asked questions. One thing at a time, I thought. I just wanted to go home to my basement hideaway.

Jarek disappeared, soon replaced by a talkative older gal with big breasts and a big heart who rolled in a cart bearing my lunch. "You hoo, and a big 'boo,'" she announced. "Happy Halloween." Whatever lived in her cart, it smelled tasty, and I relaxed. I could stand this for another day. Mrs. Biddy set up my dining experience, turned on the TV, and, except for her rather grating high-pitched voice, I welcomed the company. As I ate some boring hospital food and endured boring TV, I recalled Kathy's early morning visit. A smile may have crossed my face. Possibly something was happening between us. Who knows? Into the unknown, we ventured. What the hell? We're all adults. We'll work it out. I hung on to these optimistic, rational thoughts, but remained wary. Life is never simple. And I understood nothing.

Chapter 31

The next day, I awoke in Hell, unaware of my crime or the trial, judgment, sentencing, and confinement. I couldn't see. I couldn't move. At the moment, it would be so easy to slip through the cracks in my skull and disappear forever into the nothingness of sleep. But I forced myself to the surface. Something was stuck in my throat. I thought I could hear, but only the sounds of the rhythmic operations of the ventilator. They clogged my head. One sound of air pulsing in and out, in and out. Was I breathing or was it breathing for me?

Terror struck me. I knew what was happening. Chinese organ harvesting. I had read about these places. Derelicts picked up out of the gutter by the tens of thousands. They would take out my organs one by one. I didn't need eyes to see. I imagined the entire scene around me, every image in vivid detail. The expansive warehouse room with a ceiling full of hundreds of blinding bluish fluorescent lights resembling a cheap used car lot with row upon row of naked bodies lying on metal carts, some twitching and writhing in pain, others like mine dead and still. Chinese men milled about wearing little white caps, clear plastic visors with blue trim, white face masks covering their mouths, and thin yellow plastic gowns all stained with human blood, and people screamed while the body mechanics surgically removed their organs without any anesthesia. The surgeons held the purloined parts in two rubber-gloved hands as if carrying a baby bird, and laid the steaming, bloody meat into stainless steel bowls ready to be transplanted into waiting customers. I wanted to cry out for Kathy to save me. But she wasn't here. No one was here. I was all alone in the hospital room, my mechanical breathing the only sign of life. Alive and dead at the same moment.

Once before, I had been lost in the depths. I dug back into my memory and remembered the Madalena River, the home of the Alligator Man. My crew and I were headed downriver, through a section of violent rapids in an inflatable, six-person boat, overloaded with supplies and equipment, and all of us hanging on as our bodies bucked up and down. The river wanted to drown us. We hit a massive whirlpool and flipped. Thrown into the water, I was agitated like dirty laundry in a washing machine. I had no idea about up and down. Those simple markers had disappeared. I gave up hope of returning to the surface. Underwater, I was still alive yet dead in every sense of the word, almost relaxed and accepting of my fate. One fleeting moment in a thousand, I was able to detect brightness, and I sensed the light above was my salvation. I dug out of my underwater grave like a frog caught under a rock, pushing hard off the bottom with my legs and reaching for the sky. With this remembrance that I had beaten death once, I willed myself to escape the Chinese organ harvest, and in seconds, I was breathing above the depths of my nightmares. Yes, I was on a ventilator. I knew not why. But now, at least, I had an understanding of the physical aspects of my current existence while remaining in the dark as to their cause.

I stopped asking "What" and focused on "Why?" For an unknown period, I pitied myself. This was a literal dead-end trail. I knew I would go mad chewing on my questions. I had no answers. I remembered the concussion. I remembered where I was, righted my mental kayak of life, and quieted myself. I listened beyond the ventilator sounds, and they became the background. I searched for the foreground. I yearned to move above the surface. Until I heard it, faint at first, then louder and clearer. "*Attention visitors: Please note hospital visiting hours are between 10 AM and 8 PM. Thank you for your cooperation.*" This message was repeated twice and is gone. I lay there in my bed waiting for it to return. And it did. I thought it repeated every fifteen minutes. It was only a guess, but I was buoyed by the thought that I was tuned into reality. I kept count of the number of times I heard the message. After a while, I was able to pick up other background sounds. Toilets flushing, blinds being raised, footsteps, and in time, I heard actual human voices.

Two people, most likely nurses, entered my space to argue about their jobs in Spanish. My presence didn't hinder their conversation. They knew the man on the ventilator couldn't hear. So they argued about who should be doing what and when. I knew enough Spanish to interpret their dialogue. "But it's your job to deliver the bathcloths, not me. It's not my job, Maria." So it went, and I was delighted. I knew I was a human rock, a lump of unmoving flesh in a coma, but I was a rock that could hear. It couldn't see, talk, wink, or wiggle. But it could hear. I was an invisible private detective. I proceeded to monitor these inane conversations for what was, I guess, an entire day. Also, if I listened intently, I was able to sense the presence of loners. They moved about my room like mice, but noisy enough for my senses to recognize their existence when doing their jobs: checking devices, staring at me, and maybe replacing items I never used, like tissues and water bottles, according to a hospital schedule.

I waited for someone to come visit me, a thrilling event for the rock. First, it was my buddy Nurse Darone. He stopped by simply to talk to me, a friendly gesture. "Mr. Reinhart. How are you doing? Hope you can hear me, man. I don't know what happened to you. You were all ready to take off and bust out, and then you went down for the count. Lots of talk about you out here. But it's just talk. The Doc, he's not talking. He thinks you're in a good place. My ass...a good place. What a load of bull. Something happened to you. But no new scans. No new nothing. Hang in there, Mr. Reinhart. You're my ace."

And after it was quiet again.

I dozed off, but now the PA messages were as loud as church bells. Four "visiting hours" messages later, I reopened the use of another sense. I heard someone enter the room, and not long after, I heard the sounds of a woman crying. In addition, something awakened deep inside, a primitive emotion of elation, unraveled by my sense of smell until it became recognizable as the smell of a woman, my woman, Kathy. I lingered on the smell, rolling it around in my head, until it unleashed its power and filled my being.

She was near now, so close that her every whispered word was loud and clear. "Alex. I don't even know if you can hear me and understand what I am saying. But I'm so upset to see you here like this. You must feel alone and abandoned. You are not. I am here, and I love you."

Her words, mouthed to me, a half-dead man, gave me new life. Something grew inside me that wanted to get out. But I didn't know how to do it. Nothing worked. I couldn't open my eyes. Even if I could speak, my mouth was filled with plastic parts, rendering it useless as a communication device.

"I'm holding your hand now, Alex. Can you feel it? I'm squeezing it. Can you feel that? If you can, try to wiggle your fingers. Just a little. Can you move them, Alex?"

I tried. I tried hard. This simple task was impossible as a short man hoping to grow taller, or a bone-dry farmer wishing the sky to rain; I tried, but I couldn't move anything.

"That bastard, Jarek." I heard her say it. Seconds later, she cried, deep, heavy sobs a dead man could hear. I felt sad, but there would be no emotion from me. No sniffles. No weeping or wailing. I was useless. I had the woman I loved begging me to respond to her entreaties, but it was impossible, a one-way street of communication.

She stopped crying. I didn't know what she was doing. Until I heard her blow her nose. A bit later, I thought she had left the room, but I heard her sniffling again, her nose blowing, and then silence. I waited for another announcement from the PA system, and when it came, I assumed she had left. But I was wrong. I smelled her nearby again. She whispered a single unforgettable sentence: "Alex. We're going to have a baby."

At that moment, I was a baby, floating in a womb of darkness, deprived of sensations and ignorant.

Chapter 32

Gorger and Jarek stared at Alex as he lay on the hospital bed, immobile, his breathing mechanical, and his eyes closed.

"Does he ever move?" asked Gorger.

"We induced a coma, Jan. A strange thing about these concussions. Everything can appear normal in the images, but then the patient will have a relapse. Vomiting, weakness, slurred speech, confusion, and memory problems. Light sensitivity and pain. It was all going in the wrong direction. That's what happened to Alex. For a time, he was on his way to be discharged. I would have no reason not to allow it, but he was regressing. To save him from himself, we quieted him. As you can see, he's doing well now." Doctor Jarek smiled weakly. "So, Otto mentioned you would be checking on Alex."

"Yes..." Jan Gorger attempted to decipher the information. "Otto wanted me to stop by every day to monitor his brother's condition. I hope you understand. When will he rejoin the living?"

"When I say so." Jarek nodded, looking past Gorger.

"I understand. I used to work for the medical examiner in Milwaukee. I studied a lot for my embalmer's certificate. I guess I'm suggesting that you and I are both in the body business."

Jarek appeared to resonate with his statement. "You call them bodies...we call them patients."

Gorger chuckled as he became more comfortable with the conversation. "Different names, same people." Gorger nodded. "Poor Alex. Today he's your patient, but soon he could be my body. That's life."

"So it is. Did Otto mention anything about the future?"

Gorger tried to guess the meaning of this question. "Businesswise...now that Frederick is gone?" He was uncomfortable as Jarek continued to stare at him.

"Let's take a seat." Dr. Jarek guided the veteran embalmer toward two guest chairs near the window. Outside, darkness fell. Inside, the windows in Alex's hospital room began to blacken and fill with interior reflections as the view of the outside world appeared to disappear. "Sit down, Jan. We need to talk." They sat next to each other. A few feet away, Alex, a living ghost, breathed in and out, more machine than man. Jarek turned his chair to face Gorger. "Otto informed me that while he is gone, you will have my total trust." He paused as if seeking affirmation.

Gorger smiled. "I've been with the Reinharts for many years. In fact, Otto's father mentioned several times that I might become a more valuable employee."

Jarek wanted to make Gorger think he was delivering crucial information. Eyebrows raised and eyes shifting, he asked: "Can you keep a secret?"

Gorger nodded. "Dead men don't talk, but embalmers keep many of their secrets. Part of the business, if you understand what I mean?"

Jarek's expression was rigid. "Privacy, security, confidentiality. That's the key, right, Jan?"

"For certain." Gorger tried hard to follow.

"Possibly you are not aware of it, but Otto and I are going to start a new business."

Gorger shook his head to indicate a lack of such knowledge.

"Otto may not have remembered to bring you up to date. But, for the record, we are going to open a tissue recovery bank. We think it will be a perfect fit with the funeral business."

"He didn't say. No. That's news to me."

Jarek looked surprised. "Oh. I might be speaking out of turn. But Otto will be back from his little 'vacation' soon, and he will explain everything. In any event, Otto will be busier than ever. And with the start-up business, he will need more busy hands and minds. I think you see where I'm going with this?"

"I hope so," he said, nodding, his deeply recessed dark eyes searching Jarek's face for understanding.

"Well, that's Otto's business, but I'm only suggesting you may play a bigger role in the company, exactly as Otto's father intended."

These words appeared to fill Gorger's head and gut with a combination of pride and satisfaction.

"You're smiling..."

"It's just...it has been many years. I was losing hope. Hard work, loyalty, and all that...does it pay off?"

"Understood. Now, I have an important question for you. Take your time with your answer."

Gorger waited.

"This involves all our futures. Myself as Otto's new partner, and you are his loyal employee. And it requires your total cooperation, confidentiality, and discretion." Jarek swung his head back. "Starting now." His eyes focused on Gorger. "Can we begin?"

Seconds passed as the Reinharts' straw boss digested Jarek's words. "My lips are sealed."

"Good," he paused, "as you are aware. Otto is suffering from his heart condition."

"Yes." Gorger lowered his look to confirm his recognition of this fact. "I'm pulling for him."

Jarek ignored his statement of sympathetic resolve. "He needs more than prayers. He requires a heart transplant...soon. However, the system...as great as it is...is sometimes slow and unpredictable...an unacceptable state of affairs for your boss. Otto has decided to go around the medical institution and have a private procedure."

"A transplant?"

"Yes. Soon, he is to be operated on in your building. In the remodeled area. Have you seen the contractor installing more equipment?"

"I did but..."

"But you've been told to stay out of there."

"Right."

"Well, that's all over. Otto is going to need you to manage some of the elements of this project. Bringing the surgical team to the funeral home, driving them to and from the airport, and providing comfort, food, and support for a medical team member who will stay behind after the work is done. Are you OK with that?"

Gorger didn't hesitate. "Whatever it takes. I'm in...one hundred percent."

"Excellent."

"Otto is the star of this show, but he will be in no position to make decisions related to the funeral home business. You will have to take over as he is recovering. And maintain the secrecy of the event. A couple of weeks or more, during the actual activities, and thereafter... forever. Never to be mentioned. Any issues?"

"None at all, Doctor. None at all." Gorger thought for a moment. "When is this going to happen?"

"Good question. Be prepared to begin working on this, as of now. I will direct you. And from now on, and until Otto is recovered enough to rule the roost again, you will follow my rules as it relates to his medical condition. Understood?"

"Yes."

"I'm not talking about day-to-day funeral operations. My role is to put the surgical team in place and follow up. Otto assured me he would inform all the players that you would be the man in charge during his absence. But remember...no one, and I mean no one, must know Otto is taking this route. Not even his wife or family. People near him will believe he traveled to Mexico to have the transplant. If the topic ever arises, consider it a personal question outside of your authority or interest. Right?"

Gorger grunted and nodded. "Got it. Mexico," he said. "I'm on board."

To signal the end of their meeting, Jarek stood. He put his arm around Gorger's shoulder, and they walked past Alex Reinhart, who lay, eyes closed, face white, breathing with the help of the ever-present ventilator.

Gorger stared at Alex and asked. "Can he hear anything?"

Stopping for one last look at the man in the bed before they reached the door leading to the hospital corridor, Jarek spoke: "Nobody can say one way or the other. Those in a coma may hear something. But it's probably the same 'something' that reaches our brain when we are asleep."

"Never considered that," said Gorger. 'I'm always so tired after work, I don't hear a thing. Of course, I sleep with the television running. I live alone. It provides me company."

Jarek nodded. "Oh. One of those. Me too." He chuckled.

Chapter 33

The voices stopped, and I was in a bad way. My mind stirred with a pervasive, animalistic, primitive fear. Yet its source was unknown to me. Something chipped away at the sea walls of my tiny island of sanity and flooded me with negativity. Something happened. I listened to nothing. This emptiness returned me to my fantasy world. I awoke again. Whether seconds, minutes, or hours passed, I couldn't guess. I assumed now it was after visiting hours because the repeating PA messages were not evident. I was now able to sense the difference between dream events and awareness events. I was aware, and I recalled those voices. Someone was talking about Otto and his transplant. A voice that might be Jarek's. Was Otto near? Someone was near. She was speaking to me. I loved the way she smelled. I relaxed and listened.

"Alex. I am here for you. My fingers are on your arm. Can you feel that? My breathing set the pace of her words. "Now I have removed them." A pause. "Now they're back on your arm." This continued for many breaths. In and out, touching and not touching, according to her. While sensing her touch was beyond my ability, I wanted with all my heart to believe we were communicating. She cried again. Through her tears, she spoke. "I'm going to break you out of this, Alex. I will. Damn it."

Then I heard nothing. I waited. The sensory world slid away. In the dreams again, I found myself back in the organ harvesting room. I was terrified. A person wearing a mask and holding a bloody scalpel approached me. His head grew larger as it neared my face. I reached up and grabbed his mask, ripping it off. It was not the face of a Chinese doctor; it was Jarek wearing a hideous grin.

In time, I escaped the torture again, finding a way out of the organ harvesting factory. I forced my mind to think of Kathy. I wanted her to return. She was the key to my sanity.

Chapter 34

Kathy had fallen asleep on the lounge seating at the base of the window. Deep in her sleep, a nightmare arrived. In her dream, she tried to stop a man with a knife from killing another man. Reaching out her arms, with small movements, she punched the air in front of her. In her dream, she shouted, but in reality, she was mumbling loudly in anguish and fear.

"Mrs. Reinhart. Wake up. You're having a nightmare. And it's way past visiting hours," said the nurse, Darone.

She accepted the words as they freed her from a painful world. Deep sobs turned to deep breaths. She rotated her body and sat upright. "Sorry...I...I fell asleep."

"It's late, Mrs. Reinhart. Time to go home," he said in a sympathetic voice.

She looked up. A young man with a kind face studied her.

"Sit for a moment. Get your act together."

She smiled at him. "My act? That's a good one."

"Sorry, I didn't mean to offend you. You need a moment to compose yourself."

She tried to shake off the nightmare. "Stephan. In my dream, he had a knife in his hand. He was smiling, and blood was dripping off it."

"Who?"

"Dr. Jarek...oh, forget it...I just had a bad dream."

Without asking permission, the young man sat next to her. "Is he your husband?" He made a quick glance in the direction of the only other man in the room. "My patient."

"You mean Alex? No. He's my brother-in-law. I'm waiting for him to come out of it. He doesn't respond at all. It's so distressing."

"You can't wait for that. He's down by design. A medically induced coma. Dr. Jarek is his doctor, and he will give the order to bring him out of the coma, and no one else. Only when he's ready."

She stared into space, looking at the man on the bed. "When who is ready?"

"Dr. Jarek. Your brother-in-law is in a protective mode now. The doctors will ease him out."

"When?"

"Who can say?" His voice was sad and anxious. "I don't like it when they keep family in the dark. Sometimes they're so busy. But...still...we have to find out. I mean. It's too much not to know."

"Do you see this often?"

Darone rolled his eyes. "Happens. Sometimes a little bit of info makes a big difference."

"Well. I know the man. He must give me straight answers."

She looked at the young nurse for more, but he did not follow up. From her days of working for Jarek, she knew the pecking order must be maintained. Sucking up was part of the job.

"Just be patient, Mrs. Reinhart," he said as he stood. "Time to go now. Say goodnight to Alex. Come back, and you can ask the doctor about when Alex will come out."

She stood, brushed down her skirt, took a couple of steps to the bed, leaned over, and kissed Alex on the forehead. Still holding a tissue in her hand, she wiped her eyes. "I'll be back tomorrow, Alex." Then she whispered something in his ear and left.

In her car in the parking lot, Kathy Reinhart sat for a few minutes simply thinking. Mountains of doubt filled her mind. Something about Otto's story didn't make sense. She understood the need for secrecy, suspecting some part of Otto's scheme to receive a new heart was not legal. But the idea of Otto going to Mexico on his own didn't make sense. He was always uneasy about traveling to other countries. He didn't speak Spanish, and he didn't like ambiguity. Maybe, without informing her, he was traveling with someone else. She needed help and didn't care if she might end up exposing Otto's activity. She called Terry Walker. Once she explained Otto's story about the Mexican transplant, Terry said he thought something weird was going on. He told her such surgery might be an illegal activity and might involve the illegal sale of human organs. He would attempt to track Otto's movements from O'Hare to Mexico City.

She went home and sat alone in the living room. After kicking off her shoes, she contemplated having a glass of wine, then, remembering she was about to become the mother of Alex's child, she dismissed the thought. As she tried to relax, her phone sounded and broke her trance.

"It's Terry...I've checked, Kathy. Listen...Otto never left the United States. Not as a passenger on any commercial flight and for sure not United. I checked 'em all. First thing tomorrow, I'll call my guy at the passport agency."

"All right. Can we get together in the morning?" She asked. "It's not like Otto to leave without giving me his itinerary or any details. Unless he's covering for me. Trying to keep me out of whatever he's up to...but."

"Let me think about it. Meet me at my office tomorrow."

"Nine OK?"

"Make it noon. That'll give me time."

"Thanks, Terry."

"Mañana."

Chapter 35

J an Gorger escorted Dr. Jarek from the rear parking area of the Reinhart Funeral Home into the building, through the staging room, and down the corridor to the surgical suite. Gorger keyed in the computer lock, and the two men entered. They were greeted by Otto Reinhart, who relaxed in a padded lounge chair in the entry area. The space now had the appearance of a small living room fitted out with a reading lamp, a wall-mounted television, a rolling dining cart, and a guest chair. Otto removed his earplugs, set his laptop computer on the cart, and turned to face his two guests.

"Visitors...always welcome." He smiled. "It's not the Ritz, Jan. But it will do. Can anyone outside hear noises?"

Gorger shook his head. "Almost soundproof, boss."

"I could use a couple of sandwiches to tide me over."

"Forget that, Otto," said Jarek. Chicken soup and crackers from now on."

"OK, boss?" asked Gorger.

Otto nodded. "Stephan's running this show. I'll survive. I've got plenty of water, a couple of bananas, and a winning mental attitude."

"The troops are coming into town tonight, Jan," said Jarek. "Are you prepared?"

"I'm all ready to go. I'll pick them up at O'Hare. Drop them off at the motel. And tomorrow, I'll drive them here. Bring them in the back, and they can move ahead. All the equipment is in place and operational as far as I can tell." He smiled. "Take a look."

Jarek slid open the door to the operatory and surveyed the room. It appeared as proper and well-equipped as any surgical theater. Centerstage, the operating table, an isolated slab covered in black leather, awaited the players. A hospital bed, already in use by Otto, was placed against the far wall. Mobile racks filled with computer modules, equipment carts, and two rolling chairs, with a desk and computer station tucked in the corner, completed the array. Video screens and adjustable lighting units hung from the ceiling.

"Is that it for now?" Gorger asked.

Jarek waved him on. "Good job, Jan. I'll meet with you on my way out, and we can discuss the details. Thank you."

Gorger remained silent and slinked out of the room as Jarek closed the door to the operatory. He pulled up the guest chair and sat facing Reinhart.

"We've got some issues to deal with, Otto. First, your brother..."

"How is Alex? Gorger said he saw him last night. Still in a coma?"

Jarek didn't hurry to reply. He let Otto's own words sink in. "It was a medically induced coma. He was exhibiting symptoms that were not positive."

"How can that be? I thought you said he was doing fine when he was admitted." Otto's face showed his concern.

"That's true. Yet as sometimes happens...without any obvious signs of detectable blood pooling. Damage has been done."

"Jesus. I thought he just fell and bumped his head," said Otto.

Jarek swallowed and pursed his lips. "Concussions can be tricky. What kills one man may have little effect on another. The blow to his head was severe. It didn't crack the skull or break the skin, but it was a solid blow. It shifted his brain out of alignment. To tell you the truth, I was somewhat surprised at his lack of initial symptoms. I'm glad I kept him under observation for another night. He began to have other issues. Vomiting. Severe headache. Distorted vision. So we put him under to reduce any effect or risk of complications."

"Where's this going, Stephan?" His voice was weak and shaky.

Jarek pretended to think as agonizing moments for Otto passed. "Early this morning, we reduced his sedation in an attempt to bring him out of the coma to see if his symptoms had lessened."

"What happened?"

"He's not coming out, Otto. He is unresponsive. As if he were still under."

Otto's eyes shifted around, and he shook his head. Jesus..."

"There's nothing we can do at this time. It's one of those 'wait and see' situations. Days, weeks, months, we can't be sure if or when he will wake. It's no longer under our control. He's in a coma."

Otto lowered his head and rubbed his forehead. He began to choke up. "This isn't easy, Stephan. All this shit, I'm going through. First, my father. And now Alex."

The room was dead quiet except for the rush of cool air from the air conditioning vents. "It's a lot to deal with...I understand." Jarek let him stew. "However, there's no running away from any of this. We have a situation, Otto. Forget about Alex for a moment, and think about yourself. We are ready to perform your procedure tomorrow. The down payment has been made. The two doctors and an assistant will arrive tonight. The workspace is complete. Gorger is primed to help us in any way. So everything is a 'go' except for one thing."

Otto waited.

Jarek opened his palms and sighed a deep breath. "The heart...we don't have a donor heart."

"What?"

Jarek swallowed before speaking. "We had the perfect heart donor lined up. Only this morning I got a call. The young man was about the same height and weight as you. His blood work was excellent...blood type, HLA matching, and antibody screening. A very tight match."

"What happened?"

Jarek paused to think. "He got hit by a car. That's what they said. He died."

Otto seemed mystified. "Of course, he died. That was my heart..."

"Yes. He died too early, in a messy way, and...let's say...and not in a convenient place."

Otto thought about it and threw up his hands to his face. He began to sob.

Jarek let it all sink in before speaking again.

"I didn't know. I didn't realize how they would get the heart."

Jarek steepled his hands. "Sometimes it's not a pleasant world. I'm sure you agree, Otto. Is it fair that you should be born with a defective heart? Or you would have to undergo surgery as a child? While your brother waltzed around the world chasing rainbows. Life isn't fair." He paused again. "Now Alex is beaten down. For no good reason. He simply agreed to help a friend install some decorative pumpkin lights."

Otto grimaced. "You said you had two sources for the heart. What about the other one?"

"I did, and I do. But there are always complications. That heart was sold to someone else."

"Can they do that?"

"None of this is legal, Otto. It's dog-eat-dog. They went for the sure thing. I got back to them a few hours too late, and it was gone. I'm sorry."

"Then why are we playing this game?" asked Otto. "Why are those surgeons coming if we don't have a heart?"

"Take a moment, Otto. Just listen. We've got another approach."

"OK...shoot. What's the answer?"

"First, I have requested another heart, but we can't rely on that. Time is running out. Otto, this is the toughest decision of your life."

Otto wiped his eyes, waited, and listened.

"You need a heart. Here tomorrow. A healthy beating heart meeting all the requirements for the transplant. The heart we were waiting for is not beating anymore, but we have a chance to claim another one perfect for you. Some things are meant to be, Otto. And I think this is one of those things. Remember...I gave Alex a physical about a month ago. Because he is your brother, I had some blood work done. The results were excellent. No problems. And when I correlate the factors concerning a transplant situation for you, you couldn't ask for a better donor. The documented risk of rejection is low for transplants between siblings."

Otto lowered his head and shook it slowly. He shut down and said nothing.

Jarek waited.

"That can't happen," his voice a whisper. "This is crazy." Beads of perspiration clung to his forehead, his face reddened, and he began to cough.

Jarek stood and assumed the mantle of a courtroom prosecutor, pacing the little room as he spoke. "I told you this whole thing was providential. Alex is in the hospital. He is nearby lying in a coma, and he may never come out of it. You two are about the same size. The odds of a successful transplant are high. Before Alex was admitted into the hospital, I suggested I hold his wallet for him. He agreed. I walked him through the paperwork. I checked his driver's license, and it was not listed as a possible donor, and he didn't check the box at admitting."

"So he wasn't interested in donating. I wouldn't be either," Otto shrugged his shoulders.

Jarek walked over and sat in front of Otto. He brought the chair close, held his hands, and looked into his eyes. "Do you understand what this means? I'll tell you." Jarek waited, then spoke, his tone authoritative, "If he dies, his heart will be buried or burned along with his body. Can you see that it is a waste? Your father's death was sad but expected. Alex's death will be unexpected and meaningless. You have a chance to give his life and his death meaning...accept his heart for transplant."

"But he's alive," Otto said in a shaky voice. "Am I supposed to play God and take his life away?"

Jarek released Otto's hands. "I'm only giving you the facts, Otto. Do you want him to live as a vegetable for months or maybe years? Or to die with you, refusing the greatest gift he could offer you?"

"I would be cutting off his life, right?"

"Shortening it. Yes. For how long? No one but God knows. And what is the quality of life if one is in an eternal coma?"

Otto stared at Jarek. "Let me think," he said. "I've got to think."

"Sorry."

Otto drifted, and Jarek let him. Then he smiled and bubbled up some words. "I forgot to tell you. I got the news from my father's attorney about Kathy."

"What?"

"The tests. She's expecting. We're having a baby."

Jarek didn't respond.

"All this time," said Otto. "We've been trying without success. And now. Now..."

"Great." Jarek pulled it together. "All the more reason to move ahead. The child will need both parents. Did the tests identify the father for the purposes of the will?"

"No."

"Watson said two or three days. But why do you ask?"

Jarek slid back in his chair. He looked up at the ceiling and then down at Otto. "If they tell you it's a family match, don't let them confuse you."

"How's that?"

"Well, they will say they can't identify the father one hundred percent."

"Why not?"

"Because a brother's DNA would have similar characteristics." The doctor thrust his hands to either side with open palms. "It's a crapshoot then."

"Are you talking about Alex?"

"The testing outfit would be covering their asses. Just saying. Either way, the child would be a Reinhart. Hypothetically, I mean. I'm not suggesting anything."

The younger of the Reinhart brothers appeared confused. "You doctors. Test results. Organ donors. Hypotheticals. You're worse than attorneys."

"Sorry, Otto. I didn't mean to upset you."

"Sure...but you have." His face contorted, and his eyes darted about the room as if searching for a place to run. "What should I do?"

Jarek again moved nearer to Otto. Almost in a whisper, he offered his final advice. "Otto, you control your own destiny. Whether you live or die. You can decide to extend your brother's life, but he may pass away next week, and everything will die with him. Face the fact that you may never receive a call from the national donor list. You may spend your last days thinking you had one chance and you missed it. I can't make this decision. And we are almost out of time. It's up to you."

Otto didn't speak. He stared and swallowed, but Jarek pushed on.

"From the moment you told me you needed a transplant, I knew tough decisions would have to be made," said Jarek. "And I knew you were the man to make them. I believe destiny has led you to this point. I want you to live, Otto. You deserve to live. You have worked hard all your life to get where you are."

Otto appeared forlorn and vulnerable. Jarek knew he was on the edge. One more nudge might do it.

"As your doctor, I'm extending myself here, Otto. Because we are also friends and partners. This is an impossible decision." Jarek surrounded him with words. "If you tell me to move ahead, I will. At some personal and professional risk. I'm not too concerned because it is a judgment call. You are his nearest relative. As a medical professional, I am on solid legal ground asking you to make the decision. No one will know; you might have had strong reasons for agreeing to the closure of Alex's life. But who's to say your motivation? These decisions are made by the hundreds every day. Some people might suspect you were driven by money since you are Alex's closest relative, but they will not be aware of the transplant." Jarek leaned back. "But I won't feel your emotional pain. He's your brother. Not mine. But I'm like you. We're in the business of life and death. You can say yes to end his suffering and save your life. That is the essence of organ transplants. They are all about giving and receiving."

Otto leaned forward and rested his elbows on the arms of his chair, balled up his fists tightly, lowered his head, and brought his paired knuckles into contact with his mouth. He took and exhaled deep breaths. Finally, he brought still-fisted hands out in front of him as if he were ready to hit somebody or something. But the fight was over. He spoke slowly. "What choice do I have? Everything is set up. Everything is covered. Alex will forgive me. He's always been my big brother."

"If he could think and talk at this moment, what would he say?" asked Jarek.

Otto thought. "I guess...he would say...don't be a fool, Otto. Just do it."

"And you, Otto. What do you say?"

Otto didn't say anything. Jarek held back, letting him finish the story.

"It only makes sense. Right, Stephan?"

Jarek nodded.

"OK," said Otto. "OK."

"Tomorrow's the big day...a new birthday for you." Jarek smiled, knowing his hard work and planning would soon be completed.

Chapter 36

The big day arrived, and Otto was pleased that Gorger had, early in the morning, picked up one of the three medical men, the assistant, and surreptitiously delivered him to the surgical suite. The two surgeons remained at the motel, working off their jet lag. This third member of the team, a wiry short man, his hair jet black, gleaming with gel, called himself Jerzy, spoke English, and had a perpetual smile. His attire was strange: dark blue pro basketball trunks ending below his knees, a bright yellow sweatshirt bearing the name of an unknown rock group, and expensive-looking blue and white sneakers with calf-high black socks. His final embellishment was a gold choker chain around his neck. He informed Otto that he would assist and act as an anesthesiologist. He spent a couple of hours preparing and testing all the equipment in the surgical suite. He explained to Otto that he would remain behind after the operation to monitor his patient's progress for about ten days. Otto observed every move, and as time passed, his angst was tempered by Jerzy's breezy demeanor and apparent confidence. By late afternoon, everything was ready.

As Jan Gorger reentered the operatory, Otto greeted him with a smile; he was about to embark upon the riskiest journey of his life. He extended his hand toward the embalmer. "Hold my hand, Jan, please," said Otto. "I'm afraid." The embalmer's hand was cold, and he had no smile for Otto, who suspected this kind of intimacy was outside Gorger's comfort zone. He gazed into Gorger's cold eyes. "Is this too much for you, Jan...I have no one else?"

"Don't worry about me, boss. You just need to relax." He paused and cleared his throat. "Has anyone told you about Alex?" he asked.

"No," he said, bracing himself for news he expected but was not prepared to hear.

Gorger swallowed. He pursed his lips. "Alex died early this morning. I am sorry to tell you."

Otto fell back into his pillow. He didn't say anything. But he groaned and moaned.

Jerzy, his mind presently dedicated to calibrating some equipment, was startled by Otto's pathetic sounds. He crossed the room and stood next to his patient. "What is problem?"

Gorger glared at Jerzy. "He received some terrible news. It upset him."

Jerzy separated their two hands. "You must leave, sir. I will take care here."

Gorger patted his boss on his forehead. "Good luck, Otto," he said, sounding both concerned and saddened.

Otto at first did not respond. He stared up at the ceiling, his eyes fixed. But then he told Gorger, "You are in charge, Jan. Do what you must until I come back. Make this work...and never tell anyone what you see here today. Do you understand?"

"Of course." Gorger nodded and turned to Jerzy. "And now I will leave you to your work and return with your associates," Gorger told the assistant, "but first I must show you some things."

Jerzy made a face. "How you say, one thing at a time. First, the patient." He was prepared. "This is for you, Mr. Otto." In short order and with competence, he injected something to smooth out Otto's excitement and fear. "You will be better now, Mr. Otto."

Otto closed his eyes, and Jerzy checked his work. He waited a minute until his patient dropped into sleep. Then, before heading back to work, Gorger gave Jerzy the key to the crematory, showed him how to operate the automatic door, and pointed out the organ donor lying on a cart in the crematory. The two men then retreated down the hall. Jerzy went back to the operating room, and the embalmer left the building to pick up the surgeons.

Chapter 37

Terry Walker sat in his office. He spent the morning verifying Otto Reinhart never crossed the border. He was now certain the story was a fabrication, but he wondered why she didn't call. She was anxious to meet. He checked his watch...12:18...still no sign of Kathy. He stubbed out his cigarette and placed another call. Several rings later, about to hang up, someone answered.

"Terry. Is that you?" Kathy's words slurred, her voice faint; for a moment, she may have dropped her cell phone and regained a grip on it. "Terry?" she asked.

"The meeting at my office? What happened?" Rustling sounds crept out. "Are you all right, Kathy?"

"No..."

"Why is that?"

After a long pause, she answered: "Alex...is dead."

"Say again...talk to me, Kathy."

She sniffled, only returning to speak after she blew her nose. Her voice was weak, but the message was clear. "I went to the hospital this morning. To see Alex. I went straight to his room. Empty. The bed was empty. He was gone."

"How do you know?"

"The nurse. He saw me enter the room. I talked with him, and he told me Alex died early morning. Before the nurse's shift."

"Jeez...did his heart give out?"

"I guess..." She sobbed again.

"Where are you?"

"Uh...at home..."

"I'll be right over. Hang in there."

"OK."

"Sit tight." He hung up and left his office, got in his car, and headed for her house.

As he drove, he called the hospital, speaking with several different people before reaching someone who handled sensitive questions. Aggressively, he pushed through their privacy concerns and determined Kathy's story was accurate. By the time he approached her driveway, he had gathered the basic information. The cause of death was TBI or traumatic brain injury, with an official time of death listed at 2:48 a.m., and the body picked up by Reinhart Funeral Homes. Terry pulled into the driveway of Kathy's house, parking at the entry. He stopped long enough to call the funeral home. Whoever answered told him they had no current information. He got their attention when he informed them that the deceased was the son of Frederick Reinhart. They agreed to call him with an update as soon as possible.

Rolling again, he wheeled the limo to the front of the house and brought it to a sliding stop, popped out, and without ringing the bell attempted to open the door. Unlocked, he walked inside and found Kathy sitting on the sofa facing a coffee table and a half-empty bottle of wine. She sat frozen like a statue. He dumped his body next to her on the sofa. Quiet, head down, her face reddened, streaked with tears, and her mouth quivering, she hugged him and pushed her head into his chest. They sat coupled without speaking while she struggled with her emotions. He waited, his big hand stroking her forehead. In time, she settled, still not speaking, but now under control. She raised her head from his chest; her unseeing eyes wandered.

"Are you OK now?" he asked.

She nodded and spoke. "I visited him last night. I told him I would come by today."

"He was in a coma. Right?"

"Sure. But I always believed he understood me when I talked to him. Who can say?"

Terry shook his head. "I'm a shit. I gave him the ladder."

"It's not your fault, Terry. It was an accident."

"It was. Maybe...falls like this happen every day." He shook his head. A long minute passed with the two friends quiet. Then Terry erupted. "Who knows?" he exclaimed as he shook his head as if to clear it of any negative thoughts. "I don't trust anyone. All very convenient for Jarek". He paused and pulled out a pack of cigarettes. "Can I smoke?"

"Who cares?" she said.

He lit a cigarette, took a long drag, exhaled, and put some physical distance between himself and Otto's wife. He paced the room and spoke in a soft voice as he turned back to face her. "Something's wrong with this whole Otto thing. Something stinks."

"Yes. Well...it bothered me too. That's why I called you last night."

"Otto's story is bogus. He didn't leave the country."

"He's been gone for days. He packed his suitcase and rushed out. He went somewhere," she replied.

"When?"

"I'd guess it was before Alex hit his head." She put her hand to her forehead. "I can't think now."

"I checked into it this morning," he said. "Mexico's organ transplant laws are similar to ours. You can't just order a new heart. It's the same process of application and waiting. So maybe he could have had an operation in Mexico if he had been able to get one. They've got heart doctors, too. Some might work with a hijacked heart. Fact is, he didn't leave the country."

She shook her head. "I'm lost."

Terry's eyes roamed the living room as if looking for a clue. "Come on, Walker. Think." He muttered to himself as he walked through to the kitchen, grabbed an empty wine glass from a cabinet, and continued walking into the family room. He stared out the sliding door. In the distance, beyond the grove of trees and Kathy's playhouse, the river shimmered in the afternoon sunlight, but dark massed clouds moved closer, and a strong northeast wind bent treetops. Several minutes passed as he reconciled events. He turned. Kathy stood at the doorway, her hands on either side of the opening.

She spoke and startled him. "What are you doing?"

He looked at the empty wine glass in his hand and smiled. "I'll have some of that wine now."

They returned to the kitchen, where Kathy opened another bottle of wine and poured a glass for Terry. He sucked on his cigarette and then flipped an ash into the sink. One more drag, and he turned on the faucet and extinguished the butt in the flow of water. He held it in one hand, looking at Kathy for direction.

"Just drop it. Tell me what you're thinking."

"You know this Jarek guy..." It wasn't a question; he was thinking aloud. He cocked his head to the left and returned his gaze to her...waiting.

"Of course, I used to work for him. I was Jarek's office manager for a few months before I met Otto and got married. But those two knew each other long before I got into the picture."

"Old friends?

"I would say so."

"Did you know that he and Otto are partners in a new business venture?"

"No. I wasn't told. He's Otto's regular doctor. That's all I know."

"Without Otto to dovetail his funeral business and funding into their new body parts business, Dr. Jarek remains a country doctor," said Terry as he sucked on his cigarette. "I think he's an ambitious, determined, and dangerous man. Papers were filed with the State of Illinois for a new company called Biovatex. It's supposed to be a tissue bank factory."

She gave him a blank look. "Body parts?"

He backtracked. "Legal body part sales."

"News to me. Otto and I don't share many secrets."

"Meaning?"

"It means we live together, but our marriage isn't perfect."

"Whose is?"

She shrugged. "I don't think Otto understands what Jarek is all about."

"What's that?"

"He puts up a professional front, but he's a tough street fighter. He's from a different world. I told that to Otto, but he doesn't care much what I say. Otto's a sucker for a fast-talking guy like Jarek."

"I ran Jarek's file. He's a former Army doctor with a General Discharge. I'm not sure what he did or who he pissed off, but that's not great. It's more than a slap on the wrist. But not good since Uncle Sam was putting him through medical school. And more recently, a woman claimed that he acted inappropriately as a doctor. Maybe a physical exam that went south. It was local, and the charge was dismissed. But there's a civil suit."

"I would say he's a 'grabber'," she replied. "Not uncommon. Some doctors think it's their right."

"Did he ever grab you?"

She dismissed the question. "I can handle myself, Terry."

"I hear you...the man's got a lot of issues. He's also standing on the edge of a financial cliff. His credit rating sucks. IRS filed tax liens on him." Terry was talking fast now. "Foreclosure on a building he owns in Aurora. And an outstanding judgment against him related to a lawsuit filed by another one of his patients. I would guess that case also raised some eyebrows at the state medical board."

"And Otto decided to go into a new business with him?" she asked.

"You got it," said Terry. "Jarek is on the edge financially. He needs an influx of money, and Otto must have a transplant...or he dies. These are desperate people." He finished his glass of wine. "If I wanted to go inside the funeral home to look around...could I?"

"For what?"

"Who can say? We'll find out....what about it?"

She thought. "What day is it? I've lost track."

"Monday. That's good, it's an off day. They keep someone in the office, but overall they're shut down."

"Getting in?"

"I've got all the keys to the funeral home here. Otto keeps a backup set on the wall in the back. I've never used them. But they're here." She frowned. "Why not just go in the front door?"

"We may do that." He smiled. "I'll tell you what I'm thinking when I figure it out." Kathy lost her hang-dog look. Terry wanted to reverse her negative thinking. He needed her help. "If I'm right. All is not lost. Are you with me?"

"Tell me," she said, sounding more interested with his every word.

"Otto's up against the wall," he began his story, "I think Alex became his backup plan in a scheme involving an illegal transplant. I don't think he went to Mexico. He never left town. Maybe Otto's hiding inside his business...waiting."

"Waiting for what?"

"A new heart."

She looked puzzled. "Alex's heart?" She answered her own question, and as the words came out, she recoiled. "No. Otto's not..."

"Just a possibility. I can't believe he would take his brother's life to save his own. But maybe he could be convinced. What do you think?"

"After five years of marriage, I'm not sure about him. Who understands what's going on in the mind of someone with a gun to his head?"

Her words triggered Terry. He flashed back to a night many years ago, working as a cop when some drugged-up gangster shoved a 38 revolver into the back of his neck. He was younger then, athletic, in shape, and just coming off a course in close-quarter combat. He put that guy down, but that was years ago. That was do or die. Now he chased deadbeat ex-husbands, followed wayward spouses, and ran down missing teens. He was a soft, paperweight crime-fighter now. But no matter, today he would be going into battle; mentally, he braced himself.

"What about Alex?" she asked.

"Could be Alex's heart's only a possibility, a backup. I'm guessing Otto's partner Jarek opportunistically took advantage of Alex's concussion in case they couldn't find a new heart."

"From where?"

"Look online. Everything's available on the internet. I've seen the websites. If they're real. You can buy a new organ and have it overnighted right to your door. For a price. I know this sounds crazy. Maybe...but it fits, right?"

Kathy only looked at him.

"Have you been in the back area of the funeral home?"

"No. I have no interest in that place. I was there for Frederick's wake, but I didn't stray from the viewing room except to go to the washroom."

"Have you ever seen a floor plan of the funeral home?"

"You mean here. In our house?"

"Yes."

"No."

"That's all right," he said, thinking while talking. "All buildings have them mounted on the wall for emergency purposes. I'll find one. Got to know the layout."

"What am I supposed to do?"

Terry thought. "I need you to divert attention. You go into the office. They'll recognize you. Go in and demand information about your brother-in-law. They should admit he's in the building since the hospital logs have it that way. Tell them you have to see the body. Can you do that?"

"Yes."

"If they give you shit, which I'm sure they will, you can bring up the business of burial or cremation. Whatever. I'll need time to look around. Stall them. Understand?"

She nodded.

"You can ask them if they have been in contact with Otto. Get that story going. That'll slow them down."

Kathy smiled for the first time. "Thanks, Terry."

"For what?"

"For giving me hope."

Chapter 38

Darkness and a light rain covered Naperville that evening. Terry and Kathy didn't talk much as they drove from her house north to the funeral home. With each sweep through the cold, weak, dirty drizzle, the windshield wipers chattered like angry squirrels. Terry pulled the Lincoln into the funeral home's empty lot and parked away from the entrance. Barren blackened trees of November surrounded the building and stood like sentinels in a yellow moat of water-soaked fallen leaves. Kathy Reinhart, sitting in the passenger seat, stared and sighed. She sensed she was about to inherit only an ill wind as Frederick Reinhart's legacy faded in the early evening darkness. His funeral home, a symbol of his life, appeared desolate and undefended; he was dead, his eldest son was dead, and his other son was dying.

"Buck up, buttercup," said Terry. "Are you up for this?"

"I'm ready."

"I'll text you if I need your help. You do the same. If you have to leave, wait in the car. You keep everyone in there busy while I do my magic. He reached into his shirt pocket to retrieve a car key. "Here's another key to the Lincoln. You may need it."

She stuffed the key into her jacket pocket, fumbled with her umbrella, exited, opened the umbrella, and drifted through the light rain toward the funeral home entrance about a hundred feet distant.

Terry drove behind the building and parked in a far corner of the lot. He walked cautiously as he approached the double door entry opposite the garage; the metal key ring he held, full of tagged keys, jingled with every step. He hoped the one he pre-selected would allow him to enter the building. Standing at the door, key in hand, he slid it in, turned it open, and entered the darkened staging room. Not wanting to use any of the building's lighting, he played the light from his flashlight around the room. Mounted on the wall near the door, he found an emergency evacuation floor plan, rudimentary but workable. He studied it and took a photo with his phone. Feeling more confident, he moved toward the door leading to the main corridor.

Kathy confronted a locked door and a sign behind its glass, which informed her that the place was closed for the day. Visitors were asked to call or check out the website. She leaned into the doorbell push button, and a faint buzzing sound inside the building followed. She peered through the glass. A light in the reception office glowed; after fifteen seconds, someone's head popped out the doorway, and a person appeared. A young woman wearing casual clothes and a helpful smile approached and sized up Kathy through the window. She half-opened the door, and Kathy stepped in.

"I'm sorry we're closed," said the woman as she stepped back, surprised at Kathy's aggressiveness.

The door closed behind Kathy. "You don't know me, but I'm Mrs. Reinhart, Otto's wife. I'm here to view my brother-in-law's body."

The woman spent a moment digesting her words before replying. "Oh. Mrs. Reinhart. I'm Cindy. I didn't recognize you. I'm so sorry for your loss. How...um...how can I help you?"

Kathy edged deeper into the building, looking around as if seeking a place to sit. "May I sit for a moment?"

"Of course." She took Kathy's umbrella, placed it in a stand near the door, and escorted her guest a few steps to the lounge area. They sat facing each other, a marble coffee table between them.

"I must see him...before..."

"I'm sorry Mrs. Reinhart. I'm afraid I can't help you." Possibly, she was digging deep to gain an understanding of the situation, enough to present a good front. "There is no one here at this moment. To be honest with you, I was unaware of your brother-in-law's death. Are you certain his body is here?"

Kathy gave her a condescending look.

"Sorry." She shook her head, "Of course." She stood. "Can I fix you something to drink?"

"I'm not here to drink anything. I've been drinking all day. I spoke to the hospital people this morning, and they said Alex was transported here. Is that not true?"

"I...I don't know. I only do the paperwork. Mr. Gorger is here." She paused. "He's busy working. I don't think I can disturb him."

"Cindy. If Jan Gorger is here, can you ask him to come and see me? Now."

The woman frowned and recovered. "Yes, Mrs. Reinhart. I'll be back in a moment. I'll call him. Please wait." Then she walked away at a fast pace, heading to her office.

Terry opened the door to the corridor, glanced left and right, and crept ahead. He pocketed his flashlight. Nearby, muffled machine sounds pulsed somewhere. The map identified the source of the noise as the embalming room. Two steps into the corridor, a phone began ringing. The sound of someone speaking startled him; a man's voice penetrated the silence.

"I told you never to disturb me when I'm working...Yes. Who's asking?...What?...Tell her I will be there in a few minutes. That's all. Don't say anything else."

Terry retraced his steps into the staging room and waited with the lights out. He suspected Kathy was attempting to draw the attention of the person in the embalming room. As he waited, almost hyperventilating, he worked to calm himself. He didn't wait long. Soon, the sound of a door opening and closing and hurried footsteps in the corridor informed him that the room might be empty now. He reentered the corridor and walked down the hall, putting his ear to the door. He listened and heard machine noises, but nothing else. He sent Kathy a text message: "*Keep him busy as long as you can.*" A few seconds later, he got a reply: "*K*".

The embalming room was a black hole, but the dim light from the corridor penetrated enough to reveal the room's occupants: three bodies under white sheets and one half-naked body. Sucking it up, the detective entered and latched the door behind him with care.

Gorger popped into the lounge area, a sweaty mess with beads of perspiration sliding down his face. He did his best to wipe off the moisture with a handkerchief. "Kathy," he said. Sweat drops blinded him. He squinted his eyes and blinked. "I'm sorry. I was working. I didn't know you were here. I'm so sorry."

Cindy drifted away back into her office.

"Jan. I want to see Alex. Can I do that?"

"Now?" He asked.

"Yes."

He shook his head, almost talking to himself. "When my work is interrupted, I am always disoriented. I am very focused on my tasks. You understand." He paused, looking for some reaction from Kathy, but she remained resolute. "Please let's sit."

They sat. He was sweat-soaked and nervous; she was composed and confident. "Did you talk to my husband about Alex? Does he even know?"

This question seemed to stump Gorger. "I tried. But he's out of town. Of course, you know that. I couldn't connect. I left a message to call back." His eyes widened, and he shrugged his shoulders. "I couldn't leave a message about your brother-in-law. No. It would be unprofessional. I'm sure you agree."

"No one called me," she said with anger in her voice. "Was that professional? I had to find an empty hospital bed this morning. That was my notice." She broke into tears.

"Mrs. Reinhart. I'm sorry. That was a mistake." Gorger rushed to snatch a tissue from one of the many boxes populating the lounge area. He handed several to her.

"Thanks," she said under her breath. She took her time in reassembling herself; real tears flowed, and she used them to her advantage, trying to give Terry more time.

In a room full of dead bodies, Terry used his flashlight to find his way. He viewed the poor soul on the embalming table. Flexible hoses connected to the source of the pulsing machine sounds, one penetrating the man's neck and the other snaking out from beneath the sheet covering the chest area; fluids flowed in the tubes, blood evacuating and formaldehyde entering. The detective flashed the light on the face of the corpse, exposing the face of an old man, his cheekbones tight with rubbery grey skin drained of life.

Terry moved on systematically, checking all the other bodies on carts. Lifting the white sheets, flashing on the faces, and then moving on. A total of four bodies, but Alex was not one of them. Again, he scanned the room with his flashlight. The machine continued to pulse, relentlessly replacing the old man's blood with embalming fluid. The formaldehyde smell made Terry sick to his stomach; he wanted out before he vomited. He was afraid the embalmer could return any second. Reaching the door, he eased it open and exited.

He crept along the corridor until he spotted a door on his right. A yellow tag on it read: *No Entry. Hazardous Material.* He stared at the lock. It had an electronic keypad. He tried the lever, but it was disengaged. He put his ear up to the door without result. Pausing to listen, maybe he heard voices approaching from inside. He wasn't sure. He searched for someplace to hide and entered the tiny, unlocked closet, closed the door with care, and held his breath. He waited, jumpy now. The storm outside was gaining strength. Sounds of thunder rumbled and shook the building. Rain pounded on the roof above. The muffled voices disappeared, or maybe he imagined them.

Light from his phone illuminated the utility closet as he checked the evacuation plan image on his phone. The special room was not shown on the plan. Alex could be in there, but it offered no entry. He debated leaving his hidey hole. He listened in the darkness for several minutes, but nothing happened, so he decided to move on. As he entered the corridor, only two more rooms remained ahead. The one on the right was identified as a cooler, and the one at the end was the crematory.

He tackled the cooler first. A blast of cold air hit him as he entered. He secured the door, turned, switched on his flashlight, and examined the occupants of the cold, quiet tomb. Three stiffs lying in cardboard caskets awaited their fiery destinies. The two men and one woman dressed in the official Reinhart death uniforms appeared cold but peaceful...but no Alex. Terry was confounded; he sensed his friend was near; only one room remained, the crematory. He opened the cooler door, and the fresh, warm air from the corridor gave him hope.

Kathy's conversation with Gorger got hotter, too hot for Cindy, who seemed more comfortable with bookkeeping than dealing with human conflict. She slid past the two combatants on her way out.

"Hello, Mr. Gorger...good evening Mrs. Reinhart." Gorger nodded. Kathy ignored her.

Kathy demanded to see Alex. Gorger admitted the brother-in-law's body was in the building, but refused to allow her in. "Of course, it will be made ready to view, but not until I am done with it. Until it is ready to be presented, I cannot show it," he said as if he was introducing a new model year car or the next Miss America.

Kathy remained undaunted. "I don't care, Jan. I just want to see my Alex."

Gorger was disappointed. "You're missing the point. I am only halfway done with the...embalming process. His body is in a state unfit for viewing by loved ones. I am sure you understand. Please come back tomorrow morning. Come with a friend if you can. That would be best."

Gorger's words were painful. She got the picture now. Alex really was dead. Terry was wrong. And the truth hit her hard. Gorger was in the process of draining Alex's blood. She broke down again, turned, and headed out the door.

"Mrs. Reinhart," Gorger cried out into the night, but she had disappeared into the cold, wet darkness.

Kathy ran out, her head lowered in despair, stumbling along the front walk in the driving rain, until she bumped into Stephan Jarek.

"Kathy, what are you doing here?" He shouted as he held his umbrella in his left hand, now protecting both of them from the rain.

Shocked by the impact and even more upset when she was confronted by Jarek. "I came to see the body. Alex's. Of course, you know, he's dead. Don't you?"

"Come back in. You're in no condition to drive," he said. "I'd drive you home, but I got a ride here."

"I don't care. I have to go. I'm so upset. Gorger wouldn't let me in."

"It's his job, Kathy. He's a mortician. He tries to help people navigate through tough times."

"At some point, his job is to kiss my ass." She didn't like the look on Jarek's face. "You have a bad attitude," she said. "On top of everything, Otto's brother is dead."

"I'm well aware that Alex has passed. I was there when he died. Nice man. Too young. I'm sorry for you, Kathy. I know you had feelings for him. But you have to live with reality."

He reignited her anger. "Sometimes you're impossible, Jarek. I'm leaving. It's raining, and I'm crying. I'm going home to lick my wounds."

He nodded. "I understand. All right. But take my umbrella. Please. You need to sleep tonight. Take a pill."

She took the umbrella, and he turned and walked away, heading for the building entry. After a few steps, she stopped and looked back through the windows. Gorger and Jarek conversed in the reception area. It appeared to be an animated conversation that quickly terminated. Jarek turned and strode rapidly toward the back of the building. Kathy was concerned, but she remembered Terry's instructions. She wandered through the falling rain into the back lot, found his car, entered the passenger side, and sat soaking wet on the leather seats. The cold rain pounded down on the roof. She shivered and cried, knowing Alex was dead. Shortly thereafter, she came to her senses and sent Terry a text: *Jarek is in the building.*

The door at the end of the corridor was Terry's last hope. The sensor pad on the right door jamb demanded a special key to allow for automatic operation with the wave of a hand. That key was conspicuous because of its cylindrical shape; he rattled through his ring of keys, found the special key, inserted and turned it. He waved his hand before the pad, and the wide door swung open. He took a moment to focus, and he retrieved his flashlight, but that was not needed because the room lights were activated by the door switch. The white room was filled with the glare and hum of the bright fluorescent lights.

As he turned back to face the interior of the space, the automatic door closed behind him. To his right, his eyes swept past the massive stainless steel-clad crematory and continued on to the location of a strange sound. The rhythmic noise pulsed and echoed off the walls. It came from a portable ventilator hanging from the frame of a mobile cart and connected to the face of a person lying on the cart. Terry's eyes opened wide. He found Alex. Alive or dead, he didn't know.

He rushed to the cart. The plastic breathing mask covered half of Alex's face, but enough was visible to confirm his find. At that moment, he received another text from Kathy. In response to the faint beep, he focused on reading the tiny view his cellphone provided. Behind, the automatic door opened, at first unnoticed by him. Too many simultaneous events confused Terry; finding Alex, reading the text message, and processing the sound of the door opening were too much. He started to look back when something hit the base of his skull, the cell phone flew out of his hand, and his limp body collapsed. Half-aware, almost out cold, he lay on his back atop the concrete floor.

Jarek lifted Terry's body onto the horizontal metal track with his head leading into the crematory firebox. Terry's body reacted, sending agonizing messages to his scrambled brain. His skull screamed in pain while the nerve endings in his back and shoulders were pinched by the rippled bed of metal rollers supporting his body. Nearby switchgear popped, and a motor started. Behind his head, mechanical operations vibrated the rack he rested upon, and the small steel door began opening. His mind was clouded, and he couldn't handle the input; he focused and refocused, sensing danger was imminent.

Behind him, the rush of flames igniting sequentially was startling. He felt the heat as the furnace flames in the cremation machine singed the hairs on his head. Now he was certain he was about to be barbequed. He felt someone's bony hands gripping hard on each of his shoes. He lifted his head to see his attacker. Jarek's face, red and orange, full of evil, pulsed in the light of the dancing crematory flames. Bump by bump, Terry's body slid along the steel rollers beneath, as he was pushed into the furnace of flaming death. He lifted his upper body just in time to remove his head from the doorway leading to Hell. Almost upright, his shoulders caught the frame of the opening while his body resisted Jarek's desperate thrusts.

The back of Terry's shirt burned, as did his flesh. Reacting, he twisted his body violently to the left and propelled it off the roller track. Jarek, retaining his grip on Terry's shoes, followed him down to the floor. Terry took the fall, landing on the back of his head and shoulders. He shook off his right foot from Jarek's iron grip, hinged his leg back, and then rammed his foot forward with all the force he could deliver. The heel of his shoe caught Jarek on the chin, and the impact slowed him.

Both men rose to their feet: Jarek, tall and wiry, Terry, short and powerful. Jarek initiated the action. He threw a fist at Terry's head, which missed. Terry grabbed Jarek's slashing wrist and spun him around in one quick move. He held him from behind, and in a few seconds, the former cop immobilized the doctor, crushing him down with both his arms and hands in what looked like a chokehold, but wasn't; it was a sleeper hold. It took Jarek less than a minute to lose consciousness from lack of blood flow to his brain. Terry held on to Jarek's body and looked around, evaluating his options. He saw an empty cart and carried the limp body to it, laying it atop the cart.

Terry retrieved a handkerchief from his pocket and stuffed it into Jarek's mouth. He figured Jarek would remain out cold for a short time, but he wanted to slow him down when he awakened. Prepared for anything, he had a pair of flexicuffs on him. He used those to tie down Jarek's arms to the cart. He ripped off the sheet covering Alex and placed it over Jarek's body.

The door to the furnace had closed, and its flames no longer roared. Jarek remained unconscious, and dead silence filled the room. Terry ripped open the entry door and rolled the cart carrying Alex out into the corridor. As he moved away, the door closed, the lights extinguished, and the lock reset. He returned to the cart carrying Alex, stood behind it, saw freedom ahead, and pushed. The ventilator forced air in and out of his friend's lungs. Alex could be alive, or he could be dead. The cart plowed along through the corridor's double doors and into the staging room. Behind him, Terry heard the door of the unknown room opening. He wondered whether someone was coming. He waited, breathing heavily, Alex's ventilator pumping, until he heard the automatic door to the crematory opening and closing. Whoever it was would be faced with the sight of Jarek's body under a sheet. Terry knew he was running out of time.

He moved ahead without concern for noise sensing that the storm was covering everything. The escaping duo blew through the exterior set of double doors, temporarily sheltered by the driveway roof, but soon pummeled by the falling cold rain of the thunderous storm. Alex's body jumped up and down limply as the cart rolled out into the darkness. The wind whipped water into Terry's face, blinding him as he raced the cart across the flooded lot searching for his car. He parked the cart carrying Alex's body behind the limo and raced around tapping on the driver's side window. Kathy, red-eyed and frightened, looked at him. He gave her a hand signal and shouted, "Get out."

Terry reached into the car and opened the trunk lid while Kathy discovered Alex. She hugged his body, gently pushed back his wet beard, and kissed his forehead. Terry opened the rear doors and released and lowered the seat backs. He joined Kathy behind the car, grabbed her by her shoulders, and put his face close to hers.

"We'll take him to the hospital," he shouted above the noise of the storm. "Hold the ventilator onto his chest while I put him into the trunk."

Lightning flashed. Alex Reinhart's stark white face was vacant and peaceful. His water-soaked beard glistened. The rain pounded on the trunk lid, and the wind drove sheets of water onto them as they both guided the lifeless body. Without concern for bruising, they lifted its shoulders, forced it into the trunk, and slid it across the flattened back seats. Terry rushed around to the side, reached in, and pulled the body clear of the trunk. Kathy slammed the lid. Body secure, Terry placed the ventilator box next to Alex and yelled at her: "Get in!" He slammed the rear door shut and hopped in the driver's seat.

"Which hospital?" She asked.

"Same damn hospital that killed him. Those bastards are responsible. They've gotta bring him out of this coma or else," he shouted.

The Lincoln limo rolled into the storm and headed for the hospital. Steam poured off their bodies; water dripped from their hair. The windshield wipers beat back the storm, and the headlights cut a path through the driving rain. From the back of the car, the ventilator pulsed. Then they heard Alex moaning. A humble sound, but it filled them with hope.

Terry burst out a celebratory, "Hot shit! Hang in there, Alex."

Chapter 39

Earlier, Gorger had returned to the motel, picked up the two surgeons, brought them back to the funeral home, and slipped them in through the back entrance, where they prepped themselves and waited. When the surgeons arrived, they had offered yellowed half-smiles and grunts by way of introduction. Both doctors wore dirty five-day beards, white tee shirts, and blue jeans as if someone had told them how to dress in America. Their patient was not impressed, but there was little he could do to improve his situation. He was about to get an off-book, illegal, discount heart transplant. Otto knew all this, and his only comfort was the thought that the most probable alternative to Doctor Jarek's unusual solution was death by the conventional medical establishment.

Time passed while Otto amused himself by watching sitcoms on his laptop. The two surgeons went into the prep room to clean up, don their scrubs and masks, and otherwise prepare. Otto heard them talking, making quips, and occasionally laughing. He was beginning to sense that he was making a terrible mistake. But it was too late for those thoughts. The money had been spent, the surgical suite was ready, and his body was being prepped.

Otto's anxiety peaked as he watched the foreigners go about their dangerous business. But Jerzy was prepared. He injected Otto with something to smooth out his patient's excitement and fear. In addition, Jerzy reached into his kitbag, pulled out his laptop computer, along with a couple of mini-speakers, and played soothing light classical music. Otto sensed his surgical team was about to begin.

Covered with a white blanket, lying on the hospital bed, his ring, watch, and gold chain removed, Otto, now naked as a newborn, awaited the installation of his new heart. The injection had worked. Whatever it was, Otto was no longer anxious. He was calm. Things seemed to happen in slow motion now. They moved him onto a cart, rolled him near the operating slab, and lifted him onto the table. He felt the coolness of the black leather and the flow of conditioned air blowing across his naked skin. Someone placed a sheet on him, covering his lower half. That was comforting for Otto.

Equipment was pulled into place, and connections were made. The machines announced their presence, humming and beeping. Bright white lights were activated, adjusted, and focused on his chest. A surgeon dropped his head into Otto's vision. He said something in a foreign language and smiled with his yellow, uneven teeth. The grizzled face disappeared, but the heavy smell of burned Turkish tobacco lingered.

One of the surgeons gave an order to Jerzy. Out of the corner of his eye, Otto watched the little man leave the room, and a short time later that same door swung open, this time with Jerzy pushing a cart holding a body under a sheet. The cart was parked parallel to the operating table. About six feet separated Otto from his donor. In his sleepy state, Otto was not certain exactly what was happening. He thought he heard muffled sounds coming from the gurney at his side. That couldn't be. It was Alex. But Alex was dead. Then there was movement under the sheet. Otto told himself he was dreaming, but soon he understood it was not a dream. The unseen moving arm pulled down the sheet enough to expose the crazed face of Stephan Jarek. Something was in his mouth. He made terrible grunting sounds, which alerted Jerzy that something was wrong. Otto, strapped to the operating table and drugged out, could not move. His heart felt as if it were about to explode. He tried to shout, but the only sounds he made were incoherent mumbles.

He watched Jerzy rush to the side of the gurney while Jarek freed one of his hands, grabbed the assistant's arm, and pulled him down. Jerzy wasn't a large man; Jarek was fighting for his life. Jerzy shouted out to the other two, crying for help, and they joined in the battle. The three of them attempted to restrain Jarek. By now, he had freed himself from the other flexicuff binding his arm to the cart. He reached into his mouth and removed the handkerchief.

"Otto. Tell them to stop," he shouted in a raspy, loud voice. "It's me, Jarek."

Otto peered out, drugged, stunned, and immobile. He watched the strange scene unfold.

Jarek lashed out with both fists, pummelling the three men until he was finally subdued. His head turned to face Otto. His tearful, wild eyes, blood vessels popping, met Otto's sleepy blue eyes. In some confused way, Otto understood, but when he attempted to shout out to the surgeons, his words were garbled utterances without meaning.

Jarek screamed out: "You will burn in Hell, Otto!"

The last thing Otto would remember is the grotesque scene of Jerzy injecting Jarek in his neck, freezing all of the doctor's movement, and the three men releasing their grips on the uncooperative donor, laughing loudly and swearing for several minutes. The crisis was over. Jarek was done resisting, and Otto would soon have his heart.

A surgeon dropped his head into Otto's vision. He said something in a foreign language, paused, and smiled.

"Where is Jerzy?" Otto asked in a slurred voice as he sought the comfort of a friendly face.

"I am here, Mr. Otto." His face came into view.

Otto knew what would happen next. "How long?" he asked, his words barely intelligible.

Jerzy smiled. "For you, there will be no time. But for us, it will be many, many hours. Relax. We take care of you."

He moved away to start the anesthesia, and the surgeon appeared again. He spoke: "It is time. We go sleep now, Mr. Otto."

Behind Otto, Jerzy started putting him to sleep: "Count backward starting one hundred. Begin please..."

Otto complied. "One hundred, ninety-nine, ninety..."

After about five minutes, the two men went back to their work, appearing not interested or unaware of the change in the game plan. Soon, they all found the rhythm of their work. The sound of the cardiopulmonary bypass pump and the mechanical ventilator filled the otherwise deadened room as the machines pretended to be part of Otto, keeping his body functioning, ready to receive new lungs and heart.

The imported doctors were only halfway through the operation; they did their work business-like, occasionally joking with each other, stamping their feet into circulation, ignoring the extreme mental and physical stress of their work. Next, they cut deep into Jarek's chest and carefully removed his organs.

Many hours later, they finished. Jerzy summoned Gorger. He quickly assessed the situation. The sheet covering Jarek was pulled back to reveal his face. Below, an enormous bloody void, once filled with life, was now empty and dead.

"What we do, Mr. Gorger?" asked Jerzy, his eyes focused on Jarek's lifeless form.

Gorger made a face, took a deep breath, and muttered: "Don't worry. I will take care of it." Before he returned the two surgeons to their motel, Gorger ran the crematory furnace one last time for the day, setting the controls for two hours at 1800 degrees, and Dr. Jarek disappeared forever, leaving behind only a few ounces of cremains, a few patients, a 2020 Toyota Camry, and a befuddled blonde office assistant. Otto slept like a baby, unaware that the operation was successful, and his new heart, donated by Dr. Jarek, was now efficiently pumping his blood. Otto Reinhart was a new man, his body and mind curiously adapting to his business partner's heart, ready to take on the world.

Chapter 40

"We'll be doing a teleconference today," said Edwin Watson. The aging attorney's voice sounded almost excited, like a little kid playing with a new toy on Christmas morning. "Janice, is everything ready to go?'

Watson's assistant, a sweet-looking young female attorney, spoke: "Everything is running, Mr. Watson. Should I connect Mr. Reinhart?"

"Beam him down, Janice. Beam him down." Watson appeared to be enjoying his first video conference call.

She smiled, tapped on her laptop, and in seconds Otto Reinhart's smiling face appeared on the wall-mounted monitor above the end of the table.

"Edwin...I'm happy to see and hear you—five by five. Top of the morning to you."

"Hello, honey," said Kathy, seated on one side of the conference table adjacent to me.

"Another good morning to you, Babe. And you too, brother. You're all looking good."

Otto's giant animated head hung on the wall. He sat confidently in a recliner in the bedroom suite of his home; his red silk robe, white silk scarf, slicked-down hair, and tanned face gave him a Hollywood look.

"Well, you look like a new man. Bigger than life," said Alex.

"I am a new man. And you, too, Alex. Life goes on. Isn't it great?"

Watson dismissed his young assistant with a weak smile and a flip of his hand.

"Each of us has been given a second chance in life. Something we shouldn't take lightly," Otto's voice boomed out of the speaker. Momentarily reflecting, I thought Otto was beginning to sound like our father. Maybe it was the television screen and the audio setup, but he seemed to have a new commanding presence. Kathy and I turned to face Watson.

"OK. I'm sure everyone has a busy morning lined up, so I'll get to the point." He pretended to look at his notes, but I doubted that any complications were expected. "My goal today is to complete the process of reading the will of Frederick Reinhart. We had an open issue at the time, which is now resolved. The issue was your father's conditional bequest, which opened the possibility of Kathy receiving twenty-five percent of the net estate of Frederick if she were pregnant with a baby legally possessing the Reinhart name. Certain testing procedures were stipulated in order to satisfy the provisions of the will. We don't have to go into the details, but suffice it to say the tests were properly completed. And as we know, Kathy did test positive..." He faced Kathy.

I glanced over at her. The mention of the test set her off. "I'm sorry," she said, "may I please have a glass of water?" Her voice was dry and full of emotion.

"Excuse me," said Watson, "of course." He rose from his chair, poured some from a pitcher on the counter below the window, and set the glass down before her.

Kathy's face was pink. She drank, coughed a little, and took another sip. "Are you OK?" I whispered.

She didn't respond, but she nodded.

"Otto, are you still with us?" asked Watson.

"Yes. Yes. Go on. Let's get this over with." For a moment, a look of anger flashed across his face.

"Fine," said Watson as he continued, "As I stated, Kathy did test positive, and the test indicated the child would be a Reinhart baby.

However," he made a face, "as we know, unfortunately, the pregnancy was terminated by a miscarriage. Therefore, nothing additional will be required to complete the distributions of the estate. Otto Reinhart will receive a fifty percent share, and Alex Reinhart will receive a fifty percent share. Any questions?"

Everyone remained quiet.

"Then I will call this meeting to an end. It should be noted that Kathy has assumed the responsibilities of executor as Alex is moving out of state. That said...thank you again." He slid the laptop closer to him and said, "Goodbye, Otto. Have a fine day." He pushed a key on the laptop, and Otto faded from the screen.

Kathy and I rose, offered a few parting pleasantries, and left the attorney's office.

Chapter 41

We walked a couple of blocks and crossed the bridge to the Riverwalk. On this chilly, yet sunny, early December day, we strolled side by side on the winding path beneath the bare tree branches with the sleepy river on one side and the placid lake on the other. Not so far away, the carillon bells announced the passing of time. Only a few other people shared the space. I reached out and held her hand. "Well, we got through that," I said.

"I guess," she said, her green eyes bright in the sunlight. "But now you'll be starting a new life in the Keys, and I'll be going home to Otto's house." She squeezed my hand. "I'll miss you, Alex." We stopped. She turned to face me, and we embraced. It was a friendly embrace and not one that would raise any Naperville eyebrows nor send any hearts a flutter other than mine.

I held her hands gently and looked deep into her eyes. "If it wasn't for you and Terry, what's left of me would be in one of Otto's golden keepsake hearts dangling around your beautiful neck. I owe you my life, Kathy."

"Alex Reinhart, you don't owe me anything. You gave me something I couldn't buy, paint, or pretend existed. Everything's clearer since you arrived. I can see the future now. And I won't forget our stolen moments. You'll always be in my heart."

After a long pause, I spoke. "I'm sorry about the baby, Kathy."

I felt better getting it out in the open. I held a shared responsibility for our love child's short life; it was a sobering reminder that our relationship was real yet ephemeral.

She sighed. "Me too. I was surprised and happy. The baby was ours, Alex. But I'm not sure I would have been the greatest mother.

I've still got some growing up of my own to do. First, I think I'll become a better wife. Otto needs me now. He seems to be recovering nicely, but he's different now. In a good way."

"How's so?"

"Well, I don't know if he's jealous because he suspects that you and I may have crossed the line from in-laws to lovers, or just the fact that he's feeling better...but he's taking a much stronger interest in me. If you know what I mean?" She smiled.

"I can guess. It is difficult to ignore you, Kathy. I speak from experience." I smiled.

"Yes. I would say, since his heart operation, he's a more interesting guy."

"Give it all time and space. You might surprise yourself."

We resumed our walk. "We've both learned something about ourselves. Haven't we?" I suggested.

She thought about it before responding. "Sometimes it takes an emotional earthquake to shake a person out of complacency, fantasy, and denial. That morning. When I heard you were...dead...that empty hospital bed. Anyway, I knew that life was not a game." She released my hand as her face tightened to subdue tears. "Let's go back."

I telephoned Terry and asked him to pick me up at the Riverwalk entrance. A few minutes of walking and contemplation brought us to the street. We stood across from City Hall, two old friends saying farewell, visible to all of Naperville.

"I'm going to give it a try, Alex. That's all I can say."

"Do you have plans?"

She smiled. "Plans are for people who make assumptions. At this moment, I'm alive, very wary, and I'm making no assumptions about people or things. I've been told I'm a cat on a hot tin roof. But..." Her voice betrayed some weariness.

"Is that cat gone?"

She nodded. "Let's just say the cat knows she has used up most of her lives."

"You know how I feel, Kathy...if the roof gets too hot...jump off." I wanted to be unequivocal, regardless of Otto.

"You're full of answers, aren't you, Alex Reinhart?"

"And only one question." I waited. The wind picked up a bit, and the bare tree branches high above swayed. The aching sounds of those tree limbs, with sap no longer flowing, filled the early winter air.

She wasn't following my oblique reference. "What about the box?" I asked.

"What box?"

"The little box, filled with all our dreams, the one tied with a pretty blue ribbon?"

She thought, then smiled, "Oh, that box. You haven't changed." She shook her head. "That's why I love you, Alex."

"Because I'm so lovable?"

"Yes. There's no one like you. Forever young. You take it with you to Florida. And if you wish, save it for me."

I didn't know what I wanted her to say, something more definitive for sure, more hopeful, but...I just swallowed hard and said, "I'll miss you."

For a long moment, she gave me a look, shook her head gently, and offered a small knowing smile. She shrugged. "Box or no box, you have to do what's right, Alex."

I was left to interpret her words, certain I would never forget them.

Terry's limo pulled to a stop in front of us. I didn't care if the Mayor of Naperville watched us from the top of City Hall. I grabbed Kathy, kissed her like I meant it, released her, and opened the limo door. I took one more look at the love of my life. She left me wondering. She had a smile on her face as she turned away, her head held high, a light breeze gently tossing her auburn hair. As she sashayed up the street, she looked like a New York model. Her short tan leather jacket on top and her tight skirt below were all set into motion by a pair of trendy pumps with three-inch heels. Slowly, as my eyes captured our final moment, I entered the limo. Terry and I sat quietly. I caught my breath and waited.

He shook his head. "You are incorrigible."

"What? Kathy and I are just old friends now...reunited."

"Reunited...I'd say."

"You old bastard. Take my advice, Terry. You should give Margie a few extra kisses. She deserves it, and so do you. Life's too short to ignore your friends, brothers, and lovers...may they never meet."

"Right. Whatever...your bags are in the back. Where to?"

"O'Hare. United...and better times."

Terry swiftly motored out of Naperville and onto the tollway. He looked good behind the wheel, like he and his machine were one and the same, a man in control of his destiny. Without looking at me, he said, "Feels good. Doesn't it?"

"You mean getting out of town?"

"Getting untangled. Since you arrived, you've been balled up like a big cat at the bottom of a Burmese tiger pit," said Terry.

"You mean the deluxe suite in your basement?"

He chuckled. "That too." After we buzzed through a toll plaza, he turned his head to look at me, then slid the Lincoln over a couple of lanes. "So are you done with her?"

"What do you think?"

Terry paused. He shook his head. "I think it's good you're heading to Florida. Naperville was too much for you."

"It wasn't my choice. But I can tell you I'm not coming back. I'll just have to live off my memories...including Kathy."

Terry made a face, took a deep breath, and released it noisily. "Sometimes I wonder why I saved your life." He shook his head. "You'll just find yourself in another tight spot."

"Tight spots are my business."

He gave me a hard glance. "You're only flesh and blood. You know Margie and I talked this morning. She asked me to pass on some of her motherly advice." He looked over, shook his head, and chuckled. "She really likes you, but she thinks you shouldn't be so trusting. She said: 'Tell him to wake up. Look out for yourself. Most people are no damn good...and some are just plain bad.'"

I thought for a moment. "A bit hyperbolic. You have to trust someone, right?" I studied my old and loyal friend with some reverence. "I trusted you. Did I thank you properly?"

"The answer is a definite, unequivocal, 'no'. All the bullshit I went through. And your only reaction afterward was to play nice-nice with all the devils."

"Otto is family. My brother. Nothing's going to change that. And he was backed up against a wall. He wasn't in his right mind. Jarek manipulated him, and Gorger, as usual, was only following orders."

"What about the rat bastard?"

"You and I can guess, but officially, Jarek's disappeared. Some say he ran off after I came back to life. Others think he's just another desperate deadbeat who left town, leaving a mess behind. The hospital's off the hook. They claim Jarek's lack of medical judgment was the sole reason I was declared dead. They want to remain out of the picture and bury the whole thing. Physically, I'm fine. Everyone's taking the position of...'no harm no foul'. I signed an agreement with the hospital and picked up a nice little settlement. Gorger says he was just doing his job. Very loyal. And Otto's made him the head man at the funeral home."

Terry amped up his response. "But we know Jarek's goal was to steal your heart, and eventually Otto's money, and maybe his wife."

"No more talk, Terry. That's a done deal. Otto says he doesn't know what went on. He doesn't want to go to jail, and he simply wants to keep the lid on the transplant operation. And I'm not pushing him. I just hope all goes well. He's happy with his new heart, and he must be getting better. I get the impression he's even sniffing around Kathy again."

"Good for him. I hope those two settle down. And I take it you know nothing?"

"Me? You forget. Officially, I was in a coma the whole time. Thanks to our good buddy Dr. Jarek. So, we all let sleeping dogs lie. I guess what goes on in Naperville...stays in Naperville." I chuckled.

"Good riddance to Dr. Douchbag," said Terry. He glanced over to make sure I was listening. "You know you owe me and Margie and the kids at least a lifetime of vacations at your new beach home."

"You got it," I said.

Terry laughed. "And you never paid me for my detective services."

I feigned indignation. "One second, my misinformed friend. Today I mailed a check for $25,000 to Margie." I paused for effect. "But it's made out to you. You two lovebirds get to work it out." I laughed.

Terry smiled and stared out the windshield. I could tell he was thinking. "To better times..." He turned to face me. "Right, my old friend?"

"Sure, Terry...they're just around the corner."

Epilogue

My plane is flying slowly and low over the rich Illinois farmland. The ground below is a grey-brown matte of tangled, rotting pumpkin vines. Soon, winter will bury the past under a pure white frozen blanket of snow, and then, in time, a new season will arrive with new growth.

In a state of excited optimism, I am beginning the second half of my life. My old favorite mystery novel feels good in my hand, and I'm reading it with fresh eyes as if it were the first time. Florida is my destination, first Miami, then the Keys. I am confident I will find the perfect oceanfront writer's hideaway.

I'm in a window seat, the pilot has made the turn to the south, and below are the western suburbs of Chicago. I wonder if I will be able to detect Naperville.

Out the window, I see the toll road heading west. Then the railroad tracks heading east lead my eyes to the cute little train station, next to the village square. Beyond is my father's funeral home, the old high school, the original Reinhart residence, the bell tower, and the river. I see Kathy and Otto's mansion on the bend in the DuPage River and her little art studio in the back. It's all there in one tidy package.

My old hometown looks peaceful from this height, as if nothing bad would ever happen there, but I know better. The South American jungles and the plains of Africa are filled with wild animals and terrain, but I'm convinced there is nothing more dangerous than the desperate human animals living in the middle of America. I am more aware now, and less naïve, I hope. I escaped with my life...and my future. I will never return to Naperville.

W. GREEN

All book reviews and stars are appreciated.
Thank you.
Visit Website: www.wgreen.me[1]

Also by W. Green
Becoming Irrelevant: Less is More...More or Less
Dead Wong (w/Tom Smith)
Saving JFK
X-ooming FDR 1932
X-ooming FDR 1933
X-ooming FDR 1934
Saving Trump
Happiness Wants You
Eggplant: A Different Kind of Racehorse